To Cynthia, ":Tahbut ne!":

A Legend in Time

Book One of the James Sutherland Chronicles

A Novel

By

Jonathan Westbrook

Copyright © 2010 by Jonathan Westbrook

Cover design and art work by Jonathan Westbrook.

Manufactured in the United States of America

1 3 5 7 9 10 8 6 4 2

ISBN: 978-1453648889

Printed by CreateSpace.com

A Legend in Time

Book One of the James Sutherland Chronicles

PROLOGUE

The brilliant and often funny Albert Einstein once said to me, "The only reason for time is so that everything doesn't happen at once," and the philosophic Aristotle debated with me one day, "Time is only the measurement of movement in space," but since becoming a time-traveler I have developed my own opinion … Time is an element; a precarious one that can be manipulated; where events in time can be changed, but not always for the good of mankind.

Like Einstein and Aristotle, I used to view time as it passed me by—either slowly as I watched the unmoving hands on a clock's face, or as it flew by when I was not giving it any attention.

Which brings to mind a thousand colloquialisms that I could throw out there for debate, like "Time flies when you're having fun," "A stitch in time saves nine," or "Time is money," just like I did with Aristotle atop the Acropolis, but I'm not here to recount all of the sayings about time that I've heard over the years. In fact, there are only two questions that I want to ask.

The first: If you had the chance to time travel, would you? I'm curious, because I wasn't given the chance to answer that question, not really. I don't wish to say that becoming a time traveler was thrust upon me—that would be incorrect, or, that I don't find it terribly exciting, because I do, but when I think back on it all now; the circumstances of my past; the lack of knowledge on the subject by me; the lack of tutelage on it by my mentor, they all gave me no other choice but to become what I am today.

My second question: Is fate written in stone? My mentor was fond of saying, "The future is subject to change," but at times it seems to me that my life has always been pointed in this direction. And because of that, somewhere along the way, I learned to respect time, to cherish it, to fight for it, and I'll be the first to admit it, I've basically come upon this realization ad hoc—or so it would seem.

My first adventures in time were frustrating and naïve at best. Time was just a notion, a clock on the wall, an uncontrollable passage from day to night—only to repeat itself again and again. But because of my naiveté, I think I have grown into this position well—I didn't come into being a time traveler with any preconceived ideas of it.

And so, the time has come for me to share my experiences, because ad hoc or not, I've learned a lot over the years, and if I should not get the chance to tutor my own replacement someday, let this manuscript be his or her guide.

James Sutherland

President, pro-tem, Earth Time Authority

THE WATCH

I didn't pick up the box again until a week later, and I did so with a nonchalant attitude. I had given in to the feeling that what was in the box was an eighty-dollar mistake and that it was just another trinket to add to my collection of stuff. Whether the watch was pure gold or not, it was a fine looking piece, so I sat down on a futon that served as my couch with the box in hand to have another look.

I opened up the almost forgotten package and there it was again in the palm of my hand. Its beauty matched by none of my other antiques. "I really should get this appraised," I said to my pets. I would often talk to them just to keep my sanity in check because living alone for years with only a hand full of friends, who never stopped by just for the hell of it, can do that to a person. I didn't feel so solitary by talking to my animals.

Looking again at the watch, I forgot all about the old man ripping me off for it was clear I had gotten the better bargain. I popped open the front cover and the time was still correct, which I found odd because I had never wound it, so I pushed down on the plunger and cranked it until it wouldn't turn any more. I knew that pulling up on the plunger would adjust the time but there was no need for that. I started to examine the face closer in an attempt to change the date. It read October 11th, 1964, the day before my birth. I fingered the dial below the month, and it turned freely. The months scrolled by. I stopped at July. I turned the middle dial to the correct day, the 12th. I moved on to the farthest dial on the right to change the year from 1964 to 2004, but the dial wouldn't turn to the right. It only moved to the left – backwards. 1963, 1962, 1961, I stopped after each year and tried again to go forward, but each time it wouldn't advance past 1964. I spun the dial back in frustration and it ended up on 1919. I left it there. "I guess it had to have something wrong with it," I sarcastically said, remembering my eighty-dollar bargain. I investigated the watch face closer until I found two very small push buttons along the rim at the bottom. They were so subtle it was only with luck that I found them at all for they were underneath the dials between where the glass started and where the cover snapped shut just in line with the outside edges of the hinge. I thought they were just a way to release the glass if replacing the hands were necessary – maybe that was how I could change the year. Closing the cover, but not all the way, the buttons were completely hidden, so I let the cover open fully again. With my thumb, I pushed in the button on the right and nothing happened. I didn't hear any click or see any sign that the button had any function to it at all. Then I pushed the left button and my life changed forever.

I didn't feel anything. In fact, I felt fine, but when I depressed that left button things around me changed. The futon I sat upon and other items in my house grew faint until they no longer remained. I fell to the floor and watched on as the rest of my surroundings began to fade away. I stared in awe as things disappeared in order of their age. First the TV and then the futon and coffee table vanished. I turned to see that my computer and its table were already gone. The frames that housed my antique buttons went next and then the cardboard they were mounted to, but to my surprise the buttons stayed hanging there in mid air. What seemed to be happening in slow motion quickly sped up. Everything I owned was soon gone and replaced by the previous owner's things. It took only a couple of seconds before their stuff was gone too. The room changed colors; the rug turned into hardwood; and the wallpaper border disappeared, replaced by full wallpaper top to bottom. I couldn't begin to fathom what was happening to me. Suddenly, the walls to my house began to fade. I could see the outside coming into the inside so I jumped up to a standing position. I grew concerned thinking of how I fell off of the couch when it disappeared. I thought I was going to fall down into the basement. It didn't happen that way because the house disappeared so quickly I didn't have time to fall that far. I did fall, but only a couple of feet, to solid ground. My house was gone, and I stood on a tree stump. I spun around trying to comprehend what was happening, when a large oak tree started to form right where I was standing. I quickly stepped to the side and watched it solidify before me. I watched other trees come to life out of thin air and what was once my grassy green lawn became woods and underbrush. The process seemed to slow, as I could actually see some seasons passing backwards: summer, spring, winter, fall, and then finally stopping at summer.

It was then I realized that the birds were chirping and a slight breeze tickled the back of my neck. I'm not sure if it was really a breeze or if I was just plain scared, but the little hairs on the nape of my neck stood straight up. Everything I knew was gone. I still had on the clothes I was wearing and my glasses on my face and the watch was still in my hand.

The watch!

I looked at the pocket watch, which was still running. I then looked at my wristwatch, and it had stopped running. Only a couple of minutes had past since I pushed the left button of the flea market pocket watch. I looked at the date, and the pieces of the puzzle started to come together. My house was built in 1920. The date on the watch was set for 1919, where I had arbitrarily left it.

"Holy Shit!" I exclaimed. "I can time travel." I had traveled back in time to a wooded lot, where my house would eventually be built a year in the future.

I stood there not knowing what to do. I stood there in shock. My house was gone. Keisha, my German Shepherd, was gone. My cats were gone. Everyone I knew was gone. Even my mother was gone—she wouldn't be born for another seven years. I felt overwhelmed. I felt lost.

I turned my back to the tree I almost became a part of and leaned against it. I heard a rustling in some bushes to my left and noticed a family of wild turkeys watching me from where my kitchen used to be. My knees gave way and I slid down to the leaf-covered ground. I shifted my perch and felt my wallet in my back pocket. Without letting go of the watch, I pulled out my wallet and thumbed through a life I thought I would never see again. I decided to experiment by pulling out one of my business cards and throwing it to the ground next to me. It stayed there. I thought, *If my business card from the future can stay in this time frame, then if I let go of the watch, will it stay here too? Will I?*

I laid the watch on the ground next to the business card and I tried to let go of it twice. I was scared—just like a kid who tries to jump off the second stair instead of the comfortable first one, I didn't know what was going to happen to me. The third time was a charm, as I did let go of the watch, and it, and I, stayed there. I picked it back up. I thought that if the device brought me there it should be able to take me home again. I depressed the left button again thinking that maybe the same button acted as a toggle switch, but nothing happened. I pushed its sister button on the

[6]

right. Suddenly, the birds stopped their singing and the branches stopped swaying; my business card that I left on the ground began to grow old quickly. It soon eroded to nothing and as I stood up the tree I had leaned against was back to being just a stump. Time was moving forward again, and I fell into the all-too-sudden basement that appeared below my feet. Luckily, I landed upright and was not hurt at all. Soon my house reappeared around me, but I had to react quickly in order to prevent my head from getting cut in half by a low ceiling joist. I crouched low and watched as time moved forward. As quickly as I had traveled to the past I arrived back to the present. My stuff reappeared, and everything solidified back to normal. I closed the cover to the watch, placed it in my pocket, and quickly turned to go upstairs, but the door to get up there was locked from the outside. "Not a problem." I grabbed a hammer and screwdriver and started to take the pins out of the door's hinges. My wristwatch had started again, and I saw that not a moment of time had passed while I was away. I had returned at the exact time that I had left, and I was ecstatic about the whole process. I could travel through time.

*   *   *

After some celebration with Keisha – who had no idea that I had gone anywhere but was surprised to see me coming up from the basement when I had just been in the living room—I sat down happily on my solid futon. The box, the purple velvet, and the receipt were right where I left them on the coffee table. I pulled out the watch from my pocket.

I pushed down on the plunger and felt the cover try to open into the palm of my hand. Immediately, I knew I had it upside down, but the picture of the Italian Villa was facing me. I turned it over expecting to see the train, but what I saw instead was a picture of my house. I closed the cover and looked at the backside; it definitely showed the kids playing in the street where the train used to be, but before I pushed the button, the first time, it showed on the front. I flipped the watch over again, but now, the front showed my house. "It's keeping a record of the places it's been. This is the most amazing thing ever," I said to the animals and myself. "And it's mine." I hesitated a moment until it fully came to me, "I can travel back in time but not in my lifetime. Is that it? Is that why the date won't go past my birthday?" I had watched enough sci-fi to know that Einstein's theory of having two of you in the same space time continuum would cause chaos in the universe. Perhaps his theory was true.

The old man, the Professor he called himself, who sold the watch to me knew I was its next owner. I knew then that he was just being quaint. The watch didn't know I was the next owner, he did. He knew my name. I snatched the receipt up looking for some contact information. I hadn't read it before, but its header read, "Colt Firearms, Hartford, CT. 1910."

My mind raced. I felt at a loss for information and needed to talk to the Professor. My only lead was the church where I met him. Crazed with excitement I said goodbye to the dog and rushed out to my car. I'm not sure if I believe in fate or destiny, but I do think there are circumstances beyond our control that can lead a person to a life that he never even dreamed of having. Such is the case for me. For when I think back on how I came to own the watch and the events that followed, I can truly say that things do happen for a reason. All it took was one day at a flea market, and the rest of my days were to be changed forever by owning an antique pocket watch.

*   *   *

I was an avid collector of antique clothing picture buttons. I started collecting them through the interest of an ex-girlfriend of mine, Gwen. At first I thought the hobby was a very "girlie" one, but to my surprise there were all sorts of handsome "man" buttons; of cats, dogs, lions, medieval gladiators, knights, castles, mythological creatures, Greek Gods, zodiacs, Native Americans, and dragons. There was almost anything you could think of, including the ones women liked best, floral designs, children's stories, fables, etc. Having an artistic background (I went to college for graphic design); I fast became fascinated with these small pieces of art for they were so detailed and unique. I became so into collecting these gems that I joined some local button societies, one in Connecticut, the other in Massachusetts, and went to their meetings to learn more. The love of button collecting made me want to learn more about them from my fellow button "buddies," and it didn't take long before I was going to every estate sale and flea market that I heard of to find more unique buttons. My collecting had turned into a passion. I can't say the same about the ex-girlfriend.

On one particular day of antique shopping I was at a church flea market in Coventry, CT, close to where my mother lives. I didn't find any buttons at all among the hodgepodge of items, and I was prepared to leave when an old man shuffled up to me. He was hunched over with his chin to his chest, exposing his thinning gray hair in a comb-over. He wore a tattered brown cardigan sweater vest over a light blue button up short sleeved shirt and, of course, the obligatory baggy old man pants that were worn high above his waist.

Very softly he said, as he reached out to me with a frail hand that trembled ever so slightly, "Pardon me young man."

"Yes sir, may I help you?"

"You're leaving without anything?"

"Yes. It looks like there are no treasures to be found for me today."

"Well that will never do." He gently grabbed hold of my elbow and started guiding me back toward his booth in a sweet, innocent-old-man way that was hard to resist, "Come right over here. We can't have you leaving without something."

I thought he was going to give me some sort of gag door prize or something cheesy—like a little porcelain Wade figurine. You might be familiar with the ones I mean, Red Rose gives them away in their boxes of twenty-five or more in an effort to sell more of their tea. Even though some flea market sellers have the nerve to charge four or more dollars for them, there were others that would just give them away. I thought the latter was the case this time, so I let him steer me as he willed.

As we arrived at his vendor's table, which I had missed during my rounds, he let go of my arm and slowly meandered around to his seller's side. He rummaged around in some boxes underneath his otherwise empty table for such a long time that I began to think he was stuck down there. I was about to offer my assistance when he finally came up for air from his search. With relief, he showed me his right hand, and in it, he held a purple velvet cloth, and he set it down on the table. He then grabbed a black folding metal chair that had a big fluffy cushion on it, and he sat a while until his breath returned enough for him to continue.

Eventually, he said with apparent pride, "I wish to show you this." I did not respond but looked on as he unveiled a beautiful vintage gold pocket watch. It seemed to have an inner glow that was so brilliant it reached out beyond its outside casement and grabbed my full attention. Pure gold can have that effect on people.

"It's gorgeous," I told him.

A smile appeared on his face. "It's very unique, wouldn't you say?" He reached out his hand and gestured that it was okay for me to touch it.

I gingerly picked up the watch and cradled it in my palm, being careful not to drop it. First I saw it had a typical wind up plunger on its top, I fingered the textured grooves along its circumference. There was a small chain, also made of gold, attached to the plunger by a swing arm, and I let the chain dangle down between my fingers. On its front cover in small relief was what looked like an Italian Villa with children playing on a cobblestone street and an unmanned horse and cart stood off to the side. In the background there appeared to be a castle in the mountains. I turned it over and on its back was a depiction of a steam train crossing an old wooden bridge above some roaring rapids; its smoke rose between evergreens that grew up on either side beyond the bridge.

"The artwork is amazing."

"Open it up," he said to me. The old man was intent on seeing my reaction.

I pushed down on the plunger and the front popped open revealing black Roman numerals on a white clock face with ornate black metal arms that showed the correct time. A delicate second hand marched steadily along with its rhythmic tick. Just above the XII o'clock position was the latch, and it did not look worn down at all. Gold is a soft metal and after years of the watch being opened and snapped shut, the latch, if it were pure gold would have been just a stubby nub. I couldn't tell if it had been replaced in its recent past or if it were made from brass or some other stronger metal. This made me leery that the rest of the watch wasn't made of gold. Perhaps, I thought, it was just the casement that was made of the precious metal and not its inner workings. The bottom center showed the date and three tiny dials just below that, which protruded ever so slightly out beyond the protective glass. The inside of the hinged cover was plain with a carved crisscross pattern that reminded me of a Spyro-graph picture from my youth.

I was about to close up the watch when the date made me do a double take. "Its date reads as the day before my birthday."

The old man laughed, "Of course it does. It's telling you that you are the next owner of it."

I played along, "It's *telling* me that?"

"Yes. When I first acquired it, it said the day before my birth date too." He was serious.

I waited for him to continue, but he didn't. I pondered his comment a while for it really made no sense at all. Certainly the watch couldn't have changed on its own, so how did he know what my birth date was? I never met this man before. I looked up from the watch to see a beaming face with a denture smile that reached from ear to ear. At that moment, the old guy no longer looked like he was in his eighties pushing one-hundred, and it melted my heart. I couldn't afford the watch, but after seeing that face I didn't want to turn him down either.

"How much are you asking for it?" I asked.

"How much do you have?"

That was a very vague response. I set the watch down onto the velvet from which it came thinking I'd never see it again. Looking at the watch, I thought, is he toying with me or just a shrewd businessman? I didn't like it when people played games with money even if it was just bartering. "Certainly not the kind of money that this would cost," I answered.

He shifted in his chair, perhaps realizing he was losing a sale, so he clarified, "My apologies, young man. I meant to say 'How much do you have on you right now?'"

Granted, I didn't know all there was to know about antiques, but I knew a watch of this quality could easily go for a grand, perhaps two given the purity of the gold. I only had a hundred bucks on me and I told him so.

"Terrific," he exclaimed, and started to wrap it up.

Despite the apparent great deal I was about to make, I felt like I was being taken for a ride. Either this guy was crazy like a fox, or senile, or I was on some secret camera television show. I foolishly babbled, "This can't be for real." The old guy stopped his packing and stared at me blankly. He appeared deeply disappointed by my reaction. I back peddled, "You seem very nice sir, and I can tell that you are genuinely interested in selling me this watch, at an extremely low price I might add, but I can't do it. It feels like I'm stealing it from you."

What he said to me next came as a complete surprise, "Then I'll give it to you ... as a gift." Before I could protest, he placed the velvet wrapped package into a small cardboard box and strolled out from behind his table. He handed the box to me, "Jim, this watch is yours. I can't explain it to you right now, but it is. Believe me. I want you to have it."

There was something in his eyes, a seriousness that made me question whether I had met him before, but I couldn't place it, and I didn't want to argue with him anymore. He knew my name and my birth date, somehow, and he wasn't going to take 'no' for an answer.

"Okay," I said, and I pulled out my wallet. "But not as a gift. I will pay you for it."

A smile returned to his face, "That'll be fine." From his back pocket he pulled out a receipt booklet and a pen. He scribbled something down as I paid him with two fifties. I had thought that we were done with our transaction but was wrong. The old timer had written, "Watch - $80.00"

"Here is your change young man." He held out an oversized piece of paper that looked older than he did, which it was, but not by much. It was a twenty-dollar bill from 1910. I was almost more excited about the twenty than I was about the watch.

"Sir, we agreed on a hundred."

In a playful and fun voice he said, "But I can't let you leave without any emergency funds." Then his tone grew instructional, "I mean it Jim, don't spend it until you see me again."

What a kook, I thought. I pocketed the old money and started to leave, but then turned back a moment. "Sir, how is it that you know my name?"

"W-why," he stammered, "you must have told me."

I thought not. "May I know your name?"

His smile returned, obviously proud of his title, "Professor Albert Traven, pleased to meet you."

I didn't recognize the name, so I turned to leave. "Take care Professor."

"I'll be seeing you Jim. Take care."

I didn't respond until I got outside the church basement, into the fresh air, and way beyond his earshot. I murmured, "Not if I see you first."

During the half an hour ride home, I convinced myself that the self-proclaimed "Professor" was a crackpot and that the watch was a fake, and I wondered who had stolen from whom by the time I pulled into my driveway. As I let the dog out, so she could relieve herself after being stuck in the house with the two cats for three hours, I placed the box on a shelf near the back door and forgot about it, and Albert Traven, for close to a week.

*   *   *

So there I was, back at the church where the flea market was held a week before.

"I'm sorry my Son," said Father Cory. "The gentleman you're speaking of passed away this past Thursday. Bless his soul. Such a kind man and quite the historian from what I understand."

"Yes he was," I agreed about his kindness, but I was devastated at the news. My only link to the watch had died. "I'm so sorry to hear that. We had done some business at the flea market last Sunday, and I really needed to speak to him."

"Yes, you mentioned that. His wake was this morning and the burial will take place tomorrow morning just around the corner," the priest fingered in a direction that led off to the side of the church. "But I dare say that is no time to talk about your business with him to his family. If you'd like, I could give his survivors your name and number and, perhaps in a couple of weeks they could contact you."

"Yes, that would be nice. Thank you." I gave him my business card and departed.

The same questions I had asked myself during the drive back to the church whirled in my head during the drive back home. *Why me?* repeated several times, among others like, *How far can I go back in time? Can I change history? Can I warn people about Hitler or Saddam? There is so much responsibility in owning this watch. Did Professor Traven invent it? If not, where did he get it?*

I decided I had to find the answers to these questions before I played around any more with the watch, but how? Then it hit me. Traven gave me clues. He gave me money from 1910 and a receipt with 1910 on it. He wanted me to meet him back in 1910 at the Colt building in Hartford. He knew he'd be seeing me again, just like he said. *Is that because (for him) I had already met him in the past and that's how he*

[13]

knew me? I tried not to dwell on the perplexity of the situation of, which came first, the chicken or the egg? But it lingered in the back of my mind anyway. I decided I would *have* to go back in time again to get the answers I needed, as only Traven could supply them to me. I decided to leave first thing the next morning and hopefully I would be able to find him.

A MENTOR'S FIRST TEST

Having been born in Connecticut and in the Hartford area for most of my life I was somewhat familiar with the Colt building. Having driven past it on the highway hundreds of times I've always admired its famous gold star-studded, big blue onion dome—its crowning jewel, with its gilded rampant colt finial reaching for the sky.

Sitting in my car, on what passed as a parking lot, I could see the Hartford skyline in front of me to the northwest, with the Travelers Insurance tower prominently in the foreground, the morning sun shined brightly against the metal, glass and concrete. I hopped out of the car and looked around at the time worn buildings of Colt. They were all made of brick, most of them four stories high. They looked very old and desolate, except for the blue onion dome that had been restored and was more impressive up close. Most of the windows and doors on the ground level of all the buildings were either boarded up or closed permanently with bricks and mortar, except for the main lobby. I walked over to the door and decided to enter when I saw a security guard sitting on the inside looking back at me.

"Good morning," I said. He gave a nod. I looked at the directory on the wall to the side and it had only three names on it. One was just a person's name and the remaining two were businesses, both having to do with photography. "Is this place all retail now?"

The stern looking guard stayed seated in his metal folding chair, his arms were now crossed over his chest. He said monotonically, "There are some businesses, some residential."

Personable fellow, I thought sarcastically. Just then another guard showed up from around the corner with two coffees and a bag of what I assumed to be doughnuts or bagels. I noticed a glass door with a key card lock, keeping uninvited visitors from using the elevator, so I thought it best not to ask if I could go inside. Instead I asked, "Would it be alright if I walked around the property?"

The second guard, obviously more personable than the first turned with a smile and said, "Sure." Apparently there wasn't much to guard on the outside, but if I hadn't known better, I'd have thought it was some government complex on the inside given that there were two guards posted.

I decided to walk the property even though I had just driven around it, for I wanted to find a good place to travel into the past. It had to be someplace where I wouldn't be noticed. I headed back toward my car but hooked a right and walked into what must have been a courtyard back in its day. Large buildings surrounded the courtyard with just a few smaller ones in the middle. I walked around these toward the main plant. It was 7:00 AM by that time, and I didn't know if the plant would be up and running that early in the morning back in 1910. I also didn't know if people would be milling about or not, so I needed to find a more secluded spot. I headed for the north end, because as I drove by the campus earlier, I noticed an electrical station across the street. Surely there wouldn't be anything there in 1910. I passed through the alleyway between the office and the plant, where I noticed two blocked up doorways leading to the outside, but up on the second stories of each building. I imagined a walkway that connected them over the alley, and then I continued past to the front of the office building.

Above the doors a sign read, "United States Patent Fire Arms Manufacturing Company." It was difficult to read the word "Patent" because it was hidden behind a cutout silhouette of an old style Colt six-shooter. I was becoming excited and nervous at the same time. Ahead of me across the street I saw a sign for the electrical company telling me not to trespass, "Only authorized personnel only," so I headed straight for it.

There were three strands of barbed wire stretched across a dirt driveway. The sign that was suppose to keep people like me out was attached to the middle strand of wire, and I carefully pushed down on it while ducking under the upper. I peered around to be sure no one had seen me enter and then walked back along the path until I thought it was safe enough to go for it. I pulled the watch out from my pants pocket, gave a last look around, opened it, dialed it back nine years from 1919 to 1910, and pushed the left button.

* * *

I walked out of the woods where the electrical station used to be and into a new, or I should say old, world. The weather was the same, maybe the air was a little cleaner, but other than that it was the complete opposite from what I had left. The first thing I noticed was that the highway was gone. The second thing I noticed was that the buildings were intact and beautiful, there weren't any paved roads yet, no broken windows, smoke rose up from two high chimneys, and there were a handful of workers unloading supplies from a steam train.

The locomotive was sitting on the tracks about a hundred yards from me with twenty cars for a tail. The engine stared sternly ahead with its one eye while its supply of steel was being taken away by hand to feed a hungry factory. Food was also being unloaded to feed an equally hungry work force. I walked on down the dirt pathway and into a range of looks from the workers as I passed them. I saw looks of bewilderment and surprise as they whispered and pointed. I hadn't spoken to anyone yet, in fact I had no idea why they reacted that way, but it made me feel uneasy. I picked up my pace and headed to the office building where I quickly hopped up the three steps and in through the front door. An old brass bell rang above my head as I entered.

When I closed the door behind me, the bell rang again, and I smiled at the thought of the advanced red eye laser monitors that let store owners in my day know that someone had just entered their establishment. In front of me was a large wooden bench that stood a foot below my waist height. It was darkened from oil with pits and grooves in its top – a true workman's bench. A short, stoutly man, not much older than me appeared from a doorway just beyond the front counter. He was big bellied, completely bald, cleanly shaven, and wire rim glasses adorned his nose. He stopped short, peered over his glasses and hesitated. With obvious apprehension, he continued toward me, "May I help you?"

"I certainly hope so. I am looking for Albert Traven."

"We haven't anyone here by that name," he said rather smug. "Perhaps you've got the wrong place?"

My heart sank but I pressed on, "No, I'm pretty sure it's Traven, Albert Traven, and I am definitely sure of the place." The salesman straightened his back along with his coat tail and turned to leave the room. "Sir?" I asked before he could get away. Without saying anything or even turning around he just stopped his exit and waited. "Maybe Albert isn't exactly correct, but don't you have any Travens working here?" The penguin of a man just grunted under his breath loud enough for me to hear and then left the room. I was amazed. I would somewhat, although shamefully, expect that kind of service in my day, but I had always thought that being polite to the customer was the most important mainstay to the past working class. I wanted to leave and go find someone else, but I stood my ground and waited. To the left, carved in wood and hanging on the wall, I read, "'There is Nothing that Can't be Made by Machine.' ~ Samuel Colt." I heard footsteps approaching, and someone else walked into the room. Mr. Penguin was right behind her.

"Yes?" she asked annoyed. Clearly older than the penguin or myself, she was short, standing there at the counter at five-foot nothing in height. Her large sagging breasts almost touched the counter. She was doughty looking; her hair up in a bun, with a frilly white blouse buttoned up to her neck, an unshapely black skirt. She had high cheekbones and her face was thin and gauntly. She gave me a suspecting half-crooked smile as if she couldn't be bothered talking to me at all.

My patience grew thin, "Have I done something to offend you people?" I gave a glance to the portly fellow. "I'm just looking for someone and all I'm getting is an attitude."

She was taken aback by my being so forward, and she put her hand delicately up to her chest. "What is your business with Mr. Traven?"

"So he *is* here. May I speak with him please?"

"Wait here *please*."

Her saying "please" was so phony I almost laughed in her face. Instead I watched as she and the man walked back the way they came. On the opposite side of the foyer from the woodcarving I saw a newspaper article. As I approached it I saw it was from the *Hartford Daily Times* dated September 29, 1847. I read the headline: "Hartford's Own Ingenuity." The article below it stated, "Mr. Colt, born of Hartford, has ingeniously invented machinery that turns, and cuts, and drills, to the greatest perfection. All of his work is finished in the best manner, and his invention is of vast importance in war and in defense." The article went on to say a proposed factory was going to be built in the South Meadows of Hartford.

"Hello," a happy baritone voice said from behind me. It seemed to fill the room.

I turned to see a middle aged man with a great toothy smile on his face and a welcoming hand outstretched. He had a head full of dark brown hair, parted to one side (almost to the point of a comb-over but not to that extreme, yet), and he stood upright. It wasn't difficult recognizing him. It was Albert Traven. "Hi," I said with equal enthusiasm, genuinely happy to see him.

We shook hands and I noticed him nod his head slightly to his left and even less to his back. I followed his motion and saw Ms. Grim and Mr. Penguin peering from the safety of the doorjamb behind the counter.

"It's so good to see you again," Traven smiled. "It's been a long time."

I followed his lead, "Yes, yes it has. It's great seeing you too."

He placed an arm around my shoulders and started guiding me behind the counter. The suspicious looking couple moved out of our way, and as we passed them, Traven said, "This is my nephew returning from overseas. He was studying abroad in Japan."

"Ah," they both said in unison, like they had never met anyone whom had traveled to Japan before.

Traven and I headed up some stairs still within earshot of his co-workers, "So how's your mother? Have you seen her yet since your return?"

"Yes I have. She sends her best."

We traversed a couple of corridors in silence until I was motioned to enter an office. The Professor shut the door behind us, and I walked straight over to the windows. From there I could see a wide path in the trees made by the Connecticut River winding its way north to south, and looking down I saw the top of the steam train. It was overwhelming not to see the highway there or any tall buildings across the way – over in what I assumed was still East Hartford. I turned back to see Traven staring at me.

"Who do you think you are showing up here like that?" He exclaimed.

I was immediately confused, "Like what?"

"I had to make up that whole story about you being overseas just to cover for you."

"What's wrong with me?"

Traven glided toward me. His voice boomed, "Look at you. Just how dumb are you? Sneakers haven't been invented yet! And look at your clothes. There's nothing like those anywhere around here and your glasses are much too modern. What were you thinking?"

Before I could respond he continued in a lower voice, "Give me the watch." He held out his hand, palm up, and just stood there in front of me waiting.

I did as he asked because, ultimately, he was the one who gave it to me in the first place.

Grasping the watch tightly in his hand he turned from me and paced the room shaking his fist and the watch in the air. "Who trained you?" he asked the room like I wasn't there. "Who gave this to you?"

"You did."

"I gave this to you?" he asked. I nodded. He calmed himself down to the point of contemplation. "This is unprecedented; the same watch, my watch, co-existing as two separate watches in the same time and space. How could this be? It could only mean that this 'copy' must have been calibrated to your signature before ..." the professor caught off his words. "Why didn't my older self instruct you properly?" he asked me.

I responded with a simple, "You couldn't."

He stopped his pacing and turned, "What?"

"You couldn't because you didn't have the time." I hesitated, "You died."

Traven plumped down hard into a brown leather chair, his face scrunched up in thought.

"You sold it to me before..."

"Whoa, don't say anything more." Traven looked up at me. "It's better if I don't know the details, or the year you're from, but by looking at you, I can guess it's somewhere around 2004 or 5." I was amazed at how he had guessed just from my appearance. He placed the watch into his lap and then his chin onto the tops of his knuckles, both of his elbows rested on the arms of his chair.

I leaned against his oak desk waiting for him to come out of his thoughts again. It wasn't too long before he broke the silence. "I sold it to you?"

I told him everything from meeting him at a flea market to my trying to find him again but not any details of the year or where, per his request, and then of my deciding to visit him in that present time line. I held out the twenty-dollar bill and receipt for him to look at but he seemed disinterested.

Traven stood up and said, "I'll be back shortly. Don't go anywhere or talk to anyone." He held up the watch in front of my face, "I'll hold onto this for now." And he left the room.

As soon as he left I felt bad. I should have known better than to have worn sneakers into the past. They must have looked like big white moccasins. I had on a pair of Old Navy Cargo pants that were black with big pockets on the sides, and now that I was in 1910, they did look totally out of this world. He was right. I wasn't thinking. My shirt was pretty nondescript but it's no wonder everyone had acted funny toward me. I must have looked like an alien to everyone. I was just in such a hurry to speak to the man; I should have researched my outfit more carefully. I had to chuckle when I thought of the stares I received outside and from the reception twins downstairs. I looked down at myself and shook my head. "I won't make this mistake again."

I turned to look out the window. The sun had risen into a bright and clear sky. Men down below were still unloading the boxcars, and a man on a horse rode up to the front of the building. I watched him dismount, tie up his steed, and then disappear beyond my sight into the entrance below. Seeing him, his horse, and the train made me think about how I hadn't seen any automobiles. *When were cars invented? 1904?* I looked closely at the dirt road below and did notice a few wheel ruts that I had not noticed when I was down there. Some were a tad wider than the other wagon wheel ruts, so there must have been at least one auto to visit the factory during the recent past. I turned my attention back to Traven's office which was small and plain looking. In it was a six-drawer desk with nothing on it and its lonely looking companion—a wooden swivel chair. There was a swing back brown leather chair against the wall where the door was, an empty tree stand stood erect in the corner, and a tiny, two-leveled table stood off to my right with some books on it. I walked over to tiny table, squatted down, and ran a finger over some of the binders that laid flat on the top tier. They were Mark Twain's three Tom Sawyer books and his classic masterpiece *The Adventures of Huckleberry Finn*. I was about to pull Huck out from the pile when Albert Traven returned.

He saw me hunkered down in front of his books. "Those are first editions," he stated as he swung the door closed, walked over to his desk, and placed a good-sized package down on it. It was a brown paper bundle secured with string. "I met Samuel Clemens several times at various events here in Hartford, but nothing compares to when he gave me those in person after I received a personal invitation for afternoon tea with him at his house. He used to live right over on Farmington Avenue not too far from here. He was probably the smartest man I have ever met, such wit, and without any proper form of education no less. Can you believe it? The most famous, if not best in my opinion, writer this country has ever had, and he had to quit school as a lad to help support his family." I couldn't tell if he were boasting or just making conversation, but then he just blurted this out, "He just died a few months ago, April 21." There was no indifference at all in Traven's voice. I found it difficult judging the man.

The professor motioned for me to join him at his side next to the desk. "I have these things for you," he said sounding like he did at the flea market.

An idea popped into my head as I stepped up to the desk, shoulder to shoulder with Traven, "Did you influence Mark Twain to write *A Yankee in King Arthur's Court?*"

"I never came out and told him of my travels, but I sometimes suspected that he knew. You must always remember..." Traven looked to me and hesitated, waiting for me to fill in the blank.

"Jim," I answered.

"You must always remember Jim that no one must know about these." He pulled out two watches, his and mine, and placed them on top of the bundle. "If word got around that time travel was possible, the world as we know it would no longer exist."

I asked, "You mean if a whole lot of people just started traveling back in time it would interrupt the natural flow of things?"

"I mean if the wrong lot of people knew about this, the less likely they would be to have respect for it. There would be greed and jealousy over it instead. There is a great amount of responsibility that goes along with owning this watch and we must never forget that." Traven laughed as he looked down at the two watches, "I speak of it as one, but there are now two in front of us, aren't there?" He handed me one, picked up the other and walked around to his chair behind his desk, "Mark Twain, uh, Samuel Clemens, once said, 'Human history in all ages is red with blood, and bitter with hate, and stained with cruelties.' How true he was. If only people listened to him more closely, but he was mostly known as a humorist. He said, 'History may not repeat itself, but it does rhyme a lot.' And so, it is my philosophy to learn about the mistakes in our past in order to prevent the same mistakes in our future." Traven sat down and looked to me.

"Um, that's all very nice," I said, "but I believe this one is yours."

"Good, very good." He stood, we exchanged watches, and he sat back down. The swivel chair made an awful squeal, but Traven didn't seem to hear it or was so used to it that it didn't bother him. "That was a test," he said. "I'm glad to see that you noticed the differences in the pictures. Now getting back to the responsibility issue, take you for an example. Without proper teachings you could have gone and messed up history beyond repair. Imagine if a lot of people traveling did the same thing. Luckily, your first trip was to come and find me. Not many people would have." He fell silent, thinking, staring at his watch.

"So you're saying that history shouldn't be altered?" I asked, but Traven didn't respond. "Professor?"

"Yes? Oh yes, the package is for you. Open it up," he said with the same look of anticipation as when he wanted me to look at the inside of the watch at the flea market.

I was eager to see what the bundle consisted of, so I let my question go. I untied the string, unfolded the brown paper, and saw clothes. It was like receiving underwear for Christmas as a kid from your mom when all you really wanted was the latest toy. On top of the pile was a thin corduroy, long-sleeved, olive colored shirt. I unfolded it and noticed the buttons ran up off center like an old Texan cowboy shirt or chef's coat, and I noticed it had been used.

"They're mine," Traven said about the clothing. "I suspect they will fit you."

Underneath the shirt was a pair of jeans, faded and tattered, and below those was a pair of cowboy boots, also previously worn. Traven swiveled in his chair with another squeak, his back toward me, and let the sun shine hit his face. I felt a little at odds with changing in the guy's office but did so anyway. The button-fly blue jeans ended up being a tad wide in the waist but the length was good and the boots felt comfortable. The shirt was a little short in the sleeves so I just rolled them up, and I didn't button up the front all the way, which left a triangular flap hanging down onto my chest. I asked the professor, "How do I look?"

Albert spun around with and stood up. His chair rolled back to knock against the windowed wall, "Except for your glasses, like you belong here. Do you ever wear contacts?"

"I haven't for quite a while, but I could."

"Good. Do so next time or buy a thin gold colored frame," he ordered and then headed for the door. "Those are second generation Levi jeans you're wearing, which Levi Strauss and a Nevada tailor named Jacob Davis patented in 1873. My apologies for their not having a zipper. Zippers were invented back in 1893, but they won't become popular until the nineteen-twenties, so you'll have to do without." Traven opened his office door, "Pick up your things and come take a walk with me."

The professor patiently waited at the opened door to his office as I bundled up my stuff using the same paper and string that my new apparel came in. I followed him down another corridor, and as I had suspected earlier, to a walkway that connected the office building to the factory. I could hear the faint sounds of manufacturing getting louder as we approached a big green door. The professor slid it open just enough to fit us through.

"This is the third floor of the East Armory that was built by Samuel Colt in 1851 and finally became operational in 1855. As you may know, no name in the history of gun-making can surpass the magical Colt." We passed some workers on lathe machines and drill presses, all hooked to a belt and pulley system on the ceiling. All the machines had a guy working them. The factory was in full production. This time, the workers heeded no particular attention in my direction. Traven narrated as we walked on, "Colt's first patent was issued in 1836 when America only had twenty-five states in its Union and was only in its sixty first year of its independence. The first Colt firm was called the *Patent Arms Manufacturing Company* and was located in New Jersey of all places but ceased operations in 1836 due to a lack of sufficient funding. Luckily for Sam, the demands of the 1846 Mexican War revived the subject of the revolving pistol design, when Capt. Samuel Walker of the Texas Rangers came east to visit with Colt. He swore to Colt that his design made for better combat than the old single shot rifles, so with the Captain's help, Colt designed the 'Walker', the original six-shooter, which was eventually sold to the U.S. Military."

Traven and I reached a flight of stairs, and when we arrived at the top to a closed door, he slid open for me, which revealed some metal stairs that marched up along the inside diameter of a curved wall. "Watch your step," he told me. The sun light beamed down into the stairwell before us. My gaze followed the beams up and up until I saw white columns about fifteen feet above us in a circle supporting a structure I knew could only be the blue onion dome. I headed up first, and as I came upon the circular landing, I could see the east banks of the Connecticut River. I set my bundle down on the circular railing.

Traven stood behind me, "After receiving a thousand orders of the 'Walker' revolvers, Colt turned to Eli Whitney Jr., son of the inventor of the cotton gin. You may recognize the street by the same name, Whitney Ave in New Haven. Anyway, together they designed a way to make mass production models of the 'Walker,' and it became the largest production that Colt ever made. It became an overnight success. In 1851 Colt started buying up parcels of land here, and because they were often flooded, they went cheaply. If you look closely you can see a two-mile long dike down there near the river that Colt built, which by the way, cost him more than the 250 acres that we're on right now. He started a new company, the 'Colt Patent Arms Manufacturing Company.'" Traven walked over to the opposite side of the dome, and I followed him to see the two smokestacks churning out its billows. The courtyard was alive with people. I watched their milling about while Traven pressed on. "By 1856, he was producing over 150 weapons a day, and Colt's success made him a pillar in the community. He favored the use of gold inlay and engraving on his showpieces, and he consistently won prizes at various international trade shows. Many of the showpieces were presented to heads of state like Czars in Russia and the Kings of Denmark and Sweden. He had sales offices here, and in New York City, and London, England too.

"Although Colt died January 10th 1862, the factory ran night and day with more than a 1,000 employees, in an effort to supply the insatiable demands of the Civil War, which Colt only supplied to the Union forces. In the late sixties to the late seventies, muzzle loading weapons transitioned into breechloaders using cartridges. Out of all of Colt's revolvers, none have had such fame as the Single Action Army, a

.45 caliber, with a 7-½" barrel. It had a blue and casehardened finish with oil stained walnut grips. It was the gun that won the west. Government contracts and individual purchases number above thirty-seven thousand, and the redesigned 'Walker' soon developed nicknames like; Peacemaker, Hog-Leg, Equalizer, Thumb Buster, Plow Handle, Frontier, and of course, the Six-shooter. The 'Who's Who' of action oriented individuals of the late nineteenth and early twentieth centuries who used the Walker were Buffalo Bill Cody, Theodore Roosevelt, Wild Bill Hickok, Wyatt Earp, Pat Garrett, Billy the Kid, and the Dalton Boys.

"Following Sam's death, control remained in the hands of his widow, Elizabeth, and her family until 1901, just nine years ago. Today, this place is owned by a group of investors and thus the sign out front, '*United States* Patent Fire Arms Manufacturing Company', instead of Colt, but I'll tell you this … the name Colt will live forever."

I looked at Traven, and he had an air of pride about him as he finished his story. "That was very nice," I said to him. Though I was more pleased at his finishing so we could get back to the matter of the watch, I appeased him anyway, "Thank you for sharing it with me."

"You're welcome." He turned and confided in me, "If you want to know more about the name Colt though, you'll have to travel here yourself, for I'm almost done with this time."

"What do you mean, 'almost done'?"

He gathered his thoughts for a couple of seconds and then answered, "You see, we are still aging right now in the past. When we travel we should only go in short stretches because our loved ones and closest friends back home will see that we've aged if we don't."

I scowled a little at him.

"Let me clarify. If we travel for a year, our bodies age for that year. When we return to the time we had originally left from, we're no longer the same age as when we left, and there are people that will notice the difference. My advice to you is not to travel for more than a couple of months at a clip, because you must be careful that no one notices. Let's say that over any given span you've traveled twenty years worth of time, okay? People may think you're only sixty-five back home, but your body will actually be eighty-five. The more you travel back in time, the less time you'll have at home, understand?"

"Yes sir, I believe I do. So that's why you said 'almost done' because your stay here is at its end."

"That's right," Traven paused. "That's good, you now know our limits as travelers."

"But if there's no one at home to see that you've aged, does it really matter?"

"Everything matters. Haven't you been listening?" he answered without really answering at all. "What else have you learned?"

That was easy, "To research where I'm traveling to so I don't make any faux pas with my accessories like I did today?"

"Very good Jim. I can see you're a fast learner. Do you have any questions for me at this time?"

I didn't need any time to think about it, "I have tons. Like, where did the watch come from?"

"It was given to me in very much the same fashion as I to you. From a friend," he replied, but I got the feeling that there was a whole lot more to it that he wasn't telling me. I let it go in order to get the rest of my questions out to him.

"How far back can we travel?"

"The date window on your watch only allows four digits, so you can go back as far as 9999 BC. It is believed that the user can will himself back even further, but let me point out that if you wish to see the beginnings of our fair Mother Earth, you'll end up in molten rock. Also, you can choose a date at a whim but not the time. The actual hour must remain as it is when you leave."

I must have scowled again.

"Okay, in layman's terms … if it's ten o'clock in the morning when you leave, it will be ten o'clock in the morning when you arrive wherever you go to. It's a limitation of our tool and it prevents us from choosing exact times in history. If you wish to see a certain event, you must arrive a day earlier or plan your timing. Got it?"

"I think so. How do I pay for things in the past?"

"Well, you can do as I do. As you travel, you can acquire items of value like my Mark Twain first editions, bring them back home to sell, and with that money you can buy antique monies from the time period you're interested in. But heed this warning; don't waste your time purchasing land or something equally non-transferable. If you buy land in your name back in time, how could you possibly claim it in the future? The watch is not to be used as a quick get rich scheme, so don't be greedy, understand? Go for untraceable items."

"Can I bring anybody with me when I travel? Can I bring anybody back home with me? Can I let..."

"Slow down, Jim, all in good time. I may not be here much longer, but you can be assured that we'll see each other again. Do you see those white three story houses over there?"

"Yes, they're called Colt Estates in my time."

"Yes they are. That's where most of the plant workers live, and I'm staying at number 28C, the third floor of building 28 off to the right there. If you need to see me again, come and visit me prior to today. Just be prepared to explain everything to me all over again if you decide to do so because I wouldn't have met you yet."

"That leads me to another question. In the future, did you know that you were going to see me for the first time now, so he, excuse me, you, gave me those clues on purpose or because you knew your time was at an end?"

"Sounds like both," Traven answered without a care and then started to walk away.

My insecurity surfaced, "So why me?"

"Jim, you've been given a great opportunity here. Why question it?" I didn't respond, so Traven continued, "I don't know if you were destined to own the watch or if it was an old man's fancy, but one thing is for certain. If the watch didn't think you were worthy, then you would not be able to operate it."

There it was again, him saying that the watch seemed to have a mind of its own. I didn't understand his meaning, and I didn't think I would even if I pressed on. I decided to switch gears to something more important, "Can the future be affected by changing the past? Can I do that? Can *we* do that?" I asked. Traven had been avoiding that question since I first asked it in his office.

"I really need to get back to work," he said, avoiding the question again.

I pressed on, "You asked me if I had any questions, but you're avoiding the biggest one. Why is that Professor?"

"Maybe because I don't have an answer for you. Maybe it's up for you to decide," the professor said somewhat angrily. Then he said the following to me in the teacher voice I had come to know, but it seemed like there was a lot more to it, like he had personal knowledge about the answer. He continued, "Tell me, do you think that if you went and changed history that it wouldn't have some profound effect on something else further down the timeline? Remember what Twain said, history has a way of repeating itself Jim; you can't really change it at all. If you were to remove a catalyst of some major event in the past, don't you think that some other catalyst would surface in its place? Do you think that removing one person, say Hitler, who, although was completely insane; was just a leader that others followed, and that maybe one of those followers wouldn't step up in his place? Maybe that replacement would be worse? Maybe the replacement would have massacred twice as many people instead of the original millions? Maybe the allies would have lost the war if Hitler hadn't been such a crazy militant and power hungry? No Jim, it's best just to leave history alone. Just observe and not partake, understand? But like I said, you'll have to decide that for yourself."

I stood there a moment and watched the Professor trod down the spiral stairs. Was it possible that someone existed before or at the same time as Adolf Hitler, and Traven took that person out only to have Hitler take his place and end up killing the millions that he did? I felt the professor's troubled soul still lingering in the air, so I went after him, forgetting my bundle of clothes on the rail. Traven had reached the door leading to the passageway connected to the office building by the time I caught up with him. "Professor? I don't mean to offend you in any way but it sounds like you have some personal knowledge about," I looked around to see no one in close proximity, "affecting the future?"

"We must learn from our mistakes Jim." Traven turned to face me but left a hand on the doorknob. He looked at me with serious conviction on his face, "Where are your things?"

"Crap," I said. "I left them up in the dome. I'll be right back, and I wish to discuss this more with you."

I sprinted back through the shop to the dome as fast as I could in my new used boots, and when I opened the door to the spiral stairs I saw a large hulk of a man at the top of them crouched over my belongings. He held them in his hands and rummaged through them as he descended toward me. He wore black ankle boots that clanked against the metal stairs, a sign that they might be steel-toed. He also had on jeans and a tight black shirt that showed off his flexing muscles. His face was scruffy with a week old beard and the length of his hair on top of his head not much longer. As he got closer, I could see his hands and forearms were splattered with grease, and he smelled bad.

"Thank you," I said, "for finding my things."

"That's right. I did find them mate. They're mine now," the English machinist said as he reached the bottom of the stairs.

Traven told me to be careful. If this guy sold my sneakers to someone who invented them before they were supposed to be, what would happen? Could my secret be discovered? "I must insist that you give me back my things, sir."

The man stopped in front of me since I was partially blocking the doorway. He stood six inches taller and a foot wider than I did. "Sir?" he said in a gruff. "I ain't your poppa, boy-o." He raised a hand to push me aside, so I raised one of my own. "What are ya', crazy boy-o? I could squash you. Now git outta me way." He went to shove me.

I grabbed his wrist and spun it around to his backside, but I couldn't hold it there. The grease on his arm made it too slippery. I backed up to the bottom of the stairs as he turned to face me. "So you want to 'ave some fun, do ya' mate?" He snickered and dropped my things to the floor.

As he approached, I backed up onto three treads of the stairs. The difference in height now gave me the advantage. I stood my ground until he was close enough then I grabbed hold of both of the metal railings and with both feet I kicked him square in the chest. He was a big lout, and he moved too slowly to block me. The impact of both my legs sent him flying backwards against the brick wall next to the closed door. He hit his head against the wall, crumpled to the stone floor, and grasped for breath as I had knocked the wind out of him. I gained my bearings and was about ready to run for my things that were two feet from his head and in front of the door, but he started to stir before I could get moving. He groaned, reached up to the back of his head, and his hand came away with blood on it as he knelt there with one knee down. I will never forget the look he gave me. It was a wild eyed, crazy, and menacing look. I felt scared. I felt even more scared when I saw that he had produced a gun out of his inside left boot. As he was in the process of standing, I took action and leapt over the left rail to the center of our "arena," lunged for my clothing and sneakers, and threw them at him in an effort to distract him. It worked. I was partially blinded from his view, and when I saw the gun being raised to block the incoming articles, I jumped to his left side and kicked him as hard as I could perpendicularly to his knee. I heard it give way with an awful crack as he dropped the gun and fell onto the floor. And this time his moans were blood curdling loud, like an animal stuck in a steel jaw trap. I quickly went for the gun. It felt heavy in my hand, but I pointed it at my would-be assailant as I gathered my stuff. He didn't move except for the grasping of his knee, which I could see was broken and bending sideways in the wrong direction. With my things tucked under my arm, I placed the gun into the waist of my pants, covered it with my shirt, and opened the door, which I quickly went through and closed again.

Without creating attention to myself, I hurried along as fast as I could down the long corridor of the East Armory and into the office building. I had a little difficulty finding the Professor's office, but when I burst in, it was empty. I closed the door and stood in the silence a moment. My heart raced, and I could feel beads of sweat trickle down my forehead. I wiped away the beads with my old shirt and sat down into the swing back leather chair until my heart reached its normal rhythm again. I must have been there a good ten minutes, but it felt good just to be sitting. My eyes were closed, and I felt relaxed, but my mind was a flurry of images from the attack. I played the scene in my head a couple of times before I opened my eyes to see some items on the Professor's desk. I remembered his desk being void of any objects on it earlier so I got up to take a look.

On the very top was a note…

> Dear Jim,
>
> If you are reading this, then that means you have answered your own question. Since you did not die by a gunshot wound out in the dome, you can affect the future, your own future. Be advised. It is still not a good idea messing with anybody else's outcome. I know. Thus, that is my reason for not being

there to help you, and one of my reasons for leaving. Please accept my apologies.

On a lighter note though, did you know that Thomas Edison developed the "kinetophone" this very year? I'm off to go check it out.

Happy Trails,

A. Traven

PS Use these books as revenue like we discussed.

PPS Use the twenty I gave you to buy some cartridges for your new gun before you leave.

DECISIONS

Was I supposed to die, or wasn't I? "Unbelievable," I said to myself as I sat in my car back in my original time in the makeshift parking lot of the decrepit Colt building. I stared up at the onion dome. *How could Traven know about everything that had just happened to me and not what the outcome should have been? Why did he decide not to help me?* I read the note again.

It sounded to me like he was trying to say that there are multiple possible futures and that we really only have the power to change our own lives. Correction, we (the owners of the watch) have the ability to change the outcome of everyone's future, but we should avoid that if we can and just protect our own interests. *Could that be right?* I questioned myself. It sounded pretty selfish to me. I mean, if the roles had been reversed, and I knew that someone was about to be killed, I would try and stop it. *Wouldn't anybody? Why was the Professor being so vague?* I tossed the note down on the passenger seat along with the two boxes of 100 cartridges, my clothes, sneakers, and the Twain books.

Underneath my shirt, the gun that would have killed me had I not prevented it was digging into my gut. I pulled it out and kept it low so no passers-by might see it. It was a six-shooter like the Professor had told me about. Except this one wasn't a breech-loader. This one had the swing gate at the back of the cylinder for loading and unloading the cartridges, an added design to the original Colt 'Walker' as I had learned only recently. I placed it underneath my pile of clothes, turned the key to start my car, and I went home.

*   *   *

I didn't touch the watch again for nearly two months because immediately following the incident at Colt, I had grown to disliking the idea of possibly dying in the past. I was only thirty-nine, I had a house and animals to care for, and I wanted to live my life in the present. Besides, Traven didn't help matters by exiting when he did. Maybe he was jealous that I was the new owner, or maybe he thought me unworthy. Whatever his reasoning was, I didn't care for it. Or him for that matter.

During the two months after the Colt incident, I basically returned to my mundane life, until my father's 80th birthday when my family converged on the cottage at the lake for an afternoon of gift giving. But the draw of the watch was too strong for me to ignore, and it was there, at the one place I called a constant in my life, that I decided I would travel again.

*　　*　　*

August 22nd, 2004, a Sunday, the day before my dad's actual birthday, was boiling hot and most of the family was in the water staying cool. My youngest nephew dove for fresh water mussel, and his twin sister hung out on the raft with her two older cousins. The adults sat on the lawn, and I was somewhat by myself having always been kind of a misfit in my family. I was the youngest of four, and my closest in age brother is ten years my senior. I never really had anyone while growing up to talk to or to feel close to, except for my best friend Spencer. Sure there's the usual small talk with my two brothers and sister with the annoying question of, "So, are you dating anyone?" It always felt more like prying than caring. So this time, I had brought Keisha with me to keep from being bored, and we swam a couple of times throughout the afternoon. Don't get me wrong, I'm not totally unsociable, for I feel close to some of my family, especially my two oldest nephews, but they weren't there; one had to work and the other was off on his honeymoon, having been married just a week before. So knowing that they weren't going to show I brought the dog to keep me company.

It was just prior to dinner, birthday cake, and the giving of gifts that I took her for a walk up in the woods. I didn't tell anyone where I was going other than I'd be back in time to eat. After a short hike, the dog and I stopped at an old play spot of Spencer's and mine, the place where we had planned on building a tree house, and where I had my first beer. I laughed out loud as I sat down on top of a huge boulder that was accessible from only one side, and Keisha cocked her head at me like she

[36]

was trying to understand the joke. I reminisced about all the good times hanging out there.

*   *   *

Every weekend of every summer growing up I could be found romping around in the woods with my best friend Spencer. Spence, for short. I met him when I was five, he was six, and he's been my best friend ever since.

I don't recall how we met exactly, but our fathers both had cottages on the lake in East Hampton, CT. Spence lived three doors down from me and from day one we became inseparable. There were, of course, differences growing up where we had our times apart. For example: Spence liked to water ski and I did not (it wasn't until years later at the coaxing of a girl I had just met that I even tried it, but that's the way it was with me; women always had a strong say in my actions). If the fair sex showed any kind of interest in me, I would do almost anything to win them over. Is that why I was still alone? I appeared too eager? Anyway, Spence was somewhat upset at me when he found out that I had learned to ski while he wasn't there, but given our history together he didn't stay mad for long.

I can't tell you at what point we started doing skits, or why, but I suppose every youngster plays Army, or Cowboys and Indians, or climbing trees for that matter. But that's what we did, every weekend of every summer growing up—that was our history together as kids. Our own made-up slogan was "Grace under pressure," and we carry it between us to this day.

Our childhood skits became elaborate as we pushed the envelope of our imaginations with amazing detail. Spence or I would read a book during the week apart and bring the whole story line with us for the next weekend. We would then tweak the story to our own desires and since there were only the two of us, we could follow our multiple story lines note for note or swerve away from the plot and make things up as we went along. Mostly, we just made up scenarios to suit our wants and to create a stronger friendship between us. Playing army turned into dramatic scenarios of spies saving the country or the world. King Arthur and Sir Lancelot became choreographed fights using our wooden sticks as swords, and running around became riding on imaginary horses. Ordinary wizards became "Gandolf the

Grey," who fought off ogres and other horrific monsters. We would take turns playing the bad guy or the closest tree would suffice—one good whack and that tree was dead! We always had a hero at the end of each skit too—a lonesome desperado who may or may not have ended up with the damsel in distress. We were kindred souls, weekend heroes, who had honor and charisma. I learned what it was to have pride, respect, and distinction. I learned to associate these traits with Spencer, and I, for lack of better words, respected him for it.

Because it was only the two of us, we took turns being the villain and dying while the other saved the day. We stole lines from Conan the Barbarian, saying, "Today is a good day to die," and any given day you could hear one of us screaming out a Tarzan yell – calling to our imaginary animal friends of the jungle. Actually, swinging on wisteria vines made playing Tarzan that much more fun and exciting. We'd get as high as we could with our swing and then let go only to land on the path and take off running in search of the fair maiden that was in need of rescuing. Discovering these vines and making use of them for play made our roles as Robin Hood and Little John more exciting too.

Not all the vines held us however. I remember one in particular because it broke while I was swinging on it. We found a vine that we could swing from one tree to another, where we would push off with our legs and then land back on the perch where we started. It made for great amusement and it was a good workout too; we would hold on as hard as we could while twisting, turning, and doing crunches in mid-air. The problem was we didn't pay attention to how high we were or to what was below us – a briar patch and I landed in the thick of it when that particular vine eventually gave way. I was lucky not to have gotten seriously hurt but I did receive plenty of prick marks all over me and it was hard getting out of the thorny bushes. I survived and later on it made for a good laugh.

We always laughed. One time, we had a great idea to build a tree house, so I stole a bow saw out of my dad's tool shed. I don't remember why we didn't ask to use it other than we were afraid he'd say no, or he'd want to help. In retrospect, we could have used his help because as we began to build it, I almost cut my thumb off. I started to cut a piece of two by four using my thumb as a guide. Heck, I'd seen my dad do it that way for years but after a few back and forths the blade slipped out of its groove and onto the back of my thumb. Immediately, there was blood everywhere. As Spence and I headed back to the cottage for some much needed medical attention, I stuck my thumb in my mouth thinking I could save some of my lost blood by drinking it down. Spencer told me to put pressure on it, so I stuck it under my armpit. "No," Spencer said, "Direct pressure!" I grabbed hold of it using my right thumb and forefinger, and I squeezed. That's when it really began to throb. I didn't like that at all so back in my mouth it went. It turned out I didn't need stitches or a ride to the hospital, just some hydrogen peroxide and bandages, but at that age, I thought I had lost it for sure. I was bummed that I didn't end up with a cool battle scar, but to this day we still laugh about that one.

No matter what skit or role we were doing, you could find us wearing cutoff jeans, slit on the outside seams up to our belt line making for the most flexibility possible, plus it made us think we were hot shits. Most times it only succeeded in showing our jockey shorts from underneath. That is of course, if we weren't going commando, which we did often. Another attempt at being cool – we cut the bottom halves of our T-shirts off to expose our torsos and removed the sleeves for our arms to show. On the really hot summer days, we would shed them off completely and tuck them into the front of our shorts—we called them loin cloths. We were always bare foot too and it didn't take long for the soles of our feet to become like leather. By the end of each summer, our feet were tough enough to withstand the hottest heat on the road at the top of hill. This road, Bay Road, separated us from where our cottages were and the woods that were our playground.

*   *   *

One particular weekend event has stayed with me all through my life, as important events often do, and it was the most serious event we experienced to that point in our lives. Spence and I were 12 and 11 respectively when we came across a grave up in the woods.

It was a normal summer's day, not a cloud in the sky, hot and humid. After our chores, we started the afternoon with a swim and then headed up into the woods with our staffs, only this time we ventured further than we had ever gone before and came across an area where the underbrush was vacant. There were plenty of tall trees with thick canopies that kept the sun from nourishing any under growth, and the cover kept us cool. We thought it was a great new place to hang out because it was off of the beaten path and away from our normal stomping grounds. There was plenty of room to run, and we didn't have to worry about catching a branch in the eye. We decided it would become our new place for adventures. Little did we know that we would never play there again.

During this sixth summer together, Spence and I tried to get really serious in our acting skills, which was difficult most times because we would always crack up laughing at ourselves at some point or another. One of us would see a silly smirk appear in the corner of the other guy's mouth, and that would be it. We'd laugh so hard until our cheeks were sore and our abdomens strained in pain.

I don't remember now what skit we were playing on that day but it doesn't matter. Whatever it was, after a while of running around we found a pile of rocks planted between two trees. These medium sized rocks were stacked a foot high in a three-foot wide oval and five feet in length semi-covered with leaves and moss. They looked like they had been there quite a while – probably longer than the two trees that grew at either end had been there.

"This is odd," I remarked.

"Looks like a grave," Spence stated.

I replied, "If it is, it's an old one."

Spencer was usually the first to take a conversation to an extreme. He said, "Maybe it's an Indian grave."

I followed suit by saying, "Maybe there are artifacts under there."

We both thought of buck knives and arrowheads. "Let's find out."

Just then I had a terrible feeling wash over me. It started with a quiver up my spine, and then I felt like I was going to throw up. I tried desperately not to let it phase me, and I didn't let Spence know that I was feeling ill either. I was one, excited about our possible find, and two, I didn't want to show any weakness to my best friend.

As we started to remove the rocks, we fooled with each other about finding skeletal remains along with the prizes we wished for, but the joking didn't bother us. If it turned out true it just would have been that much more exciting to us.

"Hey," I said to my fellow gravedigger, ignoring the lump I had in my throat from feeling sick. "What if this is an ancient Indian burial ground and we're disturbing their Spirits?" I was half kidding, half not, due to my feeling ill.

"Yeah, there could be a curse like with the Egyptian tomb raiders." Spencer said, unaffected by any obvious symptoms. We both stopped working to look at each other. That's when we noticed how dark it had gotten.

Because we were so engrossed in our task, we hadn't realized the sky had turned cloudy and stormy. It came on too quick, and before we knew it, it was almost as dark as night in those woods. It was creepy. We had been in the woods after dark before but this was different. There was an eerie yellow color to our surroundings.

I saw a shadow move. "Did you see that?"

"See what?" Spence asked with apprehension though he thought I was only kidding.

"There." This time it was off to my left instead of my right. It was way too fast to be caused from the same thing, animal or person. If something was moving around us, it didn't rustle any leaves on the ground or crack any sticks from its weight. I became scared.

Spencer said, "I saw it, but I have no idea what it is."

"Whatever it is, there's more than one of them."

We both grabbed up our staffs and stood with our backs to each other poised for confrontation. Our hearts raced, our breath quickened, and our feet and eyes shifted from side to side. It seemed to get darker, and the wind picked up, rustling the treetops above us. Another shadow passed in front of me. It seemed to be close and yet far away at the same time, and that's when we heard it. I don't know how to describe it other than it was a laugh. It wasn't a cackle or a snicker. It was low toned and barely audible but it was a laugh just the same. We both heard it. It sounded evil and not human. We decided to get the heck out of there. Spence took the lead, and we were gone as fast as our feet would take us. Just before leaving the clearing we heard the same sound again only louder. It seemed to be right behind us, but neither of us looked back. It was all we could do to make it an all out sprint, running through branches and bushes, until we reached the safety of Bay Road. I don't remember being so frightened about anything else.

As soon as we stepped foot on the pavement; the skies cleared, the wind died, and the sun came out, and I immediately felt physically better. It was freaky. Spencer and I dubbed that area in the woods "The Graveyard," and we made a pact not to ever go near there again. I don't think my best friend ever broke that vow. But I did, twenty-eight years later. I was thirty-nine.

*   *   *

"This is where I grew up Girlie," I said to Keisha. To myself I said, "This is where I grew up the most anyway."

That's when I decided to travel again. I wanted to see the lake and the woods before anyone else had. I longed to visit there before all the cottages came to be or before any paths were made in the woods, but most importantly, there wouldn't be anyone around that could cause me harm, or I to them for that matter. I hadn't any interest in the history of the place. I had no particular reason at all other than my life was simple here when I was younger, and it forced me to imagine how much simpler it would be to visit here before anyone else had. Screw Traven and his researching the past before traveling. If I had had the watch with me then, I would have just traveled right then and there, but I didn't. The watch was back at home because of my recent indifference to it, so I had to wait.

*   *   *

After work the following day, I let Keisha out then went upstairs and pulled down a box from the single shelf in my closet. In it were the clothes that Traven had given me, and I changed into them. There was some trepidation to putting on the clothes that I could have "died" in, but the feeling of anxiety faded after I convinced myself that I was overreacting to a situation that hadn't happened. "Don't be such a baby," I told myself. I fingered the watch that had stayed in the front pocket of the jeans since my return from the Colt building and then I stared at the six-shooter in the bottom of the box. I thought about not bringing it. I mean, I thought I would have no reason for it until my mind turned to the time I found a deer carcass up in the woods, which had been ripped apart by what I assumed at the time, was a pack of

[42]

wild dogs. I then remembered the time Spence and I found bear tracks down by the frog pond toward the back boundary of these same woods. I had planned to go back in the past for only an hour at the most, but I decided to bring it along anyway. *Better safe than sorry*, I thought. Plus, this little trip would be a great chance to target practice, having never shot a gun before. I checked to see that it was loaded, by opening the gate and spinning the cylinder around six times, which it was, and placed the two boxes of bullets in my other pocket. I looked at myself in the full-length mirror, disregarded my glasses, because of the short amount of time I had planned, and thought I was as ready as I ever was going to be for my third trip of time traveling.

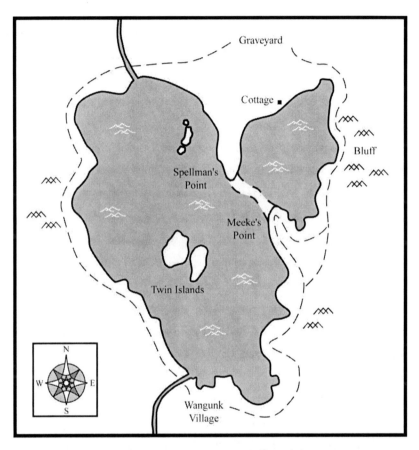

Graveyard

Cottage

Spellman's
Point

Bluff

Meeke's
Point

Twin Islands

N

W   E

S

Wangunk
Village

POCOTOPAUG - DIVIDED POND

DIVIDED POND

Pocotopaug, a Wangunk word meaning "divided pond," was once two lakes divided only by a strip of land prior to the town of East Hampton putting in a dam at the southwest end of the larger lake back in 1920. This strip of land, which was wide enough to hold a single lane road, stretched out to connect what are now known as Spellman's and Meek's Points.

The first large group of settlers immigrated to this area by sea in 1610 from Eastham, Massachusetts along Cape Cod, into Long Island Sound, and then up the Connecticut River to Middle Haddam, a name derived from its two adjacent towns, Middletown and Haddam. Chief Terramuggus saw great profit from selling his lands to various white men and among them was Thomas Wright, originally from Watertown, Massachussettes, a recognized man of high standing from Wethersfield.

James Wright, Thomas' son, received from his father an island on the Connecticut River of thirty-two acres and eventually purchased properties in Wethersfield, Middletown and Portland and became the first settler in Easthampton when he purchased more land on the shores of Lake Pocotopaug from Chief Terramaugus in 1675.

James Wright decided to build a house and barn near the shores of the two lakes on what is now called Spellman's point, and soon after, others followed him. In 1767, the settlers named their growing community Easthampton parish, in honor of their origin, Eastham. And then the name Easthampton, through its long usage, became the divided East Hampton and was incorporated in 1915.

* * *

Subsequently, knowing all this, I decided to travel back to the year 1625, a nice round number, and fifty years prior to James Wright ever setting foot on the banks of Lake Pocotopaug. One lone traveler (me) visiting two acres out of a vast wilderness and coming across another soul would be highly unlikely. So the Monday after his birthday, I drove back down to my Dad's cottage and pulled in under his carport at the top of the hill at 4:30 PM. I didn't walk down the hill to the cottage. I didn't even look to see if my Dad's car was in the driveway down below because an hour was all I thought I would need to explore the past in this area at the lake. I thought for sure that I would be home in time to cook myself dinner and without having to explain why I was down there two days in a row.

I shut off the engine, left the keys in the ignition, and stepped out of my car back into the shadows of the open-aired carport. I laughed at myself when I pulled out the watch and opened it up, for seeing that the time was still accurate reminded me of my wristwatch. I headed back to my car and started to take off my watch when I heard a familiar voice say, "Don't forget to leave your wallet behind too." It was Traven. I ran outside and around the carport to confront him, but he was no where to be found. I quickly believed that I had imagined hearing his voice and didn't pay further attention to it. I threw my wristwatch *and* wallet onto the passenger seat, and backed up again into the shadows. I gave myself a final look over with approval and with the pocket watch in hand I set the date and pushed the button.

"Here we go," I said out loud, my excitement about another journey suddenly rejuvenated.

My car was the first to fade away and disappear and then the carport followed. I looked over my shoulder to see the cottages had all vanished and in turning back, I saw that the paved Bay Road had turned to dirt. Then in a flash, it too was gone. Trees came into existence all around me, but there wasn't any need to avoid them this time before they solidified. When the process was over, I noticed the weather had changed also. The hazy, hot and humid day that I had just came from turned into an overcast, kind of drizzly day. The change reminded me of a quote from Mark Twain (not to start sounding like Traven—it was one I had learned all on my own) that went, "If you don't like the weather in Southern New England, just wait ten minutes," but this was something far more extreme. In fact, this instant changing of the weather would take a lot of getting used to before I eventually took it as second nature.

I walked down the hill through the bramble and brush and came upon the water's edge. I was amazed to see how much smaller the lake was. Everything looked different. From my vantage point I could see that I was well beyond where my Dad's cottage would eventually be and I could also see the strip of land connecting what I knew as the two points, Spellman's and Meek's. Straight across the water and to my left from where I stood there were no beaches (I had swum to both of these as a kid and I never knew they had been man-made). In between the two spots where the beaches would eventually be was a high cliff that rose above the water. The cliff was much higher than I remembered. I guess this was because the water was lower and there were no houses built into its side. There were no houses anywhere within sight and it was quiet. The water made its gentle lapping at the shore, but there were no loud motor boats, no whining ski-doos, no sails, and no one was fishing or swimming. It was peaceful. It was as natural as could be, and I loved it. I felt like the first person to come upon it. The water looked clear and the trees a little more green. It was a relaxing sight and with it came silence. In my time, one would only expect to find that untouched scenery in the far reaches of Alaska, Canada or Maine, and it was wonderful. Down to my left, a place Spence and I called the cove there was a plentitude of cattails standing tall among the rushes. I followed the shoreline with my eyes back to near where I was standing and spotted several largemouth bass breaching the surface.

I wished I had brought my fly rod with me for the scene made me ache to do some casting. Not that I would have made the time to clean and eat the fish, but I made a mental note of it for future reference. The idea of fishing/hunting brought with it the Colt tucked under my waistband. I pulled it out and its walnut finish felt smooth in my grip. I fingered the trigger and using an extended arm looked down the sights across the lake and down into the water. I certainly wasn't going to shoot any fish with the revolver so I turned back toward the land with it until my line of sight came across a lonely mountain laurel branch twelve feet away. I held my breath, aimed as well as I knew how, and squeezed the trigger but nothing happened. I couldn't pull the trigger back. I looked for a safety button or latch but found none and then thought of what Traven had told me about the "Walker." He called it a "thumb buster." I cocked back the hammer using my thumb, and I wasn't sure why they called it a "buster" because it wasn't that difficult. As I did, I noticed the trigger moved back in unison, and when I went to retarget the branch, the gun went off prematurely with a loud bang that echoed back and forth throughout the tree lines that surrounded the lake. I discovered that the .45 caliber Colt had quite a kick to it.

"Hey now," I said surprised. Even though I didn't have any experience with firearms, I decided my gun had what was known as a hair trigger.

"Are you sure you know what you're doing?" Traven said as he stepped out from behind a tree. "You could have killed me. Or yourself for that matter."

Without showing any emotions I asked, "So ... you *were* just up at the carport?"

"Yes."

"What is your problem?" I said frustrated with his antics. "Why aren't you teaching me instead of just telling me what my mistakes are?" Then I remembered the incident in the Colt dome, "Or almost letting me die back in Hartford."

"But you didn't."

"No thanks to you."

"On the contrary. Those clothes I gave you, particularly the boots that allowed you to drop your opponent, saved your life, so therefore, I did help you."

"So therefore," I repeated condescendingly, "You changed history."

Traven's back straightened up. "Of course not," he quickly responded. "You would not have been there to begin with if not for me. *This*, this is your first real test in time travel. If you pass, then I will tell you more, but you must prove yourself."

I wasn't concerned. I was only going to stay a little while longer. I looked down to the gun in my hand next to my thigh, set the hammer to the Walker again, and made sure not to touch the trigger before I was ready. "And if I fail?"

"Then I shall take back the watch and you will never see me again."

I raised my head to get a look at Traven's conviction, to see if it matched his words, but he was gone.

"I'll do just fine. With or without you," I yelled with determination. *What did he mean, "First real test?"* As if almost dying when first we met wasn't test enough!

I aimed the gun roughly where Traven had stood, acquired a target, placed my index finger inside the guard, held my breath, and fired. It was a miss. I tried it again with the same result. Each time the bullet sailed into the woods beyond the one-inch diameter branch and echoes were heard that rumbled around against the hills until they dissipated. I chose a different target—a larger sized elm twenty feet away. With the same previous ritual, I aimed dead center at the trunk and fired.

[49]

This time I hit home, though a bit off to the right, so I tried it again only I aimed a tiny bit to my left to compensate. The shot went exactly where I wanted it to go, so I turned back to the branch in an effort to redeem myself. This time I succeeded in hitting the branch though it didn't break off completely. It just hung down and swayed there, but it was a success regardless, and I was pleased.

"I'll do just fine," I reiterated.

After the six shots, I knew the gun was empty. Located just under the barrel was a spring-loaded arm that kept the cylinder in its place so I pulled it out forward and swung the cylinder to the right to the open position. This method was so much quicker than using the swing gate. Instead of one cartridge at a time, the whole cylinder could be emptied at once. I emptied the spent cartridges into my palm by tilting the gun barrel up toward the sky and placed them into my back pocket. One of them, the last one shot, was a little warm. I reloaded, jerked my wrist with a snap causing the cylinder go back to its closed position, and tucked the gun back into my pants. I felt like Clint Eastwood in one of his Spaghetti Westerns. *Where was Spence to see this?* I felt like I did back in the days of playing skits with Spence; those trees were the enemy, and I was left standing as the hero. I laughed at myself again.

I took another look around at the lake and when I decided that I had had my fill, I headed up the hill, roughly back to where I had come from. I had planned on going home, but for whatever reason I kept walking further into the woods. The continued trek up the hill was slower than it was going down, but once I got past the brambles and wisteria vines it was easier. My jeans started to become soaked through to my skin due to the misty weather combined with low ground cover, but it didn't bother me. I knew my pants would soon dry out once I got up to the top of the hill because the smaller vegetation gave way to the larger and the walking became less of a chore. There were no paths to follow like I was used to in my youth so I just headed straight back and tried to use the familiar landmarks to guide me. The landscape was far from what I remembered because the larger trees that I had grown accustomed to weren't there yet. I had to remind myself that I was close to four hundred years in the past and that the trees hadn't grown to be the familiar ones that I knew as a kid. I had to use my sense of direction and the occasional boulders to guide me.

I wandered around the woods without any real destination, but there it was. The trees were scattered, but they grew tall and sturdy. The canopy was so thick that the area was dark looking and the ground was barren with years and years of fallen leaves, just like the first time I saw it. I don't recall saying to myself, "Let's go check out the 'graveyard'," but that's what I did. I ended up with it right in front of me after twenty-eight years. I stepped over that the clearly visible line, where the under growth stopped completely and separated this area from the normal look and feel of the forest, and I entered the place I had once vowed never to go into again. There was a slight breeze but not the kind to cause a chill, not during the summer months anyhow, but as I entered that area a shiver ran up the length of my back. I felt stupid that a childhood manifestation should frighten me, but it did nonetheless, so I blamed it on the mist.

I walked cautiously on, further into the site, trying not to make any noise as I stepped. I would imagine I did so out of fear of the place and my trepidation for breaking my vow, but as I came to the point where the rocks would be piled up in the future, I saw that nothing was there. I felt foolish and was about to go back when I heard a soft but close clinking sound. I had no idea what it could have been, so I looked around and saw a small patch of red about twenty yards ahead of me in the direction of the noise. It seemed to float in mid air about six feet above the forest floor. I was drawn to it.

As I got closer, the clinking grew louder and I could see other colors floating about. They were white, yellow, and brown, all hand painted geometry symbols on small tanned pieces of animal hide. Below each piece of hide were various types of feathers of different lengths and different colors. Below the feathers were small animal bones hanging down on rawhide like a child's mobile or wind chime, and it was they that made the clinking sound as they were knocked together by the light breeze. I could hear several such wind chimes, their sounds coming from deeper in the woods, and as I peered closer I could see many, many more feathers swaying to and fro. Then I noticed tiny skulls of what I assumed belonged to squirrels, raccoons, and other small woodland creatures. The skulls and feathers and bones were all tied to branches and I stood frozen by the image of it all for their multitude amazed me.

This place really is a graveyard. My heart raced as I just stood there and gaped at the beauty and awe and frightfulness of it.

It was then that I heard another couple of sounds.

Sounds of swiftness and fury.

A "swish" went soaring by just inches from my head and then a "snick" off to my right. I looked to see a shaft of an arrow sticking out of a tree next to me—its feathered end still a quiver. That's what broke my frozen stance. I ran. I ran like I did the day Spencer and I first came upon this area—this graveyard. I ran as fast as I could as I heard hoots and hollers from behind me. I tried heading back the way I came, away from the direction of the first arrow's origin, but it soon became clear that I was surrounded as the sound of blood curdling screams and a flurry of arrows tried to find their target. Some came from the sides and others from in front of me. I hid behind a couple of trees that had grown adjacent to each other and pulled out my gun. I noticed my hand was trembling. I searched around frantically but could not see anyone. If I thought I was scared as a kid being in that place, I was even more terrified at that point. I didn't know what to do, so I cocked back the hammer of the Colt.

I heard a scream from directly in front of me and saw a half-naked Native American emerge out of the woods running toward me at full bore with a spear raised above his head. It was clear to me that he had intentions of doing me in, so I aimed at his legs and fired. I don't know where I hit him, but he went down in a crumpled mass. I cocked back the hammer again and looked around from behind my V-tree coverage. Two arrows flew and lodged into one of the trees, one at the height of my neck, the other at chest level. I spun to face the trees and looked around the other side. I saw a blurred motion off in the short distance, so I fired at it. A couple more arrows came my way. One struck the ground at my feet and the other went sailing by behind me. I turned my back to the tree and tried to think of what else to do, but I had no where to go to. It seemed I was now in a stand off. I raised the gun up with my right hand, level to my face, preparing to take another look and perhaps another shot, when an arrow struck me in the right wrist near the base of my thumb. I dropped the gun out of surprise and from the sudden pain and when I tried to pick it up I found I was pinned to the tree. I couldn't move my arm and I couldn't bend down low enough to reach the gun with my left hand. I looked for the predator that let loose the arrow but could not see anyone off in that direction. I tried to pull the arrow out of the tree and free my wrist but it wouldn't budge. I was about to snap the shaft just short of my flesh and then slide myself off of it when I was hit with another arrow from the same direction. This time it was in my left thigh, and this time I screamed in agony.

Except for my heavy breathing and my heart pounding in my throat and head, everything else fell silent. I grabbed hold of the arrow in my leg with my left hand and gave it a tug, it gave a little, but the pain was too great to continue. I looked from side to side to see where my adversaries were, but I saw nothing. Again I tried reaching for my gun, but it was beyond my grasp. I went back to try and snap off the arrow in my wrist, but an Indian jumped out in front of me with a bow fully stretched back and an arrow pointed right at my throat. Our eyes met and I lowered my free hand.

His eyes were dark brown and full of hatred underneath a tight scowl. His nose was all scrunched up and his mouth snarled at me. His right arm held the bowstring back almost to his right ear, and his left arm extended straight toward me, as well as the pointed stone tip of the arrow. I saw his head was half shaven (the half where the bowstring was pulled back to), and the other side was full of straight black hair maybe three feet long. I would make a terrible carnival man, the one who takes your money for guessing your weight and/or age, but this angry man looked to me to be in his mid to late twenties. He was naked from the waist up, in superb physical form, and he had tattoos that ran down the length of his arms and scattered upon his upper body. The tattoos consisted of the same geometric shapes and arrows that were painted on the squares of hide with the feathers and bones. He wore a breechcloth, leggings and moccasins, and a feather with a black stripe painted on it was tied into the ends of his long black hair. He stood there, legs apart, still aiming his arrow, ready for me to make a move. I made sure that I didn't.

His brethren soon joined him, and they were of similar dress and stature. There were eight of them including the one I had shot who still laid on the ground unmoving. Of those seven that stood before me, one was shorter than the rest and younger too. He slowly approached me with a flint knife in his left hand and with his right he reached up toward my neck. I responded by raising my free hand in protest to being touched and they all reacted. Three bows were stretched tighter then

[53]

they had been, two spears and a ball club were raised a little higher, and the short guy, the one with the knife, jumped back out of my range with a couple of grunts. I tried to relax and eventually (reluctantly) put my arm down. The little one approached me again.

He grabbed hold of the front of my shirt and ripped it open exposing my chest and my left shoulder. The tug at my shirt caused my body to be pulled down some, creating tension on the arrow stuck in my wrist. I winced at the pain but did not try to cover myself back up again. They stared at me and had words among themselves. I did not understand them but it seemed like an argument was brewing. The short one jumped forward and slapped the back of his hand against my chest and yelled words at two of the others. One of the fellows holding a spear did the same. He approached slowly, and with a flash he jumped forward, slapped me on the chest and then jumped back as he yelled something. The one that came upon me first took a step closer; the head of the arrow just inches from my neck, and his eyes were wide and wild. The other, who held a spear in my direction, shouted out some guttural sounds. It seemed to me that they were divided as to how to proceed with their captive. Then the one who spoke last extended his spear's end toward me. I closed my eyes and felt the stone spearhead graze my shoulder and push my shirt down a little bit more on my arm. The spearhead moved away and there was another exchange of words and shouts. I opened my eyes to see they were looking at a tattoo of mine. It was a tiger's head on my upper left arm. Just then, the warrior with the ball club rushed me and struck with it. The ball of the club came down hard on my left shoulder at the base of my neck. I saw stars and then passed out.

*　　*　　*

The first time I had a concussion was in my freshman year in high school during a public swim. I was there with a bud and we had gotten close with the lady who ran things there. I think her name was Elaine. Anyway, she was a softy at heart and had let us boys get away with a lot of horseplay when it wasn't to be allowed. It's because of these shenanigans that I ended up in the hospital. During one particular evening, I was running around the pool, as we had done on numerous occasions, tried to take a corner, but ran into it instead. I slipped and fell headfirst into the corner of the wall and that's when everything went blank. People later told me that I had bounced straight backward from the hit and fell to the floor slamming the back of my head against the tile, but to this day, I have no recollection of it. I do remember being spoken to by an EMT in the ambulance and thinking it would be my first ride in one. I told my friend the combination to my locker so he could get my clothes. Then I woke up in a hospital bed the next day. To this day, that's all I remember. The public swim was soon cancelled after that.

*   *   *

I must have had a similar concussion this time because my memory became spotty after the blow to the base of my neck. I remember being dragged through the woods. Small saplings and brush whipped my face and the top of my head as the ground passed underneath me by only a couple of feet. My armpits were sore from rough handling and my legs scraped against stones and roots. I remember the sounds of paddles in the water and the sky passing by above me. Then there were lots of feet on land. Some wore moccasins but most were bare. I couldn't tell if they all belonged to men or if women and children were there too. I do remember a lot of commotion happening around me. The feet kicked dirt at me. I felt half-naked, dirty, and wet.

I remember darkness and a small fire that blazed. Animals hung above me. I remember drinking a sweet mixture and a soft and nurturing voice telling me to get some rest and to let time heal my wounds.

*   *   *

I woke to the sound of children's laughter and a dog barking. I felt warm and cozy. It took me a moment to realize where I was. For a minute I thought I was home, safe and sound in my own bed, but when I began to finally stir I felt stiff. I felt pain in my wrist, leg, shoulder, and all the memories rushed back.

I sat up with a bolt and my left thigh told me not to do it again. I tried to rub the pain out through some thick black fur, but my leg was terribly sore. That's when I noticed everything was a blur; I didn't have on my glasses, and I couldn't see much

[55]

of anything. After groping around for a bit I found my "eyes" lying behind me down where my head had been. I put them on, thankful that they were still intact, threw back a black bear blanket, and discovered I was as naked as the day I was born. Looking down at my thigh I saw a hole the size of a dime covered with a translucent brown salve. My right wrist had the same on both sides. The salve smelled of a floral ingredient.

"This is another fine mess you've gotten me into," I said to myself, in reference to the Stan Laurel and Oliver Hardy movies of old, though this time I didn't chuckle to myself as I said it. I felt I had really gotten myself into a bind this time. In no way did I think the situation humorous though—it was just a saying I sometimes quoted to ease the tension. I remember thinking how much I just wanted to be home, but instead I found myself sitting on a wooden bed covered with furs, which was surprisingly comfortable due to the multiple layers of them.

"Are you sure you know what you're doing?" is what Traven had said to me. I obviously didn't understand him at that point.

I was alone in a wooden hut that was oval in shape and the bed extended around to three sides of it. At the end of the hut to my right was a little doorway. The opening was covered by another fur and the daylight sneaked in around its sides. On the floor, in the middle, was an ash pit, and straight above that was a two-square-foot opening in the ceiling that let in a shaft of bright light. Also, above my head little furs hung about, including a squirrel that looked fully intact. It wasn't stuffed but it was all there – minus its insides. I saw bundles of corn, eight to ten ears each, shucked and dried, hanging from the ceiling, and next to them, a rudimentary pair of snowshoes. I saw a bunch of slender, and unusually straight, three-foot long sticks, used for arrow shafts I later learned, that were stacked up on a wooden shelf of sorts. All of the items were up and off of the ground, including the wooden bed, which was on legs two feet above the earth.

The hut's structure consisted of a skeleton frame work of saplings that were two-to-four inches at their base, and they were driven into the ground for support. Their tops were bent over and lashed to a companion sapling or branch coming from the other side. These formed a rafter. The middle of the hut had the longest rafters and they tapered down in size as they got closer to the ends of the oval. Along the walls, there were saplings tied horizontally to the verticals every three feet or so and they encircled the whole hut which formed a large latticework. The size of the skeletal frame was approximately ten feet wide by fifteen feet long. It was covered with sheets of bark that had been flattened out and ran lengthwise, not up and down as they grew, but overlapped like shingles. Later, when I stepped outside, there was another framework made in the same fashion as the inner ones that pinched the sheets of bark between them and kept them from shifting.

I looked for my clothes, but I couldn't see them from where I sat, so I laid down on my side and craned my neck to look underneath the bedding. I saw nothing but a couple of wooden pots. I sat back upright and without thinking I used my right hand to push myself up and noticed the pain in my wrist again. The wound itself was sore, but all my fingers worked, and I could bend my wrist quite well. It was just when I put some weight on it that it spoke up. I found standing was a more difficult task, however. I almost fell over with the first attempt but steadied myself enough to move around a bit. I couldn't place much of any weight on my left leg, so I stumbled around and looked for anything that belonged to me. I found nothing—not my jeans, not my shirt or boots, not the gun, and not the watch. I hobbled back to where I had slept, but instead of sitting and having to struggle to get back up again, I grabbed the black bear fur and wrapped it around me. I decided it was time to venture outside and find my things, but first I needed a weapon – something to be used for protection, something to help me fend off another attack.

The hut was void of anything that I could use. I tried pulling off one of the legs of the bed to use as a club, but it was lashed to the other members too tightly and I just didn't have the strength to struggle with it. I gave up, turned toward the door and cinched the black fur tighter around my waist, resolved to go outside anyway.

Using the frame of the doorway to steady myself with my left hand, I dragged my left leg through the opening, past the fur door, and into the bright sunshine. I had to squint and shade my eyes with my right hand. The summer sun felt good on my bare skin as I stood erect and took in my surroundings. There were a few people milling about and there were similar huts all around, some smaller, some larger. There were about eighty in total. I considered the village to be grander than I would have imagined, and it was located on the southwest corner of the larger lake where it had been cleared of trees and brush. I saw a stoutly woman kneeling in front of a hut twenty feet away to my left. She had long black hair tied in a loose pony tail that ran down the length of her back, and she was bare from the waist up, exposing her shoulders to the sun and her breasts to everything else. Her skin was a dark brown, almost a red and bronze mixture, and I suspected her legs were also, but they were covered. I was surprised to see a half-naked woman, but at the same time I found it natural given my new surroundings. She was working on something in front of her on the ground, but I didn't have time to see what it was, for as soon as she saw me looking at her, she picked up everything and went inside her hut in a hurried state. Before she disappeared, I noticed she wore a deer skin skirt with a beaded pattern on it, which extended down half-way down her calf and a beaded necklace which curved down and divided her ample breasts. That was all she wore. Just then three young boys came laughing and running by. They saw me and skidded to a halt. Their laughter died out and after a short while, they ran off probably to warn someone I was up and moving, but no one came.

Noticing how high the sun was in the sky, I assumed it was midday. I also assumed I had been there for one night. My eyes came to rest on the lake beyond the village, and from where I stood, I could tell I was located near where the damn would eventually be built. When I saw the water, a terrible thirst came upon me. It was about two hundred and fifty feet away, and I decided I could make it there, even with my bad leg. I knew I needed to regain my strength before I could search the whole village for my belongings, I knew I needed water and food. My stomach growled with the thought, so I let go of the hut's framework. It was very slow going and very discouraging. After about a hundred feet of stumbling, hobbling, and resting, I finally fell. I heard laughter and snickering as I came up on one elbow and saw the three boys hiding behind a hut, pointing their fingers at me, and having a wonderful time at my expense. I would have laughed with them had I not been in such agony. Then a woman came out of the hut the boys used as a screen and shooed them away. She turned to me and placed her hands on her hips; a universal sign of "Now just what in the world are you trying to do?" I watched as she grabbed a long stick that leaned against the side of her hut and headed in my direction. I tried crawling away from her—fearful of another beating, but then she just stood there next to me and offered a hand to help me up. I hesitated accepting her help because she was just so damned ugly and dirty to boot.

Her face was painted black with what looked like soot or charcoal and her hair was ruggedly cut short, and it was matted in places, wild in others. She looked homely. She was of average build, fully clothed with a shirt and skirt, but they were torn, full of holes, and dirty. Her skin was caked with weeks of dirt, and she stunk to high heaven. I didn't want to touch her at first, but then she smiled at me when my eyes eventually got back to her face. It was an innocent smile, and her eyes showed me her middle-aged kindness. I finally accepted her hand and she helped me to my feet with her other arm around my waist. The urge to hold my nose was very strong, as I could smell urine and feces about her. The force of that smell made me stumble back a few feet, and when she came forward to offer more assistance, I held out my arms in a "no thank you, I've got it from here." She thankfully didn't come closer. We stood a while studying one another until she offered me the stick. It had a little right angle bend to it at its top, and she shoved it under my left armpit. She wanted me to use it as a crutch. I gave her a smile, said thank you, and her smile widened back at me. She motioned that I try using it, and as I did, she made a couple of sounds of approval and started to walk back to her hut. She was done with me. When she looked back I gave her a wave. She waved back. It seemed like I had made a friend, albeit a really smelly one, but I was grateful regardless.

I passed other people, clean ones, as I hitched along toward the lake with my new support, but no one paid much attention to me. I saw three older guys standing around a large flat wooden bowl and smoking tobacco out of individual pipes. In the bowl, I could make out five disk-like pieces that looked like coins only they were white and black not silver or copper, but I wasn't close enough to tell what they really were. Two of the guys to the right of the bowl wore breech clothes and nothing else. The oldest, to the left, wore one as well, but he had an animal skin cape on that covered his backside from his shoulders down almost to his knees. On his right hip, was a squirrel body tucked in and folded over the drawstring, just like the one I saw in the hut. It turned out it was a pouch for holding his tobacco. The one in the middle had short dyed red hair, which stood pointed up to the sky, and he wore a big shell medallion around his neck. He seemed very pleased with himself for he had a big grin on his face. The guy on the farthest right looked kind of familiar, and I thought he had been one within the party that had captured me. If he was, he gave no indication of it. Neither of them even looked in my direction.

I saw a couple of younger women kneeling on the ground grinding up some corn and a boy atop of a hut teasing a dog on the ground who wanted so much to be up there with him. The dog was odd looking to me. Its color was a strange light yellow, and its body shape was a cross between a fox and a wolf. It had short hair like a fox and pointed ears like Keisha's that were a bit too big for its size. I saw a little girl, not more than five years old, totally naked, run by with a doll made out of cornhusks. Off in the distance there was a woman weaving a mat out of bulrushes. She was working about halfway down a four foot long mat, which hung from a rod of sorts between two poles. The top half looked finely woven, and the bottom half just dangled in strands about a foot shy off the ground. I saw yet another woman weaving a basket out of wood splints. Everybody seemed so carefree, so quiet except for the exuberant happiness of the children and the barking dog. It was so peaceful, but I still felt ill at ease.

When I reached the water's edge, I found out why…as I turned back for a moment to take in the grand scale of the village, I saw a man that I hadn't seen before, perhaps a little bit younger than myself, and he stood back ten paces. In one hand he held a spear taller than his body. The pointed stone was high above his head. Tucked into his breechcloth was a ball club. He wore leggings, a breech cloth, moccasins, and his top was bare, exposing black linear tattoos that were similar in style to that of my captures back in the woods, but they were oriented differently, like he didn't belong to this particular tribe. He just stood there watching me and he looked solemn about it. I felt a little leery turning my back to him, but my thirst outweighed my caution. If he had followed me from the hut to the lake and hadn't done anything to me then I felt my chances were good that he would continue to leave me alone.

It was cumbersome getting down to the water for a drink, for it took me a while to figure out how best to get close enough without the ability of squatting or kneeling with a bad leg. I ended up lying down on my belly, perched up on my elbows and scooped the water up with cupped hands. It felt good on my face. It tasted fresh, clean and cold and I splashed my face several times in between mouthfuls. I didn't taste or smell any contaminants (due to the lack of motorboats), so I slurped down as much as my stomach could hold. After filling up I managed to pull myself upright using the crutch and felt a strong urge to urinate. I started to walk west along the edge of Pocotopaug, headed for a line of trees. My man shadow followed along.

Out in the middle of the lake, off to my right, I could see the familiar twin isles. In my day, there were houses out there, and when I was a kid, a Cub Scout camp, but now they looked more beautiful than ever, lush and untouched. I looked back over my shoulder. "Beautiful sights you've got here," I said to my companion. He didn't react, other than to keep my pace as I continued on as quickly as I could.

Just before my bladder burst I reached the line of trees, and with one good leg, I quickly hopped behind one to relieve myself. My shadow kept his distance of ten paces as I spread apart the fur skirt and let the hot liquid exit my body. After everything was extricated with a big sigh of relief on my part, I heard a whispering come from deeper within the woods. I turned to see two young boys, with their backs to me, aiming a small bow and arrow at a target. From their gestures I could tell that the elder boy was instructing the younger on how to shoot. I advanced quietly on their position to see what they were hunting, and as it is with most hunters, my approach was slow, steady and silent, even with my wounded leg they did not hear me coming up behind them. Their target was a squirrel. It was seated on a branch, gnawing on an acorn, apparently unaware of its being preyed upon as the younger boy made ready to fire. The scene reminded me of Spence and I when we were their age, but we always shot at inanimate objects or "bull's eye" targets with our slightly bevel-ended arrows. This was the real thing, granted on a smaller scale, so I sat down and watched with excitement.

The younger boy was ready. There were a few more whisperings from his older friend, and the bow was raised slowly into position. It was then that I noticed, and found it odd, that the end of the arrow was squared off flat. There wasn't any pointed stone head attached. Instead, it was carved a little bit wider and heavier two inches at its end for balance and greater striking. The shaft was let loose and it went sailing by the squirrel—a miss. There was sorrow on the young boy's face as the squirrel scurried closer to the trunk of the tree, but it didn't disappear out of sight. The elder boy exchanged a handful of blunted arrows, sans one, for the bow his friend held, as it was his turn. He had obviously done this before because after notching his arrow he didn't hesitate. He quickly took aim, let the arrow fly, and downed the squirrel without any effort. He looked at his companion with an air of

[61]

confidence, slapped him on the shoulder, and ran off to gather up his prize. He returned with the squirrel dangling down by its tail from his hand and the arrow that had done the deed. With some words and gestures, he exclaimed to his partner that since he didn't make the shot he had to go find the first missing arrow. The younger one ran off to find it and then the elder turned to see me sitting there watching. I smiled at him and gave him a silent applause. He looked at me strangely and then approached. I attributed his lack of being afraid of me to the shadow I had acquired behind me. He held the dead squirrel out in front of my face, and I saw how accurate the shot had been, for the arrow had broken the neck but kept the body intact. Like the other dead squirrels I had seen it was going to be used as a pouch, and it was meant to remain whole. It was a very clever use of the blunted tipped arrow, for it caused no "harm" to the skin of the smaller animal. I smiled again at the boy.

He then held out the bow and the one arrow toward me. "Bushkwa," he said.

"What?" I shrugged my shoulders and held out my hands in confusion.

"Bushkwa," he repeated, again gesturing that I take the bow and arrow. His young friend returned and stood watching us with as much amazement as I did when I first came upon them.

"I'm sorry, I don't understand," I said.

"He want you to shoot," I heard from behind me. It was a woman's voice.

I turned to see the most beautiful woman I had ever seen in my life standing next to my man shadow. She was tall and lean, in her late twenties I imagined, dressed from head to toe in a beaded deerskin shirt, skirt, and moccasins. Her face was soft and symmetrical with big brown eyes and large dark pupils that were accentuated by her long black hair. Her hair was off her right shoulder and tucked behind her ear, but it hung down in the front on her left, extending down to her shapely, slightly exposed waist. Her dark skin was smooth and her eyes inviting. Her hands were cupped together in a stately manner, like a queen, showing a certain patient and demure nature. I was thunder struck.

I stood up quickly and almost toppled over. The elder boy held out his empty hand to steady me. He had placed the squirrel under the tie string of his breechcloth. I smiled again at the boy, gave him my thanks, steadied myself with a hand on his shoulder, and turned back to my new encounter. "Hello," was all I could think of saying.

"Hello," she replied. Her sultry lips were full of vibrancy as she smiled back at me.

I cinched up my fur to be sure it wouldn't fall and approached her, but as I got close my man shadow took a step forward and shoved the spear shaft between us. She waved him off, but he did not leave her side. Her hands returned to being complacently cupped together in front of her hips, and I stood my ground not advancing further. "You speak English," I stated.

"Is that what you are wonnux, an Englishman?" she asked in a business like fashion.

I didn't know what "wonnux" meant or how to respond to her question other than yes. What if her and her people had been in battle with English colonists, and it made me an instant threat? But she had no apparent bad reaction to my answer. She gestured that I walk back toward the village with her.

From behind us, the elder boy yelled out, "Bushka!"

She turned back to him and said, "Ne sewortum. Bahkeder zob." Turning back to me she said, "I told him sorry for taking you away, and maybe you would shoot tomorrow." She started walking again.

"Could you tell him thank you for me?"

"You can say yourself. Say, tahbut ne."

I did my best with it. "Ta-butt nee," I said with a wave of my free hand. The boy waved back and took off running with his friend into the woods.

"Nice kid," I said as I rejoined the fair woman.

"What is your name, Englishman?"

"Jim Sutherland," I replied.

"You have Inchun name. You were born south of land?"

"Um," I hesitated. I knew that my ancestry led back to direct relations with William the Conqueror, but I thought it best not to mention it. "My forefathers lived in a shire in England called South Land. I suppose through the years that our last name was acquired for whatever reason because of that."

"I like that name, south land."

"And your name is?"

"Namoenee. My father is sachem here."

"I don't know what sachem means."

"Pard-on me," she said with complete innocence. "It means he chief of tribe. Terramuggus is sachem too, he first chief, does not live here."

I understood her meaning even though they didn't have a word for "second in command." It turned out that many factions or communities, within the same tribe they had their own sachems, and her father was one of them. "So that means you would be a princess." I stopped walking, turned toward her, and held out my right hand. My shadow stepped forward meaning to intervene again, but one look from her stopped him short. She took my hand very softly, and we shook, "It is a pleasure to meet you, Princess Namoenee." I wouldn't say that it was an obvious ploy on my part at being charming and sophisticate, for that's just not in my nature, but I needed an ally to retrieve my belongings. Plus, it was a true heartfelt moment. I was grateful that someone spoke English, and the added fact that she was elegant, graceful, and a long legged, long haired beauty certainly stirred things up for me. My attempt at winning her over may have had some affect on her too, for I received another warm smile.

"It pleasure from me as well," she said and then we continued our walk.

She didn't have more to say at that point and neither did I because by the time we reached the first hut on the outer boundaries of the village I was getting tired and my hobbling had slowed to a snail's pace. Namoenee didn't seem to mind. She kept her strides slow and even with mine and by the time we got back to "my" hut, my armpit ached from the weight of my body supported on only a stick. My leg was so sore I thought it might fall off. I knew I needed medical attention – modern medicine to be exact. I needed to go home.

"Do you think I could get my belongings returned to me?" I asked.

"I will ask," she said. "You should rest now."

I recognized her voice just then with the word "rest." It was her that took care of me during my concussion, and I was even more grateful to her than I had first realized, so I told her so. She told me I was welcome and reiterated my need for down time before she left me to my own thoughts. I watched her until she was out of my view and before I entered the hut and plopped down onto the comfortable furs to resoundingly fall asleep, I used my remaining strength to walk back to the ugly woman's hut, the one that gave me the crutch.

I knocked awkwardly on the side of her entrance, and when she appeared I shook the stick gently and said, "Ta-butt nee. Thank you."

*   *   *

I awoke to the smell and sound of fish being grilled over an open flame. I opened my eyes to see that Namoenee had started a fire in the ash pit within the bark house and was cooking some freshly caught fish. I noticed it had turned to dusk outside, and the flames from the fire made shadows dance along the inside of the hut. The brightness of the flames and the glow of the coals made her look absolutely ravishing, and again, she took my breath away with her beauty. I laid there and admired her for some time before she noticed I was awake. When she did, she brought the food to me and knelt on the ground beside my bed. I sat up.

"I hope you enjoy," she stated in her quaint broken English.

I could tell that the fish were perch because they weren't filleted but split down the middle, gutted, de-boned, and still had the skins on them. They were delicious. Between bites, I said, "I do indeed enjoy. Thank you very much." It didn't take me long to devour my meal, leaving only the two sets of scaled skins behind. My caretaker switched out the wooden bowl with a wooden cup filled with water. After I gulped it down and handed her back the vessel, I wiped my mouth with my forearm. It felt barbaric in a way but natural in another, and she didn't seem to mind. It definitely felt manly, and except for my injuries, I was beginning to grow comfortable with my new surroundings. I reclined, rested on my elbows and chuckled. Namoenee looked at me slightly puzzled.

"Could you tell me about my escort today?"

"Escort?" she asked.

"The man who followed me around."

"He is to keep you from harm."

I had a feeling it was the other way around, to keep me from harming anyone, but perhaps that's what she meant. "What is his name?" I asked her.

"Gowanus. It means young pine."

"And what does your name mean?"

"She that is curious."

[65]

That raised a bunch of new questions for me to ask, but before I could form the words, Namoenee set aside the bowl and cup and produced from off of the dirt floor yet another item. At first, I thought it was dessert until she started to move back the black bear fur I still wore about my waist and legs with nothing underneath. I grabbed it just in time before she exposed my privates. "What are you doing?" I asked, surprised at her lack of humility.

"Do not worry Jim south land. This will make you better in couple of days." She dipped two fingers into the bronze jar and came away with a string of gooey salve and rubbed it onto my leg wound in a circular motion. Again I could smell its floral ingredients. At first, the ointment was cool to the touch, but as she rubbed it into my skin, it became warm. After an even application, she placed her fingers in her mouth and sucked and licked the salve remnants away. I thought I would lose my mind from the sexiness of it, and yet she had no idea that she was being so seductive. To her it was just a natural way to clean her fingers.

As my manhood came to life, I threw the fur back over my legs and tried to think of something else. I would have felt awkward if she had noticed because we had just met that day. Then I remembered that I had woken up completely naked so maybe she had already seen all of me. Someone had.

I cleared my throat. "You are very kind," I said, and she smiled again. It was time to get to the matter. "Did you ask about my belongings?"

"Yes," she replied. From the dirt floor, out of my sight line, she produced my pants, boots and torn shirt. Still kneeling on the ground, she handed them to me. I didn't see the six-shooter, and I didn't ask about it. I also didn't go rummaging through my pants pockets looking for the watch either. I waited until she left.

Namoenee gathered her cooking utensils and the bowl and cup and stood. "Good night," she said and then turned to leave.

"Namoenee?" I caught her. She stood before the fur doorway with her back to me. "What happened to the man I injured before I was taken?"

She turned to face me, stood there in her stately manner with the fire light shining on her face, and just blurted it out, "He dead." I first got the impression that was all she was going to say, but I had a slack jaw expression of surprise that turned to horror, so she elaborated. "I do not blame you Southland. Yes, you may be cause but not reason. Gertuhmah wanted nothing more than be with his dead wife and daughter, who are with the Great Spirit of the Sky. And, if the Spirit did not want him, he would here have stayed." She looked around the hut and then stepped out beyond the fur door.

Her looking around the hut told me that I was in a hut that belonged to the man I had killed. I needed to get out of there. I threw my tattered shirt and boots to the floor and unfolded my jeans. I quickly reached my hand into the right front pocket. There was nothing. I did the same with the left, nothing again. Even the cartridges were gone. "Great!" I exclaimed in disgust and threw the pair of jeans to the ground next to my other stuff. The terrible thought of not finding the watch gave way to worse news. "How could I have killed another person?" I asked aloud to no one but myself. I was stunned at the idea but ultimately knew it only happened out of self-preservation. *Perhaps the Wangunks realize it too.* I bent down to look under the bed, like I did earlier that day to see if Namoenee had any other hidden items down there, but it was a black hole, void of anything except dirt and the timber frame of the bed.

"How could these people treat me so well?" I asked myself, considering no one had threatened me in any way throughout the day. Except for my shadow, I was left to do as I pleased, and I didn't understand.

I sat there for a long time poking at the fire—lost in thought. This was partly out of guilt and partly from worrying that I'd never get home. However, the crackling of the fire and the constant music from the crickets and the occasional hoot of a distant owl outside (all hidden underneath a blanket of silence) made me sleepy, and I eventually went back to bed. Before falling asleep, I decided that the next day my persistence to regain *all* of my belongings would pay off. I would just have to work on Namoenee some more.

SHE THAT IS CURIOUS

"Weegwasun Gowanus," I would say to my escort each day. After a month of saying good morning to him, I would have thought he would have at least smiled once but never did in the whole time I knew him. That's the way it was with some of the Wangunks and their reaction to me. Some tolerated me and others wouldn't even look at me or remain in my presence. There were some that liked me, especially one in particular, and I had gotten to liking her just as much in return.

Namoenee and I spent all of our days together. We explored all that we could about each other. The Princess was innocent, sexy as hell, and refined. I enjoyed our conversations and moments of silence together. We exchanged everything. I learned a lot of her language, of her, her background, and that of her people. She was born on the banks of the Connecticut River near some early English settlements "twenty-eight summers past." Her mother died giving birth to her and she had no siblings. She learned how to speak English as soon as she was old enough to speak as she was often found hanging around the English village and was often chastised by her father because of it. Her father, Tahadondeh, or Wood's Edge, was annoyed at her lack of respect regarding his wishes to keep her distance from the white man, but she would always return to them. Because of her natural curiosity, before Wood's Edge became a chief to his own tribe, the grand sachem, Terramuggus asked her father to allow her to learn the "wonnux gigetookerwong" or "white man language" and translate for him between the English traders. The English traded goods and tools to the Pequots and others on the shoreline for wampum (white and purple beads made from seashells) that were considered currency and highly sought after by the interior Native Americans. Then the English traded the wampum for furs in the interior lands, but Wood's Edge had had enough when the trading came without proper profit. He sought and received permission from Terramuggus to become sachem of his own village if he could convince others that felt the same to leave with him. By the time Namoeneee was twelve, she had learned English as a second language, and she was taken away by her father with a band of forty followers and ended up at the shores of a divided pond some twenty miles away. Wood's Edge presided there as a new sachem and his only child, Namoenee, with her abilities to speak with the English, had grown to be highly respected in her village. Since the segregation, the village grew because others wished to escape the English trade route, and the community was a hundred and twenty strong at the time of my arrival.

During the first few days of my being there, I think she was just gathering information for the protection of her people. I felt her purpose of keeping me company and extracting all that she could was to make sure I wasn't a threat, but we became friends during the process. After my leg had healed to the point of not having to use the crutch, she taught me how to hoe the garden—bountiful of corn, beans, and squash. She called them the Three Sisters. We stripped cattail leaves, dried them, and then she taught me how to weave them into a floor mats. After I finished my first one I gave it to her as a gift. One day, we went searching for turtle shells and she explained that the larger ones were used for bowls and ladles, and that the smaller ones were used for child rattles or pendants. I found one after a while that was slightly smaller than the palm of my hand, and Namoenee shrieked with glee and gave me a huge hug. Apparently it was the perfect size for a rattle and she had a friend who was about to give birth that I had not met yet.

I also discovered that the woman who gave me the crutch, Dupkwoh, had been in mourning. She was purposely not taking care of her hygiene in order to make herself unattractive to others. She did not want anyone to approach her with any idea of courtship because she was still mourning. If anyone were interested in her, they would have to wait until she got through her feelings of sorrow and was ready to move on. "Her husband die from red spot sickness after trading with the English before you came to us," Namoenee told me. Apparently, soon after I thanked Dupkwoh that first day, she started cleaning again. She let her hair grow and started to wear nice clothes again. I had told Namoenee of my thanking the old woman, and she said that maybe Dupkwoh wanted to "mate" with me. The Princess laughed afterward to let me know she was teasing me—thank goodness for that.

She and I ate most of our meals together. There were a lot of fish available from the lake, but we also ate various meats like deer, raccoon, bear, and fox. There may have been some squirrel, skunk, and bird meat in the mix, but I couldn't tell, and I didn't ask. I hadn't been shown how they hunted; in fact, I was kept away from any object that may have been used as a weapon including the tools they used to make spearheads, arrowheads, bone fishhooks, or anything of that nature. Although I had seen some of the women taking it upon themselves to hunt, my impression was that the men were mostly in charge of that. Some of the men were gone for days at a time but would return with carcasses, and there was always a celebration in the village when they did. I offered my assistance once to a woman who was scraping flesh from a deer hide that was tied to a wooden frame, and the woman placed the serrated deer leg bone behind her back so I couldn't see it and be tempted by it. Namoenee gently led me in another direction. I was allowed to work on a small fishing net one day, but that's as close to any hunting material as I had gotten. I even attempted to shoot the bow and blunted arrow with the boy that offered it to me, his name was Souch'pon, Snow Falling, but was told by Namoenee that I was not allowed to handle the weapon, any weapon in fact, per her father's instructions, so I didn't press the issue.

Namoenee also instructed me that, "Animal trails were first path to be used by Inchuns. Inchuns observe paths carefully because they offered a way to food. Using them found us grassy clearings and Pocotopaug." I translated this information as to why Native Americans were often used as trackers because of their highly tuned abilities in the wild. They used every sign on the trail to their advantage in order to find food and water, or man for that matter.

I acquired knowledge about edible roots and potato-like tubers found on the groundnut vine. We picked berries, hazelnuts, hickory nuts, cucumbers, and sunflower seeds. I also learned how to make succotash with a combination of the Three Sisters. When we went after the cattail leaves for the mat, I learned that cattail stalks can be eaten raw or cooked and that the pollen was highly sought after, but it was past season for that. During our foraging for food, I found out that a lot of what was all around us could be used as medicine like the salve that was used on me, but Namoenee asked me not to pick any of it. That was the job of the powwaw, the medicine man, and there was a ritual involved prior to doing it in order to make the healing powers all that much more potent. I was told that wintergreen leaves reduced fever and pain, and partridge berry leaves eased childbirth and insomnia.

White pine bark was used to make tea that could cure colds, and stomach troubles, and the resin from the same tree, which was used on me, helped heal cuts, burns, toothaches, and sometimes was boiled down to be used as a cough syrup. Once they were picked by the powwaw and his rituals, then they could be prepared by anyone who knew how to dry, ground, pound, or boil them to the right consistency. Namoenee added a caveat, "Of course, medicines only work if Spirits allow."

The Wangunks believed everything had a spirit and that everything should be used to its fullest potential and never wasted. Animals, for instance, were mainly used for their meat and furs, but even their sinew was used to tie things together with great strength. They would use it them when wet, and when they dried, the sinew would shrink and become tight. It's no wonder that I couldn't pull the leg off of my bed.

Animal bones were used to make hooks and sewing needles. Not all of the spearheads and arrowheads were made from stone, but from bones. Not all bones were used as tools or weapons, but some were used as ornaments like the ones in the woods at the graveyard, and I was told that Chief Terramuggus had a bear claw necklace made from each bear that he had killed.

One popular activity included smoking tobacco, which was valued for its social, ritual, healing, and spiritual uses. Socially, it was used as a relaxing activity like the three men I first saw during their game of hubbub. The pipes they used, the "peace pipes," were generally made from steatite or soapstone. They had just finished a game of hubbub, which is a game of chance consisting of five playing pieces, each white on one side and black on the other. The pieces were tossed into a bowl and depending on what colors showed; you made your score for hitting four out of five. Otherwise, you lost your turn to the next guy. And if you hit big by tossing five out of five, everyone playing would chant hub-hub-hub-hub, thus, the game's name.

For healing the terribly sick, tobacco was burned in the person's hut in order to ward off any of the evil spirits that may surround the person.

Ritually, it was used at union ceremonies of couples and the signing of peace treaties. Tobacco was used a lot in prayer, for as the smoke rose up to the heavens, it was believed that it carried the prayers up with it. Eagles were also sacred for the same reason. If you happened to see an eagle in flight while in prayer or just after, it was taken as a sign that your prayer would reach the ears of the Great Spirit in the sky.

Being native to the forest, wood was very important to the Wangunks. They used the wood as rafters in their huts, the bark for outside shingles, dug out canoes – capable of holding from two to eight men at a time, dishes, bowls and utensils. They used wood for almost any tool you could think of. In order to fall certain trees, they gathered up their stone axes and chose a tree that would fall free from entanglement. When a proper one was found, they would build fires to char only what they planned to chip away and they placed rings of clay around the upper portion of the trunk so the fire wouldn't burn the tree any higher than they wanted. Again and again, the charred fragments were chipped away using the dull-edged stone that continually left fresh wood exposed to the fire, and eventually the tree would fall on its own. The tree would be left to dry, and then all the limbs would be burned off in a similar fashion. The log would then be carried or rolled to a particular place and made into whatever was desired. They would use the same stable, yet time consuming, technique to dig out the interior for canoes.

I also learned that there were two kinds of courtship among the Wangunks, the supervised kind and the "in-spite-of-everything" kind. The supervised courtship involved a young woman, after having gone through her maidenhood ceremony, and she would choose her mate and would tell her mother about him. The mother, in turn, would try to become close friends with the boy's mom, and if that turned out well, the first mother would tell the second mother of her daughter's feelings. If both mothers were in agreement, and the boy was in favor, the courtship would then be supervised.

Of course, there was the in-spite-of-everything kind of courtship, where no matter what was done to avoid it, the young couple would fall for each other anyway and it was meant to be. If a young man announced before all the other men, "This is my wife!" then it made the union real to the tribe. Sometimes he would have a lot of convincing to do to the girl's parents and family, or perhaps even to another man who had wished to court the young woman himself. "It must be understood," Namoenee said to me. "Marriages do not happen within own clan. We must marry outside. Bear must not be with Bear but with Wolf or Turtle or some other clan." Thus, when a marriage was approved, a council was convened by the clansmen of

[73]

each tribe and assembled on opposite sides of a fire to give testimony as to why they thought the marriage was a right one. I learned that Namoenee had gone through her maidenhood ceremony, but had yet to choose a mate.

*   *   *

During that first month of my stay, I learned a great deal from the Princess, but she knew little of me. She shared great amounts with me, but with a large amount of guilt, I had to hold back a lot about me, given the circumstance. I got the feeling she realized some of my answers were very cryptic. Although she was curious, she never questioned me further on any answer. Instead, she just soaked it all in. I would have liked telling her more about me, but I thought she just wouldn't have understood. If I told her everything, it would be like explaining that the stars in the night sky were really just balls of flaming gas and not Spirits as she believed.

During my stay, I found that their life style was a pursuit of necessities and personal enlightenment and not much more. Their lives were simple and filled with happiness. There was no hustle and bustle like I was used to back in my time, and I loved it.

I had pretty much given up on finding the watch. I looked for it every chance I got during the first three weeks and had even asked Namoenee about it, but she didn't know what I was talking about. I believed her and accepted it as being lost. Especially after she lead me back to the place where I was "captured," and we retraced my steps as clearly as I could remember, but it was to no avail. I started putting notches on a post in my hut to mark the days I had been there, but I even lost interest in that. I accepted my fate that I was lost in time. Besides, I felt healthier than I had in a long time, and my new friendship with Namoenee slowly stole away my want for going home. I actually began to want to stay with her.

After a time, I couldn't tell you just when, but the sexual tension between us became so thick you could have cut it with a knife. There were times when I just wanted to reach out to her, and I got the same feeling from her, but neither one of us gave in to the temptation because Gowanus was always with me, and subsequently, with us. For instance, it rained for a couple of days, and I didn't see Namoenee very much during that time, but when I did, she and I *and* Gowanus sat in my hut. He sat there and tried to ignore us, but he always had an eye on me. Eventually, either out of boredom or because he decided that I wasn't going to be a problem, he gave us a lot of space when Namoenee and I went for walks or during my lessons. Even when I was by myself, his ten pace cushion turned into a hundred. Then sometimes, he was no where to be seen at all, but I always had the feeling he wasn't gone for long, and my feelings always turned out to be true.

But things change, as they often do.

*   *   *

One morning, I think it was around my thirty-third day, I dressed in my jeans and boots and exited the hut as I did on all the other mornings on my way to having breakfast with Namoenee, and found Gowanus not waiting there to escort me. He normally stood off to the right side of my hut's entrance and looked at me without expression and without a word. At first, I didn't believe it because I had grown so accustomed to him being there, but then I noticed that all the younger males were no where to be seen. The women milled about looking downtrodden. No one was laughing, and the children weren't playing. Even the dogs were quiet. It looked wrong and it felt even worse.

The previous night was full of dance, laughter, and bear costumes. The whole village was there, but only the men danced in full regalia and painted faces. Namoenee and I sat and watched as we had on many nights before. She was especially quiet this night and didn't interpret much of anything for me. The other nights of dance, she explained, were for various reasons: harvest time, a marriage, a birth, etc. All of which were for giving thanks to the Spirits. One dance was a boy to man ceremony where he chose a new adult name for himself, and one was for a death of an elder. I didn't think much of her silence this time around, for she would often fall deep in thought, but that morning I had the notion that this latest dance was for something big.

I ran to Namoenee's hut. I didn't bother to knock or announce myself, but I just threw back her fur door and burst in. Namoenee looked up at me neither startled nor upset at my sudden intrusion, but her eyes were full of tears. "Weegwasun Jim Southland," she said with sadness in her voice and came to me with open arms.

[75]

She fell into me, nestled her head into the crook of my neck and openly wept. I felt tears fall upon my bare chest as I held her tight, and her hair smelled of flower blossoms. I was always uncomfortable around the women in my life when they were upset enough to cry in front of me. This included my mother. I never knew what to say or do to console them, but I usually got by with a joke or two. I learned along the way that I needed to leave a tender moment alone. I didn't have to say anything. I just had to be there for them, to hold them close if they wished to be held, and listen carefully to their troubles. But this time I initiated an overwhelming concern because of my overwhelming closeness to her. "What's wrong?" I asked of the princess.

She quivered in my arms. "My father has chosen war," she replied, and her sobs grew heavier.

I didn't understand how such a peaceful society would even know the meaning of the word war. "War? What kind of war?"

"With the Pequots," she said and then broke away from our embrace and returned to sit on her bed. "The English upset we no longer trade furs with them."

I still didn't understand. The Pequots of my time had gained National recognition and had built Connecticut's first casino a number of years back. The Mohegan's, which were originally part of the Pequot Nation, had built the second gambling hotel not too long after. That's all I knew of the Pequots. "What do the English have to do with the Wangunks being in a war with the Pequots?"

Namoenee was very patient with me, even while very upset she tried to explain, "Over the seasons, English tried to talk with my father to connect trade again, but you know he had enough with them. Talk has broken. So English petition to Pequots who trade them with wampum. Now Pequots mad with Wangunks, and other tribes mad with Tahadondeh. My father sent men out to other villages to make peace." She sat down on her bed with a heavy sigh.

That would explain why none of the men are present, I thought. *But at least it had potential of avoiding what Namoenee knew as "war."*

"That's a good thing," I said.

"No Jim, that not good at all."

I sat down next to Namoenee and tried to grasp the politics of it all. "So the other tribes are afraid the Pequots will make war on the Wangunks and them if your father doesn't start trading again with the English?"

"Yes."

"Would the other tribes join the Pequots to make war on your father in order to prevent that?"

"Yes," Namoenee replied and broke down again once she knew I understood the consequences of her father's actions. I held her tight once more until she regained her composure. "That is, if men come back at all after tonight."

I took it upon myself to put that connection together. I had learned that Gowanus was a slave of the Wangunks. Originally from the Podunk tribe, he was serving time until his penance was resolved and he would be set free (thus his lack of personality to anyone, not just me). Because of this odd tradition, if the men who were sent out in an attempt to overt war ended up being killed, captured, and/or "made into slaves," then there would be no one left to protect the village and there would be no need for war. The other tribes would just come and take over the village without resistance. I understood Namoenee's fears, but the situation made me boil on the inside. I was so used to people's greed and need for instant gratification all my life that I didn't realize how bad it truly was. It wasn't until I was with Namoenee for that month that I could see how better off I was. I grew mad at the "wanting" of the white man. The English just couldn't get enough. They just had to have more and more – first wampum, and then furs and then land all in an effort to satiate themselves. This new life of mine made me realize that Namoenee's father, Wood's Edge, really had the secret to happiness, and it made me want to help her and her father's cause.

"I wish to help you and your people," I stated.

She looked up at me and wiped away some of her tears. "Why?"

Now I could have told her all that I was feeling, but the truth of the matter was that I growing to love her, and I told her so. She knew what love meant. We had had long conversations about it and its meaning. A smile broke out on her face and we embraced once more, but this time when she went to break away, I didn't let her—I kissed her instead.

At first she didn't really kiss back. Perhaps she had never kissed anyone before, let alone a white man, or maybe it was just not done among her people. Maybe it just came as a surprise to her, but I stayed there, firm yet not overbearing and not for too long. When we parted she said, "I love you too." And we went back to kissing.

After a time, the kiss subsided and we sat there in the silence. My thumb caressed the back of her hand. She lost herself in thought a while but soon perked up. "We must see father."

WOOD'S EDGE

Namoenee and I stood in front of her father's hut, which was second largest in the village only to a gathering hut, where ceremonies and meetings were held when the weather was inclement, and it was centered in the middle of the village. Before we entered, she said, "Don't look at me when I translate for father." I tried to ask why, but before I could, she took my hand and led me inside the cool and dark hut. The doorway to the sachem's hut was a foot shy of my height, because it was twice as tall compared to the other huts in the village, and I didn't have to bend myself in half to get in.

"Weegwasun Tahadondeh," Namoenee said to her father. He smiled at the sight of his daughter, but the smile disappeared as soon as I came around into view from behind her. He frowned when he saw she was holding my hand, and his eyes closed to a squint, so she let go of me and approached him. When she knelt before him, his gaze turned from me to her and his smile returned.

After a few words spoken too soft and too fast for me to comprehend, Namoenee got up and moved to kneel beside her father. "Ahupanun Jim Southland. Merdupsh," Wood's Edge said to me gruffly. Namoenee translated without looking in my direction, "Come here Jim Southland. Sit down."

I felt nervous as I approached the sachem and sat in front of him, for he was a man of stature. He was a big man, straight-backed, broad shouldered, stern and starch—he reminded me of Spence's dad. With his long black hair down his back and linear tattoos that covered most of his muscular arms, combined with his size and sureness, he commanded respect. He sat crossed legged, and his leg muscles were bulky and accentuated. He wore only a breechcloth and a choke necklace made of five rows of wampum. A bear's claw hung from the center of it and resided at the cleft of his collarbones like a crest of the moon. Behind him, his ceremonial feathered headdress and beaded cape were draped along the wall, along with his bear-claw necklace. During my stay, I had only seen him in his full regalia during

[79]

the ceremonial dances from across the courtyard, but up close he was fiercer looking than I had imagined. I found it difficult meeting him eye to eye, but I held his gaze until I saw a red glow come from the corner of the hut. I turned to see the medicine man, the powwaw. He sat alone off in a darkened corner and smoked a pipe. He studied some animal bones scattered in front of him on the floor.

Tahadondeh addressed me. "Ge chuntum woti? You want to help us?"

It was odd having two people speak to me at once, but I addressed Wood's Edge directly and did not look at Namoenee as she instructed. "Yes, I do wish to help you and your people."

Tahadondeh's daughter translated my reply.

"We shall see," he said through her. "You must understand that being a tribe member, even an adopted one, requires a certain commitment. There may be times of sacrifice and sorrow that one must endure for the goodness of the tribe. The needs of the tribe outweigh any need of an individual."

As soon as he finished speaking Namoenee stood without hesitation and I saw her motion with a slight of hand for me to do the same. I did and followed her to the doorway.

"Tahbut ne chief Tahadondeh," I said before I stepped out.

I was bewildered. Namoenee and I exited to the daylight, and I asked, "Is that it?"

"You should be pleased Jim Southland. He did not say no."

She obviously knew him better than I did given her optimism. For me, the fact that he didn't say no or yes meant that he still had trepidation about me though I made no cause for alarm during my stay and I treated everyone with respect. I was somewhat put out by his lack of caring, but was excited at the same time that he said I was "part of the tribe." It was confusing, but oh so clear however, that I still did not know the Indian way.

The whole rest of the day I felt tense, as did Namoenee, as did the whole village. There was an impending doom that hung in the air along with an unspoken anticipation for the return of the men. I felt it, but I also was upset that Tahadondeh didn't jump at my offer and say yes right away. The day went by at a slower than normal pace as I stewed over it and Namoenee and I retired early to our separate huts. Neither one of us had a good night's rest.

Wood's Edge's lack of commitment slowly burned in my belly. I remember feeling hatred toward the man though he didn't actually do anything to me directly. No, I take that back. I didn't hate the man. What I mean to say is that it was his lack of respect for me that drove me nuts. The kind of respect I had given to him and his people but did not receive in return was infuriating. I knew I shouldn't have taken it so personally, but I couldn't help it. I was offering my assistance, and I took his "we shall see" as a slap in the face. Namoenee didn't see it that way at all, and I took that as a lack of support on her part. Another slap. It wasn't until I heard an odd noise outside, sometime in the middle of the night that my thoughts turned away from Tahadondeh.

The sounds that I heard weren't like any other that I had grown accustomed to during the late nights. They weren't like the occasional raccoon rummaging about in the darkness looking for leftovers in the compost heap or a deer sneaking into the village field for corn and beans. The sounds I heard were muffled and barely audible. I think now that the only reasons I heard them was one, I was fully awake, and two, I found that my senses had been heightened during my stay without the numbing distractions like television, radio, or annoying signs posted all over everything. Namoenee had taught me to seek out the distinct sounds of nature not by concentrating on one particular item but to take it all in and then differentiate each one. One day we were sitting by the water's edge when she became quiet. I asked her what she was thinking about. "I am not thinking, I am listening," she replied. "Do you hear the humming bird behind us?" At first I did not, but with her instruction, the soft fast flutter of feathers soon became clear out of the plethora of other noises around us. I used the same techniques from that day forward and with them my hearing became exceptional. My sense of smell did as well.

Anyway, the sounds I heard that night were of a struggle. There was trouble in the village. I put out my little fire using dirt from the floor of my hut so as not to cast a shaft of light out into the dark and give warning to the cause of the commotion. I grabbed the crutch that Dupkwoh had given me and ventured out to take a look. The early morning air had a distant chill to it and a different aroma – a first sign to the Wangunks that the summer was starting to wind down. I stayed hunched down close to the ground in the shadows cast by the crescent moon as I looked off in the direction of the disturbance.

As my eyes adjusted to the dimness of the moonlight and the lack of colors, I finally saw a figure standing outside of Namoenee's hut. It was a fat man and he took a swig from a bottle as he stood there impatiently. He waved with his free arm and then two other figures appeared from out of her bark house. Another man, a tall thinner one, was carrying a woman within his arms and she was struggling to get away. Namoenee was being taken against her will. Without thinking, I went into action.

I ran barefooted between the shadows of the huts, and I circled wide around the outside of the village until I faced the way that the kidnappers were leaving. They were so concerned about being noticed and followed *from* the village that they didn't pay attention to what lay in wait in front of them just past the clearing at the wood's edge. As I hid down in the underbrush next to the path, I let the tall thin guy go past me. He still had Namoenee, who I could finally see was gagged and bound. Her screams were muffled by a piece of cloth in her mouth. As soon as he passed, I leapt out and swung the crutch with all my might into the small of his back. He and Namoenee collapsed onto the path. I let my momentum carry me and quickly jumped to the other side of the path before the kidnapper's partner could notice me. I hunkered down again until the fat guy rushed up to see what had happened to his cohort, and as he passed, I used the elbow of the crutch to hook his right foot. I swung in behind him and pulled hard with the stick. His weight did most of the work for me as he tumbled to the ground. First came the sound of his bottle smashing underneath him, and then the air came out of his lungs with a big forced "Uumph!" The smell of cheap whiskey permeated the night air. They were all down and I needed to act fast during their confusion, but I was left with a problem. The two men were still between Namoenee and me.

I hopped onto the large guy, used him like a springboard, and bounced over the skinny guy to land next to Namoenee. I quickly untied the rope at her ankles but didn't have the luxury of time to undo her hands or mouth. I picked her up and pushed her away just as the gangly guy grabbed me from behind in a bear hug. If it had been the larger guy, this may not have worked, but because it was the thin guy, I threw an elbow into his ribs and his grip loosened slightly. I spun in his arms to face him and gave him a head butt that thankfully dazed him more than it did me. He let his hold on me go and I bent down for the make-shift crutch. When I rose, I thrust the elbow end into the man's gut doubling him over and then swung the bottom end up and into his face. He went down hard. By then, the robust man was standing again, and as he tried to regain his bearings, I ran toward him, jumped, and landed both feet to his chest. He went flying and then rolled backward out into the clearing of the village. I stood and noticed my left thigh, where I had taken the arrow hit, had begun to throb, but I didn't let that stop me. I walked quickly over to the rotund fellow. He was sweating and breathing heavy. His eyes were closed. He wasn't getting up. I walked back to the first guy. He still lay there, too. I looked for Namoenee and found her standing pretty much where I had left her. I laughed under my breath as I approached her, for I realized her headstrong upbringing didn't allow her to run away from danger. Even though I had pushed her away from the situation, she had stood her ground in the same stately manner as when I first met her. The only difference this time was her hands were behind her and bound. I untied her, helped her remove the gag and we walked backed to the first guy. He was unconscious. I dragged him back to the clearing and plopped his limp body down next to his friend. Due to the disrupting noise, some of the elder men had gathered to witness the end of the scene. We all stood there and didn't say anything. A couple of them nodded their heads to me with approval, and Namoenee came to my side, handed me the stick I used as a weapon, and placed her right hand into my sweaty left. Our fingers entwined. Our upper arms touched as well, skin on skin, and I smiled. She reached across her slender body and cradled my arm with her left hand. I then noticed how fast my heartbeat was, and I chuckled again at the thought that my adrenaline was caused more from her than from the fight. It felt exciting to have her next to me. It felt great that I had protected and saved her. I think she felt it too.

We looked down on the two invaders, one thin and one fat. Both were white. Both were similarly dressed, unshaven, and dirty. They were colonists, and they were probably there word had spread that Wood's Edge had sent his best out in an attempt to negotiate peace and these two drunken fortune seekers were looking for easy cash by taking Namoenee for ransom to be paid either by her father or by the Pequots. Whatever their reason, I never found out.

Four of the elders came and picked the two men up. The thin guy was easier to carry. His boots dragged on the ground as they carried him away by the armpits. But the robust guy was still awake and he didn't want to be taken away. He fought with the two elders who tried to hold on to him, and just before some others could come to their aid, the fat man pulled a hunting knife from a sheath hidden underneath his big billowy shirt.

"Hey," I yelled out to the elders as I let go of Namoenee's endearing embrace. I rushed the fat guy with the crutch raised high above my head and screamed as I saw the blade slice through the air just missing the chest of one of the elders. "Nooooo!" I screamed. The Wangunks made space between themselves and the colonist as I came down on him in a ballistic frenzy. I first knocked the knife out of his hand by bringing the stick down on his wrist and he cried out in pain. I dropped down to my hands and swung a leg at the same time. I used his weight to my advantage once again and swept kicked him to knock his legs out from underneath him. He went down with a thud that shook the ground. I thought that would have been the end of it, but he was tougher than I realized. The first time I put him down he was just faking his fatigue. This time he wasn't going to stop for anything. He rolled over on his stomach and grabbed for the knife. I leapt on his back in an effort to get it before he could but I was too late. I placed both hands on the hairy arm that had the knife, which was clearly a mistake on my part. Having the leverage of a free hand, he used it to roll himself over and crush me with his weight. I could hardly breathe. I let go of his arm and tried punching my way out of a bad situation, but I couldn't connect with anything crucial enough to make him move. I eventually had to give up my struggle and wait for a helping hand from someone, but I wasn't altogether sure that it would come. I thought that his weight on me would probably be the end for me, but at the last moment, he decided to get up off of me, so he could see me face to face. This was no doubt part of his drunkenness and white ego.

He raised his upper body with a heavy hand on my throat, and the one with the knife in it was raised high above his head, poised and ready to be plunged into me. The tip of the blade, raised in the air as it was, seemed to touch the cusp of the moon. It looked like a child's first attempt at writing a number nine, and that image will be forever etched in my mind.

His eyes focused. "You're white," he said surprised.

I didn't respond. I thought that the image of the knife meeting up with the tip of the moon would be the last thing that my eyes would ever see again when suddenly he straightened up on his knees in shock and pain. The weight of him on me was suddenly gone. I looked to his face and his eyes bulged. The hand that had been around my throat went searching for something on his backside. He dropped the knife and started to list forward. When he started to fall onto me again, I gathered whatever strength I had left and pushed him off to the side. I then saw, in his back, standing straight and true above his heart was the shaft of a spear. The spear's head was buried deep within him.

Relieved, an answer to his statement came to mind, "Not as white as you, Casper."

I looked in the direction that the spear had come from to see Wood's Edge standing majestically fifty feet away after his throw.

*   *   *

Several hours later, when I woke up rather late in the morning after having been totally exhausted from the confrontation and had passed out as soon as my head hit the furs, I found my muscles stiff and achy. I put on my glasses, eased myself out of bed, and did some light stretching. I felt hungry, but I also felt like a new man. It was a brand new day of a brand new life, and I felt great about it. I exited the hut to go see Namoenee so we could have breakfast together, but instead I found Souch'pon, Snow Falling, sitting on the ground waiting for me. A big smile appeared on his face as he saw me, so I smiled back at him. He stood and grabbed my arm. He was intent on taking me somewhere. He took me straight to Wood's Edge's hut and motioned that it was okay for me to enter alone.

Wood's Edge sat on his bed, which was full of furs, and he sharpened a knife with a stone. I recognized the knife; it was from the dead white man. As soon as he saw that it was me who had entered he stood with a huge toothy grin. "Ah Jim Southland, seguish," he waved me in with enthusiasm. "Seguish, wigwomun."

He still had the knife in his hand, so I approached cautiously. I guess my eyes stayed on the knife longer than even I had thought because when he saw my apprehension he laughed and tossed it down where he had been sitting. "Nooger tianer?" he asked and placed his hand on my shoulder with a heavy slap. His large hand enveloped me and made me feel small.

I recognized his question; he was asking me how I was. I replied, "Borwesa, Tahadondeh. Pretty well, Wood's Edge."

"Ah, wegun, wegun. Good, good," he said, the smile still on his face. "Merdupsh," he stated. He wanted me to sit down on the bed, but he didn't ask. He more or less told me to. Maybe it was just his tough exterior, but with the big smile on his face, I accepted his invite/order in good faith.

After we both sat, he turned his back to me and picked up the knife. When it came back into view, I saw that it was sheathed, and he handed it to me saying the Wangunk's word for it, "Bunnedwong." He stood and grabbed a squirrel pouch down from a wall support that was filled with tobacco. He handed it to me, "Neitsissimou." Then he walked across the hut and quickly returned with a stone pipe, "Tummoung." He stood before me for a moment.

I finally responded and thanked him, "Tahbut ne, Tahadondeh."

"Tahbut ne, Jim Southland," Wood's Edge said. He pointed to some reed mats on the floor next to the fire pit with burning embers still glowing within it. He went and sat on one of them. It was the same one he sat on the day before when I was in his hut when Namoenee told him I wanted to help. Apparently his answer was now a yes. I mean, would he have given me a knife if that weren't the case? I sat down cross-legged on the mat as before, across from him, our knees almost touching. He produced his own pouch and pipe and began to fill it. He then grunted "bercud," for me to do the same, and with a couple of small burnt ends of sticks, we lit up and smoked a quiet smoke together. Neither one of us talked.

After several tokes I felt lightheaded and dry mouthed and I needed a drink, "Ne-goongertoon," I said. "I am thirsty." He chuckled and handed me an elk bladder full of water. When we finished our pipes and I half of the bladder, he clapped his hands sharply three times. A gung-shquaws, a young girl of maybe thirteen, came into the hut carrying a wooden platter. She set it down, scurried out, and then an elder came in and sat with us on the ground. On the tray, I saw a small container half-filled with black murky fluid, another container twice the size of the first filled with salve, a bone needle, and a small wooden mallet.

I looked up to Wood's Edge, and he was looking directly at me. He smiled and pointed to my left shoulder. I shrugged, because I didn't know his meaning. He leaned over and slapped at my tattoo, practically knocking me over when he did, then sat back and slapped at his own upper arm, "Ger-tee." Then he leaned over again, slapped my tattoo again, and then shook his head "no." He reached back behind him, and he pulled a bear's skin off of his concubine's bed. "Ger-tee you."

The Wangunks word for "this" was "you." "You do this," is what he was saying. He wanted me to give him a tattoo of a bear on his left upper arm like the tiger head that I had. Sure, I went to an art college and I could certainly draw a bear's head, but I had never given anyone a tattoo before. I became very nervous at the concept. *I don't know how to do that and tattoos are permanent. What if I mess up?*

The elder got up and pulled me over to the tray. He sat down next to me and picked up the utensils. The bone needle wasn't quite like the others I saw the women around the village use for sewing. This one was diagonally cut to a point like the sewing needles, but it was hollow in its middle. I found out this was a reservoir for the ink as the elder dipped it into the bowl of liquid. It was kind of like a quill pen. The elder held up the needle and mimed drawing with it on the skin. *Well, I could do that.* I took hold of the needle and brought it up to Wood's Edge's skin. He already had some tattoos starting on his shoulder that ran down the length of his arm. I looked Tahadondeh straight in the face and slapped his arm as he did me. He looked surprised that I would be bold enough for such an action, but then he just smiled. I paid no attention to his reaction, but instead I waved my free hand suggesting "no," and then touched his left breast above his nipple, above his heart. I then pounded my own chest and grunted to show strength. He liked the idea. He grunted and then laughed a big barrel laugh. He then pounded his own chest where I had touched him, growled like a bear and shook his head "yes." I settled in next to him and started drawing a large bear's head on his chest.

It took me two hours to do it because I didn't want to screw it up. I went very lightly at first until I got used to drawing with the needle on skin, but in the end it came out pretty well. I drew the bear with its mouth open, snarling, and pointing to Wood's Edge's left. Its tongue was showing, its teeth bared, and its eyes were mean looking. It showed strength just like Tahadondeh wanted. "It is done," I said, and returned the needle and container of ink to the tray.

[87]

The elder brought over a polished brass bowl with a flat bottom that served as a mirror for Tahadondeh to look at the tattoo in its reflection. "Done," he said very pleased. He nodded heavy and then just sat there. The elder just sat there too. We all just sat there. I looked at the chief and he showed no signs of awkwardness. I looked at the elder and he mimed hitting the needle with the wooden mallet. I shook my head at the elder and indicated that I did not want to do the next part. The elder resigned himself to doing the rest of it. He had obviously done this sort of thing before, and I was glad he took over.

The elder held up the needle full of ink, along with the mallet, and started at the bottom of my drawing. He started tapping the end of the needle, which was blunt and blood immediately came to the surface at the sharp end. The same thing happened when I got my tattoo, but with the preparation drawing in my day, the artist could wipe away the blood to see what he was doing and continue. The elder couldn't do any wiping for it would have smeared my drawing. That's why he started at the bottom and worked his way up. It didn't take long before the chief's blood was running down to his abdomen and stained his breechcloth. I stayed and watched the "tattoo artist," and after quite a long time he had gone over all of my drawing with his tap-tap-tapping—wood to bone, bone to taught skin. He placed the needle and mallet down and wiped the excess ink and blood away with a damp deer skin cloth. The bear's head tattoo came out great. I was impressed at how accurate the elder had followed my art. All the lines were there and there were no gaps in the solid areas. He even embellished in some spots. I wouldn't have been able to do that for sure. The old man then gently smeared the salve over the whole thing, extending an inch or so beyond the actual area of the tattoo to help fight off infections. He said nothing. He didn't smile at his job well done and didn't look at me at all, he just packed up the equipment and exited the hut. I suspected he was very tired after he spent hours doing it. Heck, even I was tired after that entire day of sitting around. Plus, I was famished. I figured I was done, so I decided to leave. Tahadondeh just sat there, and if he was in any pain, he didn't show it.

I got up to leave but first made sure it was okay with the chief, "Ne-getahwe?"

He replied, "Gertub." He wanted me to stay a moment longer. He got up from the mat and went to a large woven basket at the opposite side of the hut, down where

I had seen the powwaw sitting the other day. Out of the basket he produced my gun, the two boxes of cartridges, and gave them all to me. "Tahbut ne."

"You are welcome chief Tahadondeh," I said as I shifted over the items to hold them all in my left hand. The pouch he had given me was already cinched to my belt loop, the knife attached to my belt, and the pipe was in my pants pocket. I extended my right hand in an offer to shake. Wood's Edge came closer, his face discerningly not so stern anymore, at least to me after that day it wasn't, and he took my forearm in his grasp. I grasped his forearm as well. It was an Indian handshake and I had earned his friendship by saving his only daughter.

HONEY

During the day I had stayed in Tahadondeh's hut, most of the warriors had returned, but no one in the village spoke to them or they to anyone about their outcome at the offsite negotiations. As soon as I left the chief, I met up with Namoenee who was uncontrollably excited to see me. She knew that I was with her father all day and wanted to know what had happened. She could see all the gifts I received and instantly knew it had gone well, though she didn't care much for the butt of my revolver that stuck out at my waist. I told her how my day was spent and then inquired about the lack of news. She said that the scarcity of talking about it was the norm – it was their way. In order to avoid rumors being spread about the village, they would all wait until the rest of the men returned, or until it was perceived that all that were going to return had done so before giving their accounts. When the time came to hear the news, she told me, Tahadondeh would call a village meeting of the adult males, which could be as early as the following night.

While we ate dinner of sooktash and peormug (succotash and fish), we heard the news that Tahadondeh had called for a strike pole dance as soon as it grew dark. Out of all the ceremonies, I liked the strike pole dance the best. I loved to hear the stories and the humor incorporated within them. I thought it a little odd that he would call for one just then since not all the men were back, but Namoenee suggested that her father was probably trying to keep his village from worrying too much. He wanted to keep the mood light, because if there were to be a war there would be plenty of time for sorrow later. I also wondered if her father just wanted to show off his new tattoo.

After dinner, I tried to rinse the dishes like I had done every other night, but Namoenee wouldn't hear of it this time. "For the man I love, there is plenty time for you to do things like this later. Sit back and enjoy."

So I did just that. I sat back and relished in her beauty. I loved watching her subtle yet deliberate moves. I liked the way she tucked her hair behind her delicate ear whenever she had a task at hand, or the way her midriff showed whenever she bent over or stretched. Or the way she kept her knees together and her back straight as an arrow as she knelt on the ground or the way she smiled whenever she saw me. Her sense of humor was unequalled to any of my past girlfriends, and just holding hands with her brightened my day. All of these attributes drove me insane, but what did the most for me were her soft and wet lips on mine.

She was all that I could have hoped for, and although we had not spoken about it, I was hopeful that she would be mine. I got the feeling she knew I was hers.

After cleaning she laid down beside me on her bed, and we kissed a while until we heard people gathering outside getting ready for the dance. We decided it best to join them as much as it tore at us to be around others at that moment.

We approached the clearing in the center of the village, near Tahadondeh's hut, and the children ran up to me like I was a celebrity. Then they practically dragged Namoenee and me to the familiar circle of people. When we sat down in the front row with the kids all around us, I got the feeling most of the adult Wangunks were looking differently at me; like I had finally proved myself worthy of their company. I say most because there were still a few who did not look in my direction. One couple seemed indifferent and some stragglers still looked put upon that I was there though they had never interacted with me, which was fine. I was happy to be there, so I let it roll off of me like water on a duck's back. The Wangunks who seemed to actually like my presence, now more than before, had no problem showing it. I believe Namoenee noticed it too, for the restrictions of her public displays of affection toward me became very relaxed. Before the previous night, we never held hands outside of our huts, or kissed for that matter, and even then it was only because Gowanus was no longer chaperoning.

I looked around for him, Gowanus, Little Pine, and it didn't take long to spot him. He sat somewhat alone, still a victim of circumstance, still a "captured slave." I was pleased to see him for I had grown accustomed to his blank expression, which he still wore. I looked for some of the other men who had returned. There was Big Kettle, his wife, and their two boys who sat with us. Warrior's Cry was one of the guys who had captured me and he was there. He was the one that held the bow and arrow to my throat back at the graveyard. His cronies from that day were there as well: Beating Drum, Eagle Wing, Lost One, Dark Night and He Sings. Fire Maker and He Stands had returned along with others whom I had not personally met yet. At a quick glance, I had thought that ten out of the seventy men had not yet come back from their appointed mission.

"Is there a problem, Jim Southland?" Namoenee interrupted the train of thought I was having. I must have seemed solemn at that moment.

"Not a problem yet dear heart. I was just giving prayer for the return of the rest of the men," I answered.

"Tahbut ne, James," her head tilted to rest on my shoulder. Some of the children giggled at the sight.

I picked up the closest girl to me, Plump Cheeks, and brought her in close to tickle her. She playfully screamed and wiggled herself away from my teasing but soon came back into my reach, so I grabbed her and tickled her some more. She laughed and squealed. Namoenee joined in with a few tickles of her own until her father stepped through the crowd and out into the middle of the human circle. She tapped my arm lightly to tell me. I stopped playing with Plump Cheeks and placed her on my knee. I gave her a little "sshhh" with a finger to my lips and then pointed to Tahadondeh. She quieted down almost immediately. Tahadondeh must have been like a grandfather to all the children because they all settled down at his arrival. Grandfathers can have that affect on kids.

Tahadondeh was in full regalia with his beaded deer skin pants and moccasins, feathered headdress, clawed necklace, and cape. The cape was tied too tight for a summer's evening, covering up the bear tattoo and I was disappointed, at first. In his hands he carried a ceremonial spear, with one eagle and one turkey feather lashed to it, which he struck a pole on the south side of the gathering with and all grew quiet. There were four poles in total, all on the quadrants of the circle that pointed to each of the Spirit Winds: North, South, East and West. Tahadondeh raised his spear up in the air as he started, and Namoenee translated for me as she always did, "Welcome back to my brethren who have been gone. It is good to see you all again." The men in the crowd who had been gone mimed their respect back to their chief.

"First, a bit of business. I wish to offer Gowanus his freedom for his services over the past twelve moons." I hadn't been told that Gowanus had been there for a year and a month. The difference between twelve moons and thirteen months is that the Wangunks didn't count the "missing" New Moon as anything. Anyway, I was taken aback by the news. I couldn't imagine that he had been put in service "willingly" for a whole year. They stuck to a code that I had yet to fully understand.

Gowanus stood at the good news and slapped a fist to his abdomen. He said, "Thank you, oh great Wood's Edge. Now that I am free, I wish to say that it has been a pleasure serving you. And now that I have proved my worth to this great bear tribe, I wish to announce my intent..." Namoenee stopped translating as Gowanus finished his sentence.

She looked upset.

"Namoenee? What's going on?" I asked.

She swallowed hard, "Gowanus wishes me to be his."

"What?" I almost yelled. My heart dropped.

Tahadondeh looked to his daughter and could see the disappointment in her eyes, but he wasn't chieftain for his lack of political skills. He immediately said, "Well, Gowanus, let me tell you and everyone my tale, and if your intent is still true, then I will meet with your father, Gray Cloud."

My heart dropped again.

Gowanus sat back down. He produced a smile on his face for the first time since I met him. I couldn't believe I actually had started to feel happy for his freedom.

Tahadondeh had enough to deal with, and I could tell from everyone's reaction that they all thought it a bad idea for Namoenee and Gowanus to be together. I didn't know the complications of it, but I hoped Wood's Edge knew what he was doing.

He regained his composure, if he had lost it at all, and began his story. Tahadondeh started out looking directly at Gowanus, "For those of you who had been gone, and for those who were here, there has been some recent excitement, so for you all I will tell you a tale," Tahadondeh spun around for all to see him. Everyone clapped. He walked circles around the fire as he began. His massive shadow followed his trail, and fell over the crowd like a sundial over its Roman numerals. "We had quite a surprise here last night, for Namoenee, my daughter, was almost taken from us." The crowd responded with a gasp, especially some of the younger children who had not heard a word about it. Tahadondeh recited his side of the story and the crowd followed each word with anticipation. Toward the end of his tale, he mentioned my name a bunch of times and mimicked how I almost drowned underneath the fat wonnux. We all laughed at his recreation of the fight. Then he finished by throwing his ceremonial spear across the circle, through the flames of the roaring fire, right into one of the four strike poles, near where Gowanus sat, to show how he took care of the white menace. He had balls, I'll give him that much. If he had missed by just a smidgen of a degree then one of his brethren surely would have been hurt or killed.

He was an awesome storyteller, for he held everyone in a trance from after he began until he stood, just as he did the night before, majestically from his powerful and deadly accurate throw of the spear. Everyone except Gowanus broke out in cheer.

When the crowd finally settled down, Tahadondeh continued, "Now you will hear my daughter." Again, he wasn't asking but telling nicely, and no one disagreed. I found out no one wanted to, for she was as good as her father at telling stories.

Namoenee squeezed my hand quickly before standing and stepped out in front of the mass. Her father sat down in his place among his people and pride emanated from him as he watched his daughter. Namoenee started to fill in the gaps as only she could, and she captivated me. I didn't catch everything she was saying, for I had not learned their language well enough due to its complexity and my translator was the one speaking, but I was able to get the meaning of her words through her mimed reenactment. The crowd's reaction to her story was exactly the same as mine. They weren't full of cheer or laughter as she spoke to us, for as I did, they could hear the fright in her voice and were caught up in the moment. We could all feel her fear until she finished with her father's great triumph. She walked over to me with an open hand and drew me out to join her, so I did.

"Tell them your side, I will translate for you," she said to me.

I was embarrassed. "I couldn't possibly," I said as I tried to go back to my seat.

Namoenee tugged at me twice until our eyes met. She gave me a look of genuine concern and replied, "You have to. For them. For us."

I understood her meaning, it was a way for me to unite myself with the tribe, but I started with difficulty. "I heard a noise," I said as I stood there, and Namoenee spoke my words in her language. "I heard a muffled noise," I tried to embellish. The crowd quickly grew bored. I could see it in their faces. I thought of how the chief and his daughter presented their stories with animation and decided I had best do the same to keep the attention of the audience. I crouched down to the ground, picked up a hand full of dirt and threw it into the fire. Then I mimed my way out of an imaginary hut door. The crowd livened up. I ran around the fire in circles demonstrating my quickness in cutting off the kidnappers, and then showed the tribe how I dealt with them. I even took Tahadondeh's humorist approach at my near suffocation. Everyone laughed again, perhaps harder this time since I actually laid on the ground like a big bug stuck on its back. My arms and legs flailed about. "And then when I thought it was all over for me, I was saved by a great man, your chief, Wood's Edge."

Tahadondeh stood in his grandness and the tribe went nuts. He came out and joined us in the circle as everyone cheered, clapped, hooted and hollered. Again, the tribe took a while to settle down, but Tahadondeh didn't try to stop them. He waited for them to do it on their own. When they did he said to them, "We did not understand why this man came to us but now we do. If it were not for him, who knows what would have happened to my daughter. To him I am grateful, he is a great warrior." The mass joined in with his opinion as they hooted and hollered in agreement. "He has offered his hand in helping us in the future should it be necessary and I have agreed to let him. In return, Jim Southland gave me this," Tahadondeh said as he threw off his cape exposing the bear tattoo. He then walked around the edge of the circle for all to see. There were "ooos and ahs" all around. The younger men pounded their chests in excitement. The women clapped with glee. After completing the circle, the chief returned to stand between Namoenee and me. He wrapped his arms around both of our shoulders.

"For all these reasons and more," he looked at Namoenee, "it is my wish that Jim Southland," he looked down at me, "and my daughter be together." I tensed as the crowd suddenly got silent. "But I will leave it up to you, my brethren. Would you rather see my daughter with Gowanus or with the man she loves?"

The tribe stood in unison. Even the ones who doubted my presence joined in. It was a moment of truth, and I found myself holding my breath.

Like the parting of the Red Sea, the whole tribe separated themselves from Gowanus and came to the other side of the fire to stand by the three of us. Gowanus soon stood by himself with all eyes on him. His gaze was harsh across the flames.

"It is decided," the chief stated. "Gowanus, you are a strong man like your father and your people. But I think even you can see how better this union will be for all involved. What say you?" That was twice in one night that I heard Tahadondeh actually ask a question. I felt his sincerity as he stood there next to me, his arm still across my shoulders.

Gowanus's expression of hatred and surprise grew solemn once more. He answered, "It is with deep regret that I give up my claim to be with your daughter. I do understand the decision made here tonight. And with that, I ask your permission to leave in the morning to return to the Podunks, to my family."

"You may," Tahadondeh said.

With another slap to his abdomen, Gowanus left the light of the fire and disappeared into the darkness never to be heard from again, at least not by me. At least not alive.

*   *   *

The strike pole dance continued well into the night while others told stories and jokes, but Namoenee and I didn't stay for the whole thing. She pinched my arm playfully and motioned with her head, "Let's get out of here," so we departed through the half-asleep children and the rest of the captivated audience.

No one paid us much attention, but I did look back at the sachem, the chief. He was watching his daughter and me, and he smiled when he saw me look, nodded his head and then turned back to the storyteller at hand.

As we walked away from the tribe, we held hands not just as friends any more, but as a couple. It may sound funny, but that's how it felt. "I am happy," I told the princess as we reached the outer limits of the fire's light.

"I am happy as well," she said. We ended up at my hut when she finally spoke again, "Why don't you make a fire and I'll be right back?"

"Don't be long."

We kissed and hugged, and she came away with a big smile on her face. She teased me, "Well, then you better learn to make quicker fire." My fire making skill was still sometimes lacking, but I was getting better. Before I could retort, she took off running in the direction of her hut. I laughed and went inside to prepare the fire.

A random thought passed through my mind as I gathered some twigs and dried moss from a basket I kept under my bed. *I wish I had a lighter.*

It didn't take me too long to get the embers glowing this time. It was probably my second fastest time, but Namoenee still hadn't returned yet. I added some larger sticks, tee-pee style, to the kindled blaze and then two logs after that. It was an ample fire, one that would surely please my woman, but she still had not come back. I didn't worry, but I did grow antsy. Just when I was about to step out of my hut she appeared in my doorway.

"Did you miss me?" she asked with her drop dead smile and beaming eyes.

She was beautiful standing there. "Very much so," I replied. I could tell she had changed clothes, washed her face and hands, and combed her hair, but I had no idea whatever else it was that took her so long. One thing has never changed: women like to take forever to get ready for their men.

We fell into each other's embrace and stayed standing there for a long time holding each other and kissing. I started to kiss her with an open mouth for the first time, and when I stuck my tongue out she pulled away slightly and giggled.

"What's so funny?" I asked, acting perturbed.

"I never done that and it tickle," she said, still giggling.

"Would you like me to not do it?"

"I didn't say that."

We stood there kissing until a snap and a pop from the fire made us aware of our surroundings, and we turned just our heads to see if anything had come out of the fire pit. It was always a concern when living in a wooden hut. After confirming that all was still okay, Namoenee pushed me toward the bed and my knees buckled at the edge of the wooden platform. I sat down with a surprise, but did not fight it.

The princess looked at me with sultry eyes as she backed up a few steps and reached behind her for the tie strings of her deer skin top. With one pull she let the shirt fall to the floor and her beautiful, supple breasts were exposed to me. I was entranced. She came forward and knelt before me. I touched the small of her back and pulled her in close. Her skin felt warm and soft next to mine. Our lips touched with anticipation. Our breathing became heavier. I stood up, brought her up with me, and untied her skirt that was wrapped around her. At the same time, she shifted her weight from foot to foot taking off her moccasins. She stood before me completely naked, and I scooped her legs up with my right arm as I supported her back with my left, spun her around, and then placed her on my bed. She let go of me, and I stood above her admiring her golden brown body as she slowly slithered on the comfort of the different colored furs and waited for me with high anticipation. A big smile was on her face. *Do I smell honey?*

I unbuckled my belt, undid my button fly and stripped off my jeans. My excitement was evident and my feelings for Namoenee were unparalleled to any woman that had come before her. I laid down next to her and our bodies molded together. I planted kisses all over her lips, neck, and shoulders as my right hand roamed over the curves of her body. The smell of honey grew stronger.

Namoenee began to moan. I tongued her belly button and she laughed. Her stomach quivered against my scruffy face. I moved to continue, but she stopped me and pulled me back up to her.

"Let us not waste the honey," she whispered in my ear.

I whispered in return, "Why do I smell it on you?"

She chuckled, "It's not on me, it's in me."

"Why would you put honey in you?"

"It will help prevent my having your baby," she said and pulled me on top of her.

Her legs wrapped around me. Her hands went up and down my back. Oh, how she felt under me. I rose up on my hands and knees and started to lean into her. Her hands slid down to my waist and her hips adjusted to the angle of my approach. After some slight guidance from her, she pulled at my hips, and I entered her.

Our bodies became one and it drove me crazy. Our breathing became very heavy and the rest of the world disappeared. A few moans escaped her lips into our otherwise quiet surroundings, but as we got heated Namoenee forgot her English, "Nye, nye, nye!" "Yes, yes, yes!" Suddenly her body tensed and I knew she had reached her climax. Her nails dug into my back, which was a fine line between pleasure and pain, and her body shook with enjoyment. I held her tight and let her settle into her orgasm.

We were sweaty and our faces glistened by the light of the fire. After she came out of her state of bliss and back to me, we kissed hard. I moved my hips around a bit to see if she was ready to continue and she didn't complain, so I rose up on my hands and knees.

Again, I started off slow and tried to make it last, but the pace soon quickened. Our bodies looked good together. My body convulsed, and soon I collapsed onto her, and we laid there with her legs wrapped around me. We held each other tight. At one point, I thought she had stopped breathing, but I soon realized that our breath had become as one, and I just couldn't hear or feel her doing it. It didn't take long until our breathing returned to normal.

The smell of honey returned and filled the air.

I suggested that I spoon her, but she didn't know what that meant. I explained that if we lay with my front to her back that it would be like two wooden spoons lying together. She liked the analogy and the position. I kissed the back of her neck and shoulder. I held on to her with my left arm and hand and stroked her with my right. I felt every curve of her that I could reach. The curve of her waist fit into the shape of my hand perfectly, and I unknowingly concentrated my touch to that spot with an occasional grab of her pelvic bone that jutted upward as she lay on her side.

As if on cue, the strike pole dance concluded and the tribe called out its cheers. The timing did not go unnoticed by us and we laughed, amused at the thought that her kin were celebrating our lovemaking.

A fur covered only our lower halves, and we "pillow talked" a while and watched the glow of the coals. As we rested, the lingering smell of honey mixed with the unmistakable aroma of sex and all of it rose up with the smoke from the remainder of the fire to exit through the hole in the roof.

We both fell contentedly asleep.

TRIBAL COUNCIL

The next morning I felt completely rested, fresh, and invigorated. If there were such a thing as being king for a day, that is how I felt. Until later anyway.

I woke with a smile on my face as I felt Namoenee's warm smooth body next to mine. I was on my back. She on her stomach with her arm draped across my chest, and I turned to face her. Her hair was all over the place like she had been in a recent windstorm, but she never looked more beautiful. I brushed back a bit of her black strands so I could see her face better and she was absolutely gorgeous. That moment could have lasted forever if I had my way, but as soon as I started to stir a little, I felt the urge to urinate. Grudgingly, I gently moved her arm, gave her a small peck on the cheek as I got up, threw on my pants, and met the cool morning air with a renewed vigor.

As I stood at the edge of the village circle and took care of nature's call, Eagle Wing joined me a few feet away. He exhaled a big sigh of relief as he released his bladder with much more intensity than I had done. I chuckled and he laughed back. Between my knowing how he felt, and the fact of how manly it felt to pee out of doors, we enjoyed our moment.

Eagle Wing turned to me and said, "Ne sookeddung wegun."

"I urinate good," is what he was telling me, but I had learned enough from Namoenee's translations to know that what he was really saying was, "It is good to urinate."

"Nye," I agreed. I finished first and left him.

Halfway back to my hut and the woman I loved, Eagle Wing caught up to me and touched my arm. When I first met him, it was at the graveyard, and he was the one who smashed the ball club onto the base of my neck and shoulder while wild anger showed in his eyes. As we looked upon each other this time, I saw nothing in his eyes but kindness and admiration.

He smiled and said, "Ge beush peormug chaw? You come to fish?"

He wanted me to go fishing with him and that was the final piece of the puzzle that I had been looking for, male camaraderie. I wanted to tell the princess that I had finally received an offer that I couldn't pass up, so I said, "Nye, tahbut ne," and with an upward index finger, I tried to tell him I'd be right back. Quickly, I ran the rest of the way back to my hut and found my love still lying there in all her naked splendor. She opened her eyes, smiled at me, and I was immediately torn. As much as I wanted to climb back in bed with Namoenee, I did not want to pass up on Eagle Wing's invitation. I sat on the edge on the bed and told her about the offer.

She could tell I was excited about it, "I am happy for you James. Go and catch me a big one." I gave her a huge kiss on the lips and headed out to meet up with Eagle Wing. In that instant, a small twang of guilt rose up within me as I reached the door. It was a feeling I hadn't felt in seven years.

*   *   *

I was married once for a short time; it was my favorite mistake.

It's a long and sordid story, and I won't bore you with the details, except to say that she and I divorced after three years. We had terrific times together when it came to doing fun things during our courtship, but when it came time to agree on the serious stuff we ultimately weren't on the same page. She wanted to stay home if we started a family, and I didn't make enough of a salary to support a family alone, but she thought it important that a parent stay at home like her Mom did. We talked about my staying home as a Mr. Mom, but I couldn't agree to that because it would have been too much of a role reversal for me. I give a lot of credit to the fathers who do it, but I knew it wasn't for me. We were stuck on all the other important items too; both of us were too stubborn to give an inch, so we ended it. I have since heard a quote and it has stayed with me because of her, "Betrayal in war is childlike compared to betrayal in love."

*   *   *

I felt guilty when I left Namoenee to go hang out with another guy, but this feeling didn't last long. It soon changed to a feeling of comfort, which showed me again how much I cared for Namoenee. And she for me, because Namoenee actually wanted me to go. It was refreshing.

Eagle Wing stood outside to greet me, and we headed off to his hut where he gathered up two fishing poles, a deep-dish wooden bowl, and a garden hoe for digging up worms. He handed me the bowl and hoe, and we walked over to the compost heap where I dug up eight healthy sized night crawlers and a half dozen regular sized earthworms. I placed them along with some dirt into the bowl and we walked off toward the row of canoes parked along the shoreline. There were twenty dugouts that lay upside down, bark side up. It looked more like a lumberyard than a docking port. They were all different lengths too. A couple of them could hold as many as ten paddlers, but we chose a smaller one that the two of us could easily maneuver. We tossed in a couple of paddles and dragged it to the water. I was about to ask myself which end was the front, but when Eagle Wing got in and faced the length of the canoe, it was apparent that he wanted to steer, so I got into the front, and we paddled out.

The water was as calm and smooth as glass, and there were patches of mist drifting across it. The morning sun hadn't yet risen above Baker Hill to the East to heat up the morning air. Eagle Wing steered us toward the twin isles. I didn't care where we went because it was fun to be out on the water again. Back when I was a kid, Spencer and I would canoe our way around the lake without any real destination, and if we wanted to fish, we would take the motor boat and just try different spots where we felt like we might get lucky. I missed Spence. At that moment, I had wished that he were there with me. I'm sure he would have loved it.

"Yeowdi," Eagle Wing said.

I stopped paddling for he wanted to try a spot just short of the shores of the twin isles. "Here," he said again and passed me one of the poles. My pole consisted of a pliable stick with a thin line of Indian hemp tied to one end. A fishhook made out of bird bone was tied to the opposite end. The Wangunks used bird bones, either a wing or leg, because they were thin but strong. I examined my hook more carefully as Eagle Wing baited his, and I noticed there wasn't any barb on its business end. *How could anyone catch fish with this?* I laughed out loud and pulled out my hunting knife. Eagle Wing watched intently as I quickly carved a barb on the inside of the hook, and then I traded my pole for his. He looked at me strangely, so I explained through mime and the few words I had learned that because of the barb, any fish that we happened upon might have a harder time falling off. He quickly grasped the concept with enthusiasm.

As I fixed the second hook, I thought of Professor Traven and how he told me not to change history. I didn't think because I carved barbs on two bone hooks that it would do anything except to lessen some of the "huge one that got away" stories. I mean, maybe it could have increased the Wangunk's food supply but by how much, a tenth of a percent? Besides, it was already too late so I shrugged it off.

I baited the newly revised second hook with half a night crawler and tossed it into the water ten feet away from the shore. When the line became slack, I rolled the line around the pole to pull up the worm about a foot off of the lake bottom. Eagle Wing's first "cast" was to place the bait into the water next to the boat as he faced away from shore, and then he lowered it hand over hand, and didn't use the pole at all. Instead, he placed the pole under his foot at the bottom of the canoe as a security. We both smiled at each other then turned back to our lines as the wait began.

My mind was at peace as I took in the beautiful scenery. The dark green patchwork of the surrounding forests, the sun slowly coming to life just out sight beyond the hills, the placid lake water around us, the gentle rock of the canoe, and some Canadian geese honked their way by overhead. I sat there smiling and thinking, *It doesn't get any better than this.*

Eagle Wing kept his hands steady, and I jiggled the end of my pole every once in a while until I felt a nibble. My companion watched on because he knew I was close to landing one. Then it came. It was a strong hit, so I snapped my pole back in an effort to land the fish, and it worked. I raised the pole high to the sky, grabbed hold of the line, and brought the fish up by hand. The fish was a strong too. Because the wet hemp was hard to hold onto at times it slipped within my grasp. I then understood why Eagle Wing had placed his pole under his foot.

When the fish came to the surface, I could see it was a large mouth bass of good size just as Namoenee had asked for. I didn't want him to break the surface with a jump because I was afraid to lose him, so I let some line back out and waited a bit for him to tire. I eventually got the fish into the canoe and took the hook out of its lower lip. When it started to flop around the bottom of the dugout, Eagle Wing took his paddle and smashed it down on the fish's head. I found the treatment a little harsh, but without anything to keep it from thrashing out of the canoe, the fish had to be further subdued. Plus, the "keepers" were going to die anyway, so I learned that the smashing of heads was a more compassionate way of dealing with a unique problem.

So it was that the first fish that I caught was the biggest of the day at around four pounds, but it was not the last. Eagle Wing and I caught two dozen fish total (mostly perch and a small mouth bass, none of which fell off the revised hooks), and we threw back six because they were too small and not worth cleaning. It was better to let them grow up to be caught some other day, Eagle Wing told me. We tried four different locations on the larger of the two lakes, and three of them proved prosperous.

By the time our worms were gone, the sun had rose to almost noon and was hot on our skin. We beached the canoe between the twin isles and took a naked swim in the warm water canal that was at most fifty feet wide. It was easy for Eagle Wing to put his breechcloth back on while still being wet, but my jeans were a different story. They clung to my wet skin and I soon gave up with frustration. Plus, it was too hot to wear long jeans anyway, so I decided to make them cutoffs while Eagle Wing made us a small fire to cook lunch on. If I thought I had been quick with my last fire making task, he put me to shame, for he had a blaze going without any coals to start it with by the time I cut off the legs of my jeans. I was thoroughly impressed with his ability. Namoenee was right. I still needed to become quicker at building fires.

We skewered a couple of the smaller fish on sticks and we cooked them like hot dogs or marshmallows over the fire. I sat there on a log with Eagle Wing, and my new shorts started to rise up on my stark white legs. I remembered how Spence and I used to do it as kids, so I split the seams on the outsides and felt much better for it. We ate the rest of our fresh fish lunch in comfort and in silence and enjoyed the peaceful serenity of the calm water and surrounding woods of the isles. When we finished eating, Eagle Wing and I buried the remains at our feet and tossed our sticks backward in unison. We both laughed at the coincidence of the timing.

It's funny how men can bond without having to talk to one another. Eagle Wing and I had a great time together and it brought us close. And then, to top off the bonding, I passed gas quite loudly and lengthy against the log we sat on. Eagle

Wing practically fell to the ground in hysterics. It was definitely a man's day, no doubt about it.

*   *   *

During the long way back to the village, because we circled around the outer boundary of the larger lake, Eagle Wing sang praises to the Great Spirit Hobomoko for our bounty. Although the Wangunks had many spirits that they prayed to, Hobomoko was thought to be their greatest most omnipotent and easily angered one. I had asked Namoenee about Hobomoko once and wondered why they feared him so much, but all she could remember were the stories passed down through the generations. She couldn't recall one incidence during her lifetime that would be cause for such fear. Of course, I couldn't tell her I didn't believe the fears about spirits and ghosts.

It was late in the afternoon by the time my new friend and I parked the canoe and divided up the fish roughly by the pound. He tried giving me more than my share because my revision of the hooks allowed us to catch more, but I turned the offer down and said that the big fish I caught was plenty reward enough. He wouldn't hear of it though, so I took the extra fish and looked around for something to give him in return, for that, I had learned, was the Indian way. All I had to give him were the leftover leg portions of my cutoffs, and he smiled with great enthusiasm as I handed them to him. But, because the cutoffs were now more valuable to him, he offered me some wampum. I tried to tell him no, but I soon realized that I was insulting him. I accepted his terms and we went our separate ways after an Indian handshake.

I took in a deep breath as I faced the huts because it felt comfortable like I was home after a long day. I waved hello to a few of the Wangunks, and they returned the gesture before I entered my hut to find Namoenee and all her belongings there.

The hut looked full to the gills with stuff and was arranged so that every place seemed to have a thing. I saw woven baskets under the bed. There was an abundance of furs on the bed like there was in Tahadondeh's. The whole floor was covered with reed mats and some steatite bowls were randomly spread about. Over the fire pit now stood a wooden cooking rack that was used for drying out and smoking meat. In the coals, a brass pot that had boiled water in it. The walls had animal pouches, brass pots, wampum necklaces, a bundle of arrows (not just the shafts anymore) with a bow and a red fox quiver, and some eagle feathers hanging on them. Namoenee's clothes were stacked neatly off to one side with two pair of beaded moccasins. I turned and saw some elk antlers protruding from the wall, plus a makeshift pair of snowshoes, and a fur parka probably made from the remains of the elk. I saw a ball club and spear next to my crutch and firearm to the left of the doorway. My boots stood upright on the floor. There were wood working tools such as stone axes, adzes, and a gouge on the right side of the doorway along with a garden hoe. The dried ears of corn above the door had also doubled during my absence.

"Do you like?" Namoenee asked with pride in her voice.

"I do," I responded, pleased but clearly surprised. "I don't remember all of this being in your hut."

"Most was. The rest came to us as gifts from father."

I stood there confused as I held on to the fish. "To us?" I asked.

Namoenee practically skipped over to me and gave me a full kiss on the lips. She took the stick full of fish from me, and before she turned away to start gutting and cleaning them, she said, "For our marriage."

I must have seemed like a complete idiot because I just stood there and repeated her statements as questions, "Our marriage?" The thought of being married again, especially to Namoenee didn't displease me; I was just confused about when it had happened.

The princess stopped her doings, "Oh ... oh my." She stood erect and a trembling hand rose up slowly to meet with her lips. "Have I misplaced your feelings for me? Have I rushed you? We used the honey ... we were as one." Her eyes filled with tears as she turned to face me, "Are we not in love?"

Her innocence and distress tore away at my heart, and I knew there was only one thing for me to do at that precise moment. I had to fix it. "I do love you. I *am* in love with you and I don't wish to be with anyone else." I went to her and held her in the longest hug in the history of mankind until she knew that my feelings for her were true. "I never want to lose you," I said.

Namoenee relaxed in my arms and looked up into my face. Her tears had already dried on her cheeks, "Nor I you, my husband."

I still needed clarification though, "So because I'm not totally familiar with the ways of the Wangunk, shouldn't we have had a ceremony to declare our union?"

"I sometime forget you not know of our way yet. I am sorry," she humbly said to me while still in my arms. "My father gave consent, the whole tribe approved, and we spent the night together with knowledge of the village. In everyone's eyes we are married." Namoenee reached up and caressed the side of my face, "Are we not?"

I didn't need a piece of paper of legality to tell me that I was now with the woman I had been waiting for my whole life. No ring or ceremony would have made my feelings for her any stronger. She chose me and I her. We felt we were brought together for a reason and that we were meant to be.

"We are," I replied, and we kissed like it was our first kiss all over again.

Namoenee broke away with a final peck as she realized she still held on to the fish. She chuckled, "These need to be cleaned."

"Let me."

"No. You caught them. I will clean them ... husband," she smiled.

After my bride gutted the fish and showed me how to place them on the smoking rack, with the inside turned down first, I took the entrails to the compost heap. *She is my wife. How did I get so lucky?* My thoughts returned briefly to Traven and the watch and how without it I never would have come to this place in the past. Without it, I never would have met Namoenee. *I should give her a gift.* I immediately thought of the wampum that Eagle Wing had given me. *I'll* make *her a wedding gift.*

When I returned to the honeymoon suit, my princess bride and I made love again, with the use of honey again, until dusk drew near. With our lust for sex satiated, our appetites soon took over, so we ate an early dinner from the boiling pot, which contained the Three Sisters: corn, beans and squash, which had been resting in the glowing embers.

While we ate, there was talk about our day. I told Namoenee about my fishing experience and how beautiful a day it had been and she told me that as soon as I had left, she and some of her girlfriends started moving her stuff in. She showed me the gifts from her father and said that if we did have an official ceremony we could expect gifts from the whole tribe. I thought that was nice, but not necessary, as I looked again at the plentitude of stuff.

What I didn't find so pleasant is what she casually told me next, "My father and I decided to let the white man go today."

My thoughts reeled. *He might try it again, only next time with more of his white friends. What if the colonists want retribution for the dead fat guy? Would this escalate the war? How different would the outcome have been if I hadn't been here to stop the kidnapping? Namoenee certainly wouldn't be married, at least to me, a wonnux. Traven's note ... what did he say? It is not a good idea to mess around with anyone else's future, how do I know that my being here wasn't part of history?* It always came back to the question, "Which came first, the chicken or the egg?" but without the watch I was stuck in this situation. I had no choice but to see it through to the end.

Apparently, Namoenee was deep in thought as well because we sat and ate the rest of our meal in silence.

Soon after dinner, Snow Falling ran up to our hut, stuck his head in without knocking, and told us that Tahadondeh had called for a tribal council. The remaining warriors had returned and the time had come for the adult males to hear about the outcome of the visit to the neighboring tribes.

"You must go my husband," Namoenee told me, as she handed me my pipe and tobacco.

"I am interested, but I would not be able to contribute. You should come with me."

"I cannot, it is not allowed."

"But I only know a handful of Wangunk words."

"You know enough to tell me if we will war."

That much was true. Not that she wouldn't have found out from her father eventually, but now it seemed the responsibility fell on me.

I wasn't the first to arrive to the gathering hut, which was oval shaped, capable of holding at least a hundred men. It had two holes in its roof for the two fire pits that burned brightly on the floor as He Sings and I entered through one of the four doorways. Maybe half of the male population was already there, excluding the children and the immobile elderly, and no one gave me a second glance or questioned my presence. Although I didn't know what do to or where to sit, I felt accepted and welcome. I followed He Sings's lead and was about to sit next to him across the house opposite from Tahadondeh, when he, my new father-in-law, caught my eye and waved me over. As I walked between the two fires, Tahadondeh said a few words to his advisors on his left, and they parted to make room for me to sit a few spots down from the chief. I sat down on the dirt floor, looked up at him sitting on a chair above his tribe and he smiled contently at me. I smiled back and gave him a nod to say thank you.

To Tahadondeh's right, sat the powwaw, old and ominous as always. With eyes closed beneath his wild gray hair, his lips moved to an inaudible chant while tobacco burned in pots to either side of him, and a draw string leather pouch, the size of my fist, full of small animal bones laid on a ceremonial blanket in front of him. The members of the tribe gave the powwaw ample room, and no one sat between him and the chief. I turned away from the powwaw because I was unable to continue to look at him without the feeling that I was being watched myself.

It was as if he watched me through closed eyelids and it gave a chill up my spine, so instead of looking at him, I turned my gaze across the crowd of men and watched others as they filed in. I gave an idle wave to Eagle Wing when I saw him as I panned the crowd. There was small talk, murmurs really, among the males as they settled in. As soon as everyone had sat, they all grew silent and waited to hear from Tahadondeh, their chief, Wood's Edge.

Wood's Edge let the room remain silent for a long moment until he closed his eyes and began to chant. It was soft at first, but as the fifty or so men joined in with him, it became very loud. Someone had brought a drum and started beating it. The chant turned into singing and wailing. *Is this their song for war?* I thought.

Then, as quickly as it started, it stopped.

Wood's Edge said something like, "Who will war on us?" and turned to his right to see the powwaw toss the bones from within the bag out onto the blanket.

The powwaw asked without looking up from the bones, "Nehantics?"

A warrior stood up and responded, "Mud, No." He sat back down.

The powwaw studied the scattered pile of skeletal remains and nodded his head in affirmation. He picked up the bones and tossed them again, "Quinnipiacs?"

A different warrior stood, "Mud."

The powwaw affirmed the answer and threw again, "Tunxis?"

Yet another, "Mud."

This went on for quite a while with names like Narragansetts, Wepawaugs, Nipmucks, Poquonnucs, Mattabesetts, Hammonassetts, and Paugussetts. They all received a response of "No, they will not war."

Sometime in the middle of this process, as I looked back and forth from the sitting powwaw to a new standing warrior each time, I saw a glimmer out of the corner of my eye. At that time, I thought it was just the fire reflecting off of someone's bronze medallion or an ornament tied into someone's hair, so I paid no attention to it until later, when I saw what it had really come from.

Then a slight deviation from the questions and answers came when the powwaw asked about the Podunks, the tribe that Gowanus was from that lay some thirty miles to the north. The response came back as, "Ner nohwa mud. I know not." The warrior sat down, but no one seemed to react to it. I felt anxious and looked to Wood's Edge, but he just stared at the powwaw and waited to hear the rest. The powwaw neither affirmed nor denied the answer. Instead, he picked up his bones and called out another name. That's when another deviation happened as the powwaw asked about the Pequots. There was a shift in everyone's attitude as they turned from the powwaw to see Eagle Wing stand.

"Mud," he said and sat back down. I could tell that the crowd seemed overjoyed with that one though they barely showed it. We all turned back to the powwaw, and he agreed. The tribe all showed pleasure then. Everyone smiled including myself, for I could go back to my lovely Namoenee and tell her the good news.

That's when my day turned dark.

I saw the flash of light again. I focused on its origin and it came from Warrior's Cry. His head was turned downward as he played around with something in his lap. It was my watch.

He turned it over and over in his hands and rubbed his stout muscular fingers over its golden surface. The light of the closest fire reflected back to me off of it, taunting me, and just as I was about to leap from my seat, Wood's Edge stood and declared the meeting over.

As everybody stood, they broke out in song. I stood and shouted out Warrior's Cry's name, but it went unheard. I tried taking some steps toward him, but the standing crowd blocked my way. I called out his name again, but he didn't hear me. Wood's Edge came and placed a hand on my shoulder. When I turned to him he could plainly see that something was wrong. I felt I didn't have the time to explain it to him, so I broke from his embrace and tried to catch up with Warrior's Cry. If he happened to find a way to open the watch and play with the buttons, there was no telling the consequences.

When I finally did catch up to him, it was after the crowd dispersed a little outside the gathering hut, and I stood before him to prevent his progress. He had a questioning look on his face, so I pointed to the watch in his hand and shoved a palm up at him in a "give it to me" posture. He knew what I wanted, but it didn't turn out to be that easy. Warrior's Cry clutched the watch tighter as he placed it close to the side of his leg and then brushed his way past me. I grabbed his arm, spun him around hard, and stuck my other hand out again.

He got mad and pulled away from my grasp. "Nenertah! It is mine!" he yelled and turned to walk away.

By that time, the crowd from the meeting had gathered around us to see what the commotion was about.

I tried to grab hold of his arm again, but he pulled away too fast and in one sweeping motion he punched me with a right hook to the jaw that knocked me unexpectedly on my ass. Blood filled my mouth. I spat the warm liquid on the ground and rushed him like a tackle in football. I lowered my shoulder, caught him square in the abdomen, and threw him to the ground with the weight of my body on top of him. My glasses fell off. We wrestled for some time in the dirt, each of us vying for a superior hold, but we were pretty equally matched. As I tried to take the watch from his tight grip, he went to bite my upper arm, but the crowd grabbed us both and separated us before he could sink his teeth in and before I could recover the watch. Someone held my arms behind me as I stood there, and I squinted at Warrior's Cry. He was five feet away, a total blur, but I could see that the crowd held him back too. Then Wood's Edge entered the circle of people and stood between us. He grunted and the mass let go of us both. Someone handed me my glasses and they, luckily, were not broken.

Tahadondeh asked what was going on and Warrior's Cry started mouthing off about me. I have no idea what he said other than, "Nenertah! It is mine!"

The chief turned to me and grunted.

"Mud," I said, and shook my head, clearly out of breath. "It is mine ... nenertah."

Tahadondeh calmly called for his daughter.

"Good," I said to myself. "She will straighten this out." The Wangunks that surrounded me looked confused at my words.

Namoenee must have already been on her way, and she was soon within the circle of people. Because her father had called for her, she stood by his side rather than coming to mine. I understood the reason. She was acting as the chief's translator and that superseded her marriage to me. Wood's Edge pointed to Warrior's Cry first, and he spewed his tale. Namoenee translated to me that he had come upon it in the woods as he returned from the peace talks at the Poquonnucs and so that made it his. *Finder's keepers, loser's weepers? I don't think so.* Wood's Edge asked him where he specifically found it, and after Warrior's Cry response, he told his daughter not to relay the answer to me.

The chief then pointed to me.

"I had it with me the first day I came to you," I said careful not to bring up any hostilities again toward me by saying I was found in the graveyard. "It either fell out of my possession," which I seriously doubted, "or it was stolen from me."

Namoenee rendered my words into Wangunk.

Warrior's Cry yelled something back with fury in his voice, and Namoenee started to respond directly to him, but her father stopped her. He told her to just translate and not interject her own words. She submissively turned to me, "Warrior's Cry said, 'Is the white man calling me a liar?'" It didn't sound so bad coming from her, but the way that Warrior's Cry had said it was meant to be hurtful and prejudiced.

I was about to respond, "If the moccasin fits," but I was preempted by Wood's Edge. He said, "I do not believe Warrior's Cry is lying, but he did say that he found the item where you might have lost it. I therefore believe both of you and will hold on to the item until I can decide what is best to be done with it." He held out his hand to Warrior's Cry who reluctantly gave him the watch, and then he placed it into the waist of his breechcloth – the chain hung there in plain sight. Because he considered the matter over for the time being, Tahadondeh turned and exited the circle to retire to his hut.

Warrior's Cry gave me a look of contempt and then spat on the ground and grunted at me. Namoenee spat and grunted back at him as she came to my side. I didn't get the feeling she was trying to protect me from him in any way. It felt more like I was her man and she was going to stick by me. It felt natural to have her there.

The crowd dispersed, including Warrior's Cry, and Namoenee took me by the hand as we walked back to our house. We were silent until we entered the abode.

Namoenee started, "What is it you believe belong to you?"

"It's a watch," I replied, but Namoenee didn't understand. I continued, "It's a time piece. A white man's sun dial."

"Ah," was all she said, but I knew there was more to come and I didn't have to wait long. "But now you are with me. There is no need to watch the sun."

I wanted to laugh at her choice of words, but did not. I also knew that she was right, for the meaning of time had no place among them. They slept when they were tired, ate when they were hungry, made love when they felt frisky, and bathed when they felt dirty, and so on. *How can I explain this to her? Should I just tell her the truth?* I didn't think telling her the truth was plausible, so subsequently, I was at a loss for words and felt emotionally drained. I sat down on the bed.

"It's difficult to say other than it was a gift to me that I want back. It would be like; if you gave me a gift then by accident I had lost it and then saw it in someone else's possession. Does that make sense?"

"So this watch is from your first marriage?"

"No, it's from a ..." I hesitated. What was Traven to me? "It's from a friend," I reluctantly said not knowing exactly what he was. I had to hold back telling Namoenee everything. I really wanted to share it all with her, if for nothing else to relief my guilt of omission, but instead, I just let it lay the way it was. I got the feeling my bride knew I hadn't told her the whole story.

I also felt that she would have tried to help by, I don't know, talking to her father for me, but since I didn't come clean, she could only resort to one conclusion. "My father will have the answer."

"I hope so," I mumbled and lay down.

Namoenee joined me, wrapped a fur around our lower halves and snuggled in with her head on my chest. I stroked her hair and we both fell asleep.

THE CHALLENGE

"My father wants you and Warrior's Cry to meet him in the sweat lodge," Namoenee said to me around midday. The sweat lodge was a small circular wigwam capable of holding only five people at the most, and it was used much like a sauna was in my day. The Wangunks buried hot rocks partially underground with burning coals in the middle of the teepee and water was poured over them to create the steam and give off more heat. The teepee was closed tightly so that the steamy heat would take a long time to dissipate. Sometimes, people were known to stay in there for hours at a time. I had seldom seen mixed sweats, mostly just groups of the elder men, and then it was mostly the chief and his advisors. The Wangunks used the lodge for a combination of things, like cleansing the skin, but most often it was used to create vision quests. I saw a young lad of thirteen use it once. When he exited after a short time he immediately went to see the Powwaw to tell him of the things he saw in his vision. The Powwaw analyzed his visions, and soon the boy came out to announce his new adult name to the tribe, and a celebration was held in the gathering hut. Little Bird had become Rising Sun. If Little Bird did not have a vision that day or if he passed out from the heat and dehydration, then he would have made another attempt a month later. Such was the Indian way.

The lodge was also used as a de-toxifier if someone became severely sick and the Powwaw couldn't revive them with his medical herbs, which I did not see during my stay, but Namoenee had told me about it.

In this instance however, Tahadondeh wanted us, Warrior's Cry and me, to bond. I was concerned – I didn't want to bond with the man. I just wanted back what belonged to me, but in order to honor my wife and father-in-law's wishes I decided I had to go. Should Tahadondeh decide to keep me in there for a long time, I quickly drank a lot of water and ate a slice of salty venison jerky in the hope of not passing out.

Warrior's Cry and I arrived at the same time to the entrance of the lodge. We stood there a moment until I offered for him to go in first. Tahadondeh was already in there, and he sweated profusely as he told us both to sit down. I sat to his right and Warrior's Cry to his left and we waited for him to say something, but it never came. He just sat there with his eyes closed and we all just sat there. At first, Warrior's Cry stared at me, and it was uncomfortable, but I knew I was within my rights, so I stared back at him. Then, like a blast from a heated oven as you open the door, Tahadondeh poured some water on the rocks, and the heat wave hit me. I started to sweat immediately and soon forgot that Warrior's Cry was even in there with me. I had to close my eyes and concentrate on anything but the heat. It was fervid and I imagined it was like being in hell. That's how hot it was.

My mind turned to Keisha and how much I missed her, but then my thoughts switched over to why I was missing her. I had been gone for over nearly two months though for her I had only just left. Still pictures flashed through my mind as a photographic chronology covered the past months from my meeting Traven and seeing the watch for the first time at the flea market to seeing the watch again the night of the Tribal Council. It seemed like ages ago before the onslaught of heat. *Don't think about the heat.*

I changed my thoughts and concentrated on the watch itself. It's why I was there with the Wangunks, and it was the reason for my being in the "hellhole" – a new name I had given to the sweat lodge.

It is mine, but would I use it again? I have no reason to leave here. I love it here. I loved growing up here as a kid, and I love it even more now. I love Namoenee. I would be lost without her if I left. I certainly couldn't take her with me. Or could I? In my time, there is pollution, over-population, reckless murder, traffic jams, and everything has a price tag. I could never make her leave this fabulous place and expect her to be happy in my time. No. No, it is easier for me to adjust to this life, as I already have. This wonderful life with my new family. So ... I wouldn't use the watch if given the chance. So why do I want it back so badly? You know the answer to that, I thought. I was chosen by Traven to be the next operator of the watch. It was my responsibility. It is my responsibility. But why? If it is my "destiny" to stay here, then why does it matter who the owner is?

I knew the answer. *If Warrior's Cry should ever happen upon those buttons it could mean catastrophe. That's why. All he would have to do is push that right button and he would end up in 2004. He would be lost in a world of mayhem and mischief. He and the watch would be studied and prodded until the truth was discovered. The world would know that time travel existed. Traven was right. If the wrong people knew that the technology existed, then everything could change and not for the better. I need to regain possession of the watch, if for nothing else than to hide it away or throw it to the depths of Pocotopaug. I need to steal it from Tahadondeh if he doesn't give it back.*

That's when I opened my eyes and found Wood's Edge and Warrior's Cry gone. I was dismayed that my father-in-law would leave me there alone. My body dripped and my shorts were soaked, but apparently, without anyone there to tend to the rocks, the teepee had cooled enough that I was not in danger of passing out from heat exhaustion. I exited the lodge and found the sun was about to set. I had been in the hellhole for roughly four hours. Before I returned to my hut, I decided to go for a swim to cool off.

*   *   *

It was time to head home when the sunset had cast magnificent pinks and reds against some scattered clouds just above the horizon. It was both beautiful and tranquil, and I would have stayed longer, but as I floated there in the cool water admiring my surroundings, a sudden urge of both thirst and hunger washed over me. I gave up the scenery in favor of seeing my wife and eating dinner with her.

As I approached my hut, I could hear Namoenee talking with someone, and as I drew closer, I knew it to be her father. There was no mistaking his baritone voice. I turned to leave, to go with my conclusion of stealing back the watch, but my feet didn't move. *He is my family now*, I thought, but what needed to be done had to be done. Just as I was about to head off to his hut and burgle my watch, Namoenee caught me standing there.

"What are you doing? Come inside my husband," she said as she held open the flap and invited me in with a smile on her face.

I walked in and saw Wood's Edge as he sat on the floor with his back against the bed, an arm up on the rail and his legs stretched out straight. It was a very relaxed look for the chief, one that I had never seen before. In the company of his daughter, he was able to let his guard down and not worry about any impression given by his lack of posture. He still looked as big and formidable as a bear, and I never would have liked to cross him, but that night he wasn't in his position of leader. That night he was being a dad.

Maybe I don't have to steal from him, maybe I can convince him to give it to me while he's in a good mood?

I greeted him with cheer in my voice, "Aque, hello, Tahadondeh."

"Aque, aque. Sequish, merdupsh jonnow Tahadondeh," he said. Namoenee didn't have to translate his words for me. He said as friendly as could be, "Hello, hello. Come in, sit down near Wood's Edge."

So I did.

Wood's Edge was very chatty that evening because, after I sat down, not a second went by that he didn't stop talking with me. I needed Namoenee's help throughout the evening. He started casually, "I hear you went fishing yesterday."

"Yes. Eagle Wing and I did quite well."

"That's good, provide my daughter well."

"I will." There was no doubt in my response, and I think Wood's Edge appreciated it because he slapped a hand on my shoulder and shook me around a bit – like only a father could.

"This hut is nice, but when you give me grandchildren, we will have to build you a bigger one."

I just sat there and smiled, not knowing what to say and Wood's Edge let out a big bellow of a laugh. Namoenee snickered as well, and I suddenly felt out numbered, not really knowing what was so funny.

She then placed some meat on the wood rack and its sizzle and smell made me even hungrier. The meat had already been dried and smoked, so I knew I wouldn't have to wait long for it. My stomach rumbled embarrassingly loud, so I grabbed an elk bladder full of water and drank some down. I offered it to Wood's Edge but he declined. I imagined that he had had his fill between leaving me at the sweat lodge and coming to dinner.

I raised the bladder up again and squeezed out another mouth full when, down below the rim of my glasses I saw Wood's Edge pull out a golden object. I put my head down and took a quick glance to make sure. It was the watch, and it was three feet away from me. I pretended not to care.

He held it up, and the watch appeared tiny in his huge hand, "How important is this to you?"

More important than you'll ever know, I thought. "Not as important to me as your daughter is, but I still wish it to be returned to me."

He looked it over uncertain as to what it was. Maybe Namoenee had told him, but he couldn't fathom it. I am fairly certain he wanted me to show him what the watch did, how it operated, etc., but he remained reluctant to hand it to me. Instead, he tucked the watch back under the waistband of his breechcloth and I didn't see it again until three days later.

Namoenee served us our food and we all ate in silence. There was something more to Wood's Edge's visit than eating dinner with us because you could almost see the wheels spin in his head as he ate. I was sure he was still pondering the situation over the watch. I kept quiet in the hope that I would be in his favor and I wouldn't have to do any convincing at all.

It wasn't until after dinner and my sharing of tobacco with him, that Wood's Edge spoke again, "I have made a decision."

Namoenee set down the wooden dishes that she was in the process of cleaning and we both waited for his answer.

"I will call for the challenge."

I had no idea what he meant. I looked to Namoenee to clarify the translation.

She answered, "The challenge is used to settle disputes, my husband. You and Warrior's Cry will participate in three distinct tasks to determine who the owner of the watch will be. These tasks can be a test of physical or mental strength, or both, depending on what father chooses."

"But I am the rightful owner," I said to Wood's Edge with an embarrassing whiny undertone that surprised me when I heard it come out of my own mouth.

Wood's Edge continued, "I will call for the challenge that has been used since before G-oogernos…"

"Um, sorry," Namoenee interrupted, "What is words? Ah yes, 'thy … grandfather.'"

"And it will consist of wolf/fish, deer hunt, and the red wrestle. Do you accept?"

I turned back to Namoenee for more clarification.

"My father has chosen all physical tasks. The wolf/fish is a race of run and swim. The deer hunt means you and Warrior's Cry must each bring back a deer, the larger one winning that task, and the red wrestle is a wrestling match. The best two of three wins gets possession of the watch. Do you accept?"

I scratched the back of my head and spoke directly to my bride, "Do you think I could win?"

"It is not up to me James."

She was right about that. I didn't know if I could beat Warrior's Cry, but if I lost then I could always fall back on the idea of becoming a common thief and take it from Warrior's Cry instead of my father-in-law. "I accept," I replied.

"Good," Wood's Edge exclaimed as he stood up to leave. "If Warrior's Cry accepts also, the challenge will start tomorrow and will last three days."

I stood as well, "Three days long? Just what kind of tasks are these?"

"Not to worry my husband, the tasks are split up one for each day," Namoenee said to me and then explained to her father of my concern that I would have to perform for seventy-two hours straight. Wood's Edge bellowed again, shook his head, and then hugged his daughter. I felt small from their laughter.

*　　*　　*

The first day of the challenge consisted of the wolf/fish, a running and swimming race. When I accepted the challenge, I had thought of a small sprint of maybe a hundred yards into the water and then a swim to the nearby twin isles, but I was thinking too small. Namoenee explained to me that Warrior's Cry and I had to run (three miles) to the opposite side of Pocotopaug and then swim (one-mile) back to the village. She pointed past the twin isles to the other side of the larger lake to where canoes would be waiting, and said that we weren't going to do the smaller lake. Thank goodness for small favors.

"Here, my husband, you will need these," my wife said as she handed me a pair of thick soled moccasins and a pair of leggings.

"Thank you my beautiful bride."

She blushed, gave me a kiss, and helped me tie on my leggings. The moccasins were a perfect fit, like they were made for me, and I told Namoenee that I thought so.

"That because I did make them for you," she casually said.

"How did you know what size to make them? When did you have *time* to make them?"

"Well, I measure your feet while you sleep and I start them just after we turtle shell hunt because you walk so tender along rocky shore."

It took her three weeks of her spare time to make the moccasins for me. During that time, my feet had grown tough enough that I thought I could run without them, but it was better to be safe than sorry. I didn't want to lose the race because of cuts and sores on my feet.

"You're the best, honey," I told her while she was still kneeling down at my feet.

She didn't quite get the whole nickname thing, or maybe she did but didn't let on, "Win race first, honey will come after." Namoenee quickly finished the adjustment of my leggings, but her innocence with the word honey suddenly made me want to take her back to our hut and bed her down.

"Okay, I hope it does," I mused about the smell of honey again.

Warrior's Cry and I were called to the start—there was an "X" drawn out in the dirt close to the water's edge—one line ran perpendicular to the shoreline and the other was parallel for the finish. We lined ourselves up at the starting line heading west. Wood's Edge wasn't at the start because he was in one of the canoes that had already headed across the way. He wanted to watch the action up close as we swam home. Except for those who also chose to be in a canoe, the whole village was at the start to cheer us on. I don't think many knew what our dispute was about, and I don't think anyone cared. They were just excited for the competition. Maybe they had a favorite champion they were cheering for, but I didn't hear anyone calling out our names. It was good clean fun for them. For Warrior's Cry, he was in it for the gold. For me, it meant saving the future, as I knew it.

Snow Falling walked out twenty yards in front of us as our starter. Namoenee approached me and kissed me on the cheek, "Your honey loves you too."

Snow Falling raised both arms into the air, held them there for a second or two and then thrust them down toward the ground. I laughed out loud as I took off running because Namoenee was playfully wicked at times. She did understand the sobriquet, and she knew I had no time for a retort.

Warrior's Cry took the lead with a quick sprint, and I kept up with him until I realized that I was no runner. I needed to pace myself. "Keep him in sight, but don't wear yourself out," I said, as I chugged along. We followed an animal path that Namoenee and I had walked several times together, so I was familiar with its layout. But there is a huge difference in walking a path and running on one. I mean, the path barely fit two side by side because the undergrowth wanted to take it back for its own. Without the leggings I wore, my shins would have been torn up a minute into the race. I thanked Hobomoko for giving me a wife as wonderful as Namoenee.

I've always heard that a five-minute mile is pretty good for amateurs, but that's on a track or a road race. We probably doubled that as we ran through the woods with all its twists and turns. There were sharp corners and uneven ground to traverse, branches to dodge, but most of all, I was not in shape for running. I developed a cramp in my side about three-quarters of the way to the where the canoes rested and I came to an almost complete stop. I was out of breath, and I winced at the pain. I lost sight of my opponent, and I felt immediately defeated.

I heard cheering off in the distance. Warrior's Cry had reached the canoes, so I pushed on. As I came upon a straight away that ran along the shore, I could see off to my right the first canoe had started its way along side my adversary. A big red flag that was strapped to the front of the canoe flapped high in the wind. He was only about a hundred feet from shore. I wasn't so discouraged any longer. I looked in the direction they had come from as I ran and saw a big blue flag urging me to hurry up, but the cramp reminded me to keep an easy pace.

The big flags on the canoes were for the villagers back at the other side of the lake to determine who was in the lead. In my mind I could see a disappointed look flash across Namoenee's face as she saw the red flag moving first. I pushed on some more.

By the time I got to my flag, Warrior's Cry was perhaps a hundred and fifty yards ahead of me. It didn't look like he was going very fast, so I took a few moments to catch my breath while my guys by the canoe were practically screaming at me to get going. I looked at them and saw Wood's Edge stoically standing there. He chose to be in the canoe that would follow me, but he looked grim at his decision.

I slipped out of my moccasins, tore off the leggings, placed my glasses carefully into the front pocket of my shorts, and then walked into the water. My blue flag started to wave as they gathered into the canoe, and one of the men grabbed my stuff from the shore to bring with them. *Will I have to compete to get those back as well?* I laughed sarcastically to myself and walked out to where it was deep enough to start my swim. I submerged myself and started in on the last leg of the race. Ordinarily, swimming a mile at a relaxed pace was not a big deal for me. In fact, back in high school it was easy because I used to swim five miles a day during team practices, but this experience was grueling. This time, the water was choppy so just taking breaths was work on its own, and I didn't have any goggles to keep the water out of my eyes. My running cramp had left a residual pain, but I couldn't afford to relax, so I just kept a steady pace while I kept my eye on that blurry red flag.

It had been a long time since I swam competitively, and trying to win this one brought back memories of my days on the high school swim team when I broke the 500 freestyle record. I was seventeen, a junior, and I didn't want to swim it. I hated it because it was long and boring.

*   *   *

The swim meet against Lyman Hall was at 7 PM, so this gave me time to go home after school and do some chores, eat a light meal, and take a nap. I needed one because I didn't go to bed very early the preceding night, and I wanted to be well rested.

As I arrived at the school, the tension and nervousness grew as it usually did right before a meet started. My adrenaline flowed and the butterflies in my stomach were restless as I changed into my suit and got ready to warm up in the pool. That's when Charlie, my coach, asked me what I wanted to swim, so I told him the usual. I wanted to swim the 100 and 200-yard freestyle. I secretly had my eye on breaking one, if not both, of those records. I started off by swimming the 100, and though I didn't set any record, I did win the event. My attitude was high and confident to try for the 200, but half way through the meet, after the diving challenge, we all stood in the locker room. This break was comparable to half time in a football game. Charlie told me he wanted me to swim the "5," and I was immediately pissed off. I thought that doing the twenty laps was tedious, and it made me put my back up. I told myself I had to relax, so I went to my locker and pulled out some juggling balls to take my mind off of the impending boredom.

After "half time," there was the 50-yard freestyle swim, two laps worth of sprinting that lasted only twenty-five seconds or so, and then came the 500. I was moody and distracted prior to the 50, but during, I was caught up by the excitement of it. By the time it was over, I was ready for my event. I stripped off my sweats, and as always, I felt somewhat exposed in my little Speedo. I walked to the starting blocks.

I heard Mr. Parmelee, the head referee and coach of the women's swim team, tell us to take our positions. I told myself to keep pace with the clock and not the guy next to me.

"Swimmers take your mark," Parmelee called out. He raised the starter's gun – filled with blanks – and held us bent over for what seemed a long time. I used to think that he liked to let us hang there for a little while before he pulled the trigger.

The gun went off and I lunged into the water.

I got off to a fast start. At least that's what everybody told me afterward. I didn't really know how I was doing until the last four laps. At the sixteenth flip-turn to start the last 100, I could see my teammates on the side of the pool waving their arms and towels in circles in the air. As I took my strokes, I looked under my armpits at both adjacent lanes. I didn't think anyone was around me, and I knew no one was ahead of me. I thought I must be on record time. It became a fight against the clock.

I went wild. I pushed myself. I pulled as hard as I could, and on the nineteenth flip, I told myself, "This is it!" I sprinted to the finish, and as I hit the wall and looked up, I saw all my friends and teammates jumping up and down with excitement.

I knew. I didn't have to look up at the clock. I knew I had beaten the record.

*   *   *

But this race wasn't against the clock. Half way from the twin isles to the village I had pulled even to Warrior's Cry. I switched up my strokes and watched Warrior's Cry's canoe and flag very carefully, for all I could see of Warrior's Cry were his arms flailing about twenty feet away to my side. I did take it more easily then, I admit it, knowing we were even, but I also made sure to keep my stead even though my arms felt like lead and my feet barely kicked. Toward the end, I forced myself to pull ahead.

It seemed to take forever to make it to the shoreline, but I raised myself up onto a pair of wobbly legs and crossed the finish line first. I had won and the tribe clapped and cheered.

Namoenee practically knocked me over as she jumped on me and ravaged me with loads of kisses and hugs while I tried to put my glasses back on. She was very proud of her man, and she couldn't stop touching me. She kept asking her friends if they had seen my come from behind win. She was on the edge of gloating. I was a little embarrassed, but I reveled in her excitement. She left me for a bit but quickly returned with my moccasins and leggings, and we stood together, and held hands among the crowd while we watched Warrior's Cry finish. He looked as tired as I felt.

Tahadondeh had already exited his canoe, and he came over to me with my blue flag. He passed me with a smile on his face, and we all followed him to the strike pole dance area where he inserted the shaft of my flag into the top of the west-side pole. The crowd cheered again. It was one to nothing.

My wife couldn't hold back her enthusiasm the whole time, so finally, I picked her up, twirled her around, and started running toward the water with her in my arms. At first, she laughed and waved to her friends, but as we neared the water she told me to stop. I didn't listen.

"No, Jim, no!" she screamed in my ear.

I stopped just shy of the water and saw her crying. Her body quivered in my graspe d.

"What's wrong?" I asked her.

She quickly calmed down and said, "I no swim."

"You don't know how to swim?"

"No."

I set her down. As we hugged, I realized that she and I had never swum together, and then it all became clear why. Sure, we had waded in the water before, plenty of times. We even bathed together, but we never went deeper than her knees. I had never met anyone before that didn't know how to swim, so I never questioned it. Namoenee told me she had a terrible fear of the water since she was a child, and no one had encouraged her to learn.

Because Namoenee was clearly upset and I was tired, we retired to our hut where she fed me an early dinner. Her fear soon gave way to complacency and then to excitement as the thrill of my win returned. She kept on re-living it, and though I was excited about it too, after I ate my eyes grew heavy, and I couldn't hold a conversation with her. I went to bed out of plain exhaustion while the sun was still up, and I fell fast asleep.

*   *   *

There was a green grass lawn that surrounded a crushed stone walkway and within that laid an underground pool filled with stagnant stale water left over from winter. It was dirty with the previous year's fallen leaves on its bottom, and the mildew that grew up from the muck along the sides desperately tried to reach the air and sunlight.

In my dream, I was back at the house I lived in during my high school years. "If we find it, I'll split it with you," I said to someone that I knew and yet did not.

She stood at the edge of the pool poised to jump in, and she did not hesitate. After she was fully submerged, a familiar voice from behind me said, "Look how she starts right in the very center," but she soon came up empty handed.

I found myself under the murky water. *How could she have missed it?* As the question passed through my mind, I saw it. I also saw something else a little bit beyond my original goal, but it didn't register.

I stood next to the pool, and I showed her the water soaked wallet. Then I dropped it. We both noticed that four twenty-dollar bills had fallen out. They were larger than normal because they were from 1910. *Was the wallet what I was really looking for?* No, it was the other object that was still lost in the depths of the pool. I had to go back in. I had to have it back. It was the watch and it belonged to me.

[129]

I woke sometime in the middle of the night and instantly knew the woman in my dream was Namoenee even though the woman swam and Namoenee didn't. I looked over to her as she lay next to me, and I could just make out her shape against the darkness. Her warmth was so inviting, and I felt bad that I had pretty much passed out on her.

But I was no longer sleepy. I knew I had to get up early anyway to go hunting by first light before the deer started roaming. I decided to get ready for my day instead of laying there listening to Namoenee's cute, barely audible, rhythmic little snore.

The second day of the challenge consisted of a deer hunt. Whoever brought back the biggest deer would win the day's event, and if I won, then the whole contest would be over. "*When* I win, there will be no need to have a day three," I said under my breath as I strapped on my blade and put as many arrows into my red fox quiver that would fit.

"Save the heart and liver," was the first thing she said to me like it was the most important, so I grabbed the leather pouch she told me to place them in. The previous day, in the morning before the race, Namoenee solemnly explained to me how to hunt, kill, and gut a deer since I told her I had never done it before. "And don't cut the bladder, you spoil the meat," she instructed. Normally, a hunting party of five or more men would be out as a group and could carry back the whole deer. Since I was to do this alone and would have to carry the remains all the way back to the village by myself, she told me to just gut it where it fell and leave it for the raccoons and crows. "But keep the heart and liver," she reiterated.

"And you cannot use that," she said, pointing to the revolver. It seemed the playing field had to be as even as possible during the contest, so I was not allowed the advantage of the gun over Warrior's Cry. I looked at the gun and then at my bow and arrows, and I winced. "Too bad," I whispered as I left the hut.

"Follow stream until the big fallen tree that lay across it, turn right." I forged my way through the woods toward the spot Namoenee told me to go to. The dream stuck with me as I walked. I was never good at self-analysis where my dreams were concerned, so I soon shrugged it off. I thought Gwen would have had a field day picking it to pieces. She was good at making something out of nothing, like her reasons for calling it quits with me. I no longer minded, really, for if it weren't for her getting me into antiques, I wouldn't have ended up where I was – truly in love. *In love in the middle of the woods in the middle of the night,* I mused and laughed. Luckily, the sky was clear and the late moon was bright enough for me to make my way.

"Continue following stream and turn left at the three boulders and set up on the hill. Many deer come to drinking in the morning there."

I sat on that hill for a long time, waiting and watching, but because it was hours before dawn, my body became chilled. My muscles started to stiffen, so I got as comfortable as I could by resting my back against a tree. It didn't take long for my eyes to grow heavy once more.

I must have fallen back to sleep because I have no idea how long I sat there, but when I heard a rustling I opened my eyes to find the first morning light had finally showed itself. The rustles in the woods were deer starting to stir, and I watched intently as some approached the stream below my perch. It was so serene that I just sat there mesmerized by the natural order of things. Their tails twitched as they walked gingerly along the water's edge. Their ears were ever aware of the littlest noise as they rotated front to back and flickered when a fly came too close. Their big brown eyes looked like dark circles, which accentuated their black noses. They moved slowly and purposely, and I almost forgot why I was there because of the sight of it all. I cleared my head, and I slowly lifted my bow with a notched arrow. I was ready, but I had to wait for the right one to come along. *Be patient,* I reminded myself. *The biggest one wins the day's event.* All the deer I saw seemed small. There were doe watching over their fawns as they drank, but I didn't see any bucks. I wanted … I needed a big buck.

After a while, I didn't know what to do. I started to get impatient and anxious at the thought of going home empty handed because I waited too long. I lifted the bow several times and struggled with myself at every attempt to draw the string back. I couldn't bring myself to shoot any of the doe.

The birds were fully awake. The squirrels started playing "follow the leader" with each other. I saw a rabbit off in the distance foraging for its breakfast. That's when I heard him. A buck was among the trees to my left, and he was being very noisy as he began a rub. I looked over ever so slowly and saw him rub his antlers against the branches and trunk of a larger sized oak. I had learned from Namoenee that the male deer often do rubs in an effort to remove the velvet off of their antlers and to leave a scent for the perspective mates. She had showed me signs during one of our walks, but it was exciting to see it firsthand.

He was a good distance away, but he looked big, so I waited. The doe tracked him for a moment and then returned to their drinking. When he finished his rub, he gave a proud couple of barks and headed down toward the stream. I tracked him with my eyes and slowly lifted the bow with the arrow still notched as he drank fifty feet away from me. He was a six-pointer. I knew I had to do it right. I didn't want to wound him and make him suffer. I knew it had to be done with one shot to the heart. I took aim, stretched back the bow's string, and waited for him to lift his head again.

A squirrel somewhere above me started to scream. That's the only way I have to describe it, but whatever the correct term is, he was upset that I sat under his tree. He gave warning to all his fellow woodland creatures that I was there. The buck lifted his head, and he looked back in my direction.

A bead of sweat rolled down my face as I tried with all my might not to move.

The squirrel still screamed and I wanted to scream back, but soon the deer didn't seem to care anymore. The majestic buck turned back toward the water and exposed the perfect spot. I let loose the arrow.

In a second it was over. I had taken another life.

The beast fell straight down next to the stream and didn't move, but the commotion sent all the other deer running. It didn't take long for the doe and the young to scatter out of sight, and suddenly it was quiet again. I gathered up my quiver filled with arrows, sans one, and solemnly headed down the hill to see my prey. He didn't look real as he lay there, for there wasn't any movement. He looked stuffed and I immediately felt bad. When I reached the animal's side I knelt beside him and prayed to Hobomoko. I prayed once for the good fortune and once for forgiveness because I took the creature's life. With my eyes closed, I reached out to him and felt the warmth of his body on my hands.

"When in Rome, huh Jim?"

I looked up without being surprise, and saw Traven standing there in all his smugness. He leaned up against a tree with a hand on his hip. The other hand held the watch with the face open to him. I saw that his thumb was poised over the "exit" button. He was ready to pull another disappearing act, and at that point, I didn't care if he was there or not, but I came out with what I thought he should know. "I've lost the watch."

"Yes, I know. So you need to find it then, haven't you?"

"I know where it is, but I have to win this challenge in order to get it back."

"Yes, the Native Americans of this time period were ..."

"Ya' know what Traven?" I exclaimed. "I don't want to hear another history lesson right now. In fact, your popping in and out is becoming annoying to me and I wish you would knock it off. If you're not going to give me the help that I need, I wish you would just leave."

Traven pushed off of the tree, "So be it," he said, and with that he faded back to wherever he came from. It was like a surreal dream. I didn't need his input, and I'm not sure why I said what I did, "If you're not going to help me..." because he really was unwelcome in my life just then. I guess what it boiled down to is, he reminded me of my old life and I cared too much for my new one to be bothered. Plus the fact that if I was to succeed him, why the hell didn't he teach me anything? I grew tired of his nonchalant attitude and it felt good to finally tell him to leave me alone – however coy I was at saying it. Besides, I was happy in my current situation.

Thinking on my new life, I remembered Namoenee told me not to let the deer body sit for too long because I had to gut him before rigor mortis set in, so I shrugged off Traven's visit and thought nothing more of it. I pulled out the arrow from the buck's chest and followed her instructions. I propped the body up on its back with the shoulders higher than the hips. It was dead weight and hard to maneuver, but I got it to what I thought was the correct position. I started the field dressing by my making a cut with my knife just above the genitals and continued up to the rib cage – careful not to cut too deep – I only wanted to cut through the hide and the abdominal wall. When that was done, I let the buck fall back onto its side and allowed the guts to spill out on their own. But they didn't come out all the way. That's when it really got messy. I had to reach inside the cavity and cut away at the fat located near the spine careful not to puncture the bladder as I did so. Both of my arms were wet with blood and body fluids, but everything came out as my wife had promised. The guts were still attached to the animal at its two opposite ends – the esophagus and anus. I lifted its rear leg and cut a circle around its anus to release one end, but I still had to get the heart, lungs, and esophagus out.

With the intestines sprawled out on the leafy ground, I cut the diaphragm away from the chest cavity then reached up underneath the rib cage with my left hand as far as I could and grabbed the esophagus, which squished in my grip. "*Ewww*," I thought. With my right hand, I carefully slid the knife up and cut just above my handhold. Because everything was now loose, I pulled out the heart and lungs and with them the rest of the intestines came out in a fleshy pile. I wanted to vomit at the sight of it even though my stomach was empty.

I felt like the dry heaves were going to set in for a long time, so I took a break from my chore. I wiped the knife off on my shorts and placed it in its sheath and while I sat on a rock near the edge of the stream I washed my hands and arms. The water felt cool and refreshing, and I let out a big sorrowful sigh because I had killed again and this time had to deal with it on my own. It felt bad, but that's when I noticed the squirrels playing up in the trees again. They hopped from limb to limb, and scurried up and down. I noticed the gurgle of the stream and the songs sung by the birds. The serenity had returned.

"All of nature has its ebbs and tides," I said to myself. We are all born to die, and some die so that others may live. I knew this, but the reason I was most upset was because I initially thought I had killed out of selfishness—to win a contest and win back the watch. Then I realized that the whole village would profit from this death. Tahadondeh was a smart man. He designed part of the competition to benefit the tribe. Clothing for the children could be made from the hide and the flesh would feed the elderly the protein that their weak bodies needed for weeks to come. The Wangunks would not let a single piece of this death go to waste. The bones, sinews, and hide would all be used to benefit them. They were respectful of nature, even as they took from it, and I felt better after the epiphany.

"Don't forget the heart and liver," I reminded myself. The flies had already swarmed over the grotesque pile of organs and fluids as I picked out the heart and liver and freed them from the mass. I placed them both in the special pouch Namoenee gave me and then washed my hands again.

"I'm gonna win," I said with a new air of confidence. Rejuvenated, I decided it was time to bring the carcass back to the village, so I tossed the quiver across one shoulder, the bow over the other, and started to drag the buck over the rough terrain in the direction I had come. I started by taking one hind leg in each of my hands behind my back and walked on, which proved very difficult at first and then became sheer impossible from the weight alone. I tried to face the deer and walk backwards but that was worse – I only made it about twenty yards doing it that way. The deer must have weighed one hundred and forty pounds and dragging it through the woods just wasn't going to work. I decided I had to carry it.

I started to lift the carcass up by its forelegs, but the head and back legs slumped backward and remained on the ground. My back strained in protest. "I don't know how firemen can do this," I said. "How do they pick up dead weight like this?" I knelt on the ground with one knee, grabbed a leg with my left arm, tucked my right arm under its head, and grabbed the back of the neck. And I lifted. The first couple of tries the front legs kept getting tangled up with the bow on my back, so I took it off in frustration. Once I got the weight of the upper body up on my shoulders the rest came relatively easy. I just adjusted the weight with each shove until it felt centered behind my head. With that accomplished, I held on tight, picked up my bow, and gingerly stood up.

My body supported the weight quite well during my hike home though I found myself taking breaks more often than not the closer I reached the village. I eventually made it back and like the day before, everyone had gathered and cheered as I emerged from the woods at midday. To my surprise, Warrior's Cry had not yet returned. The event of the day was not over; as the outcome had yet to be determined.

I gladly handed the deer over to a couple of eager fellows who carted it away and Namoenee gave me a smile of approval. "He's a good size," she said, as we watched them carry it away. She was distracted.

"Is there something wrong?"

She grabbed my arm and pulled me away from the crowd, not that anyone would have understood her words, but perhaps she didn't want someone hearing the inflection in her voice, which was of worry. When we were alone she told me, "I saw Gowanus this morning."

"You did," I said as a statement more than a question because I didn't like the sound of her voice when she said his name—it was filled with worry.

"He came to me to say the Podunks have decided war with Wangunks."

"He told you that?"

"My father and I, yes."

I tried to keep my voice down just as she did, but some of the others could tell something was wrong. You could see it in the way that they looked at us. "So, one tribe has decided for war when all the others did not? Just because your father won't trade furs? How can that be?"

"It may be more than trade furs. Father thinks it to do with Gowanus not receiving me as a mate. That or because Podunks land is not as bountiful as ours and winter moon is coming."

I replayed the events to try and come to the same conclusion, "The answer first came back from the Podunks just after Gowanus had left, and it was undecided. Now Gowanus comes and says that they will. Did he have enough time to get to his village and back here again?"

"Yes," Namoenee replied.

"So, whatever news he brought back to his sachem affected the answer. And the only news he could have given was that he was free now and that he did not win your affection or that you had chosen to be with a another man." I wanted to say "white man."

"To war is not Gowanus's decision; it was his sachem, Yertum, which is his father. Gowanus came here to try and change my mind."

"About me, because he thinks he loves you and wants you for his own."

"Yes."

"So, Yertum knows that his son loves you and the union obviously would have made the tribes allies. The winter wouldn't be as harsh for the Podunks if they moved here, or if we supplied them with food for the winter." It came together for me, "But his son did not win you or the alliance during his stay and Yertum wants to make war because of it."

"Yertum is juni – crazy."

"When will this happen?"

"The Podunks could come as early as five suns from now."

Five days didn't leave much time to prepare. "When will your father tell the tribe?"

"After challenge is over day after zob," Namoenee stumbled on the equivalent English word, but she soon came up with it. "Zob means tomorrow."

I had almost forgotten about the challenge. "Well, if I win today, the challenge will be over."

"It might be, and I think we should celebrate your win while we wait, but you first must wash," she said with a sheepish grin on her face. I knew she wanted to be naked with me again but why wash? I looked down at myself and noticed for the first time that I had dried blood all over me from carrying the gutted deer on my shoulders.

I laughed, "Why don't *you* wash me, and then *I'll* teach you to swim?"

Namoenee hesitated a while and then respond, "Sound like equal trade."

I threw my hunting stuff, along with the pouch with the heart and liver in it, just inside the opening to our hut, and we headed for the water. I could tell that Namoenee was very apprehensive about learning to swim, but I didn't hear a peep of negativity come out of her. As we reached the shore, she stripped down to her birthday suit and strolled into the lukewarm water with me.

After I was clean, which was awesome having her rub me down with her delicate touch, I held her hand and coaxed her out to deeper waters. When the water reached her chest, she was breathing rather heavily, and I could see she was very nervous. I held her gaze in my eyes and I think that that gave her the courage to continue.

"The first thing you need to do is learn how to float," I said to her reassuringly. "So lay on your back to start with, and I will support you from underneath."

"You won't let go?"

I told her I wouldn't, but it took a long time for her to let go of my hand. Eventually, she ended up as I suggested.

"Now remember, any time you want to stop all you have to do is stand up. Okay?"

My bride didn't respond. She just nodded her head ever so slightly in agreement. I let her get a feel for the water around her as I supported her upper and lower back. When I sensed the tension ease in her muscles, I moved her slowly around in a circle and used myself as a pivot point. She actually smiled and told me it felt nice. After five or six circles, I stood her up.

"Now let's try the same thing with you on your stomach."

She didn't question it, but instead, she lifted her arms above her head, and waited for me to position my hands in front of her. In less time than it took her to lay on her back, she was on her stomach with my arms across her mid-section and hips. Her head remained above the water, which was okay, as I wanted her to be comfortable with the position first. And she seemed comfortable as long as I held her.

"I've got you. Now take a deep breath and place your face in the water," I instructed her. She did it but not for long. Her head came up with a sputter, and she brushed the hair and water out of her face. I wanted to laugh because her reaction seemed more like a five year-old and not like a woman of twenty-seven, but I held it back. It's not like she hadn't washed her face or hair before. I had her try it a couple more times.

"Try it again, but this time open your eyes. There's a lot to see down there," I suggested for her fourth try. I wanted her to be distracted by looking around instead of thinking of what she was actually doing. It worked because this time she kept her head down for a long time and looking at her exquisite, bare ass distracted me.

She sputtered again, "That is beautiful." She wanted to do it again.

"Alright, but this time I'm going to move you around like I did when you were on your back."

"Yes, yes. Move me. I want to see all around," the princess who had never swam before said with the excitement of experiencing something new, as her namesake suggested, and she liked it.

I spun her around twice slowly as she continued to hold her breath, but then I stood her up again because she wasn't coming up for air on her own.

She got a little whiny with me, "Why did you stop?"

"I thought you needed a breath."

"I am fine. I want to do it again."

"I want to show you something else. Lay on your back again."

Namoenee gave a little sigh but did as I asked. "Now take a deep breath and hold it." As she floated there, I told her, "See how your body rises in the water?" I barely held onto her. "Exhale and feel your body lower down again."

"What is exhale?" she asked, no longer nervous about the lesson.

"Exhale means to breathe out. Try again."

She did that for a period of time, and I only held her up using my fingertips. "Breath in and hold it," I said, and I let go. She floated there with her eyes closed and a big grin on her face. As soon as she exhaled, I placed my arms underneath her again. "You were floating," I said.

"I was," she said amazed and proud.

"Do you want to try it on your stomach?"

"Yes."

As my bride floated there in my arms, I could tell she was finally comfortable at being in the water. She was excited even as she looked around at the many fish swimming at and around my feet. When she at last came up for air, I stood her up again to teach her some basic strokes like the breast and sidestroke.

"But I want swim like you," Namoenee said as she pawed at the air trying to imitate the crawl.

She was so cute I could hardly stand it. Her eagerness and innocence were that of a child, but I didn't give in to her wish for her own safety, "First things first, dear heart. We all learn to crawl before we walk you know."

The princess gave a pause for thought, bowed her head slightly with disappointment, and then said, "I understand, my husband." She then lurched forward playfully, threw her arms around my neck and kissed me on the cheek. Her wet, naked body felt wonderful against mine.

"What was that for?" I asked.

"Because you care for me."

"I do," I confirmed. We kissed passionately as she wrapped her legs around my waist and the swimming lesson ended there as a more preferred breaststroke took its place and my hand came to rest on her chest. Our eyes met and we both smiled the same kind of smile. Without a word we agreed it was time for me to bed her down. The swimming lesson would have to continue another day. I carried her out of the water toward our hut, but we were rudely interrupted.

As we reached the beach, we heard a young boy yell out from the village that Warrior's Cry had returned. I stopped in my tracks with my bride still in my arms and her legs still around me. Everyone stopped whatever they were doing and ran to where the youngster stood. I placed Namoenee down, we reluctantly put our clothes back on, and we followed the crowd. I was nervous. I wanted the challenge to be over. *Please let him bring back a smaller deer*, I pleaded in my mind. I sensed Namoenee had the same feeling as she squeezed my hand.

The tribe began to cheer as Warrior's Cry emerged from the forest edge. He had his deer mounted to a makeshift litter that he held onto by vines that were wrapped around his torso and shoulders. We could all see that his shoulders were bleeding. No one saw his kill as he approached, but in my heart, by seeing those lacerations, I knew I had lost the day's event. The way the vines dug into his shoulders could only mean one thing. The weight of his deer was surely more than what I had carried back. He dropped to his knees and the litter went down—exposing the beast. The tribe went completely berserk.

I discovered that there are sounds of winning and there are sounds of losing, and sometimes they are one in the same. The crowd had cheered just as loud for me the day before as they did then for Warrior's Cry. He had brought back a fourteen-pointer, which must have weighed in at about two-ten, judging by the size of him. It broke my heart.

Namoenee's hand slipped out of mine as she left to retrieve the hunting pouch from our hut. When she returned, she instructed me to go and offer the heart to the winner. I did, and in return, Warrior's Cry gave me the liver from out of his pouch. It was almost twice the size of the liver that remained in mine. I knew then what I would be eating for dinner, and it wasn't going to be crow although that's sure how it felt.

Wood's Edge walked through the mass of people. He carried a red flag high above everyone's head and placed it into the east-side pole. The crowd hooted and hollered. One blue flag and one red flapped together in the late summer breeze. The challenge was tied, and all that was left was the red wrestle.

*   *   *

Milford, CT was where I had my first kiss. I was eight years old. Her name was Sheryl, and she was a long brown haired, skinny girl with whom I was smitten. We were friends though I didn't know much about her, and while hanging out on the

[140]

beach one day, she just walked right up to me and planted a full kiss on my lips. The puppy love kiss was short lived, because she ran away from me afterward – either because she was coy or nervous. Thinking back on it, I don't blame her. I remember it well because it was my first kiss from someone other than my sister, mother, grandmother, or from my Aunt Thelma—the overweight, pearl necklace wearer who always smelled of too much perfume and whose lips were always ruby red. Was Sheryl my first girlfriend? I don't think I even knew what that meant. Were we going steady? I didn't think so. I mean, we never talked about it. I liked her and she me, and when you are that age it seemed to be a lot more than it was. We rode our bikes or walked on the beach together, and it honestly wasn't much more than that until she kissed me.

Anyway, I had my first fight during this period in my life, and Sheryl was the indirect cause of it. Another boy named Vinnie liked her, and he made his interest known to the both of us. He would break us apart any chance he could when he saw us together during and after school hours. He was a real pain in the ass. He was my first real enemy and most times I backed down because I didn't know how to handle the situation – until one particular day when I had enough.

I was on my brand new ten-speed bike talking to Sheryl when Vinnie seemed to appear out of nowhere to disrupt us again. He stood next to me and occasionally leaned on my bike. When that didn't provoke me enough, he started bending the spokes of my rear tire with his left foot. That's what did it. I mean, I took his words with a grain of salt, but when he actually started destroying my property I became enraged. I reached back with a clenched right fist and punched him in his left kidney. He faltered a little, but not enough and he was soon on me. Apparently, he hadn't heard anything about not punching a guy with glasses because he started to swing with both arms. I was very upset to be in a real fight, and I didn't want it to continue. In fact, I tried to walk away, but he kept coming at me. I remember that he ran at me three times from behind and each time I just bent forward and he ended up somersaulting over the top of me. He wasn't stronger, he certainly wasn't smarter, and he didn't have the training in the woods like I did, but he kept coming. So I gathered my emotions, placed them in check, and just started wailing on the poor kid. I just kept punching him until he gave up.

Afterward, I felt empowered because I had won. Vinnie left Sheryl and me alone after that day, but I never got to know her better because my mom got a new job and we moved away soon afterward. I never saw her or heard from her after I moved away, but I came away victorious and confident.

The move brought another new place, new friends, and new enemies. I got into a lot of fights after this second move in two years. I think my mom decided then to enroll me in martial arts to try and channel my aggressions.

*　　*　　*

The son of a bitch bit me. I don't know if Warrior's Cry really hated me, or if he just wanted to make me as injured as he was because of the bruises on his shoulders, which he received from the vine straps the previous day. Whichever it was, he sunk his teeth into my upper arm, and I yelped because of it.

It was day three of the challenge, the last event, and it was the red wrestle.

Warrior's Cry and I faced each other as we stood just inside the inner circle of the strike pole area at its north end. Wood's Edge took an inch wide, three-foot long piece of leather and handed one end of it to Warrior's Cry. He held it in his left hand. When it was handed to me, I did the same and held it in my left hand – leaving my dominant right hand free. Wood's Edge then strolled to the opposite end of the arena and very ceremoniously thrust a knife into the top of the south strike pole. From our position, he stood tall between the blue and red flags. I turned back to face my opponent and he stared at me with a tremendous scowl – apparently trying to intimidate me. I returned his look of distaste to show him his antics weren't doing anything, and he immediately started to wrap the strap around his palm. I did the same until there were maybe six to eight inches between our hands. He grunted and snarled. And I laughed in his face. I wasn't afraid of him.

The object of the challenge was to wrestle each other from one end of the circle to the other and gain control of the knife in order to cut the strap that was between us. If one of us slipped out of the strap or gave up and let go on purpose, then it would be a loss. If no one let go, then the person who cut the rawhide could then retrieve the prize that Wood's Edge held in his hand. My gold watch shined brilliantly in the sunlight.

Namoenee told me that the "red" part of the match usually meant blood by any means necessary to reach the knife before your opponent did. I glanced at her in the mob of people as she sat next to her father. Her brow was curled in worry, but I gave her a reassuring nod that it was going to be okay. It would be—one way or the other. If I didn't win, then I would resort to stealing the watch.

Snow Falling stood in front of us as he did the first day of the three part challenge and I could tell he was proud to do it. He raised his arms high into the air for all to see, held them there for a second or two (just like Mr. Parmelee), and then swung them down straight.

The red wrestle had begun.

I expected both of us to just run toward the knife and have a little wrestling match as we drew closer. Instead, as soon as Snow Falling dropped his arms, Warrior's Cry lunged and pulled at me until I was close enough for him to cause me injury. Our left arms overlapped, and our shoulders touched for only a second. And that's when he bit me. He lowered his head and chomped down on my upper arm just below my tattoo. The Wangunks were very superstitious, and I didn't know if he thought he could gain power from me by sucking some blood out of my arm (or my tattoo), but it really only succeeded in pissing me off.

After my initial surprise and while he was still latched on, I gave him a roundhouse punch that caught him square in the left ear. He released his painful toothy grip and staggered back as far as the tether allowed. We stood there a moment. I was holding my arm, and he was cupping his ear. The crowd cheered. Both of our hands came away with blood on them.

The red wrestle event only got worse from there.

He pulled hard against my hold on the strap.

I pulled hard back at him.

We circled each other while looking for a weakness and the dust from the dry ground started to rise up around our ankles.

Warrior's Cry kicked some loose dirt at my feet, and I made a move. I used his pull against me to carry my momentum toward him, and I came up to his right side. I swung my right leg behind his and pushed him hard in the chest. Between my actions and the slack that suddenly appeared in the strap, he went down with ease. As soon as he hit the ground, I started tugging with all my might. I wanted him to let go and lose right there, but all I did was drag him across the ground as my yanking gave way to an all out pull.

Dragging my opponent worked until I neared the fire pit in the center of the arena. It was there that I lost my footing on some loose soil and fell. Warrior's Cry seized the moment to gain the upper hand and got up before I could. He started to do the dragging.

After I had dragged him fifteen feet, and he dragged me about five, my left hand was on fire. The leather strap dug into my flesh, and I felt it start to slip from the mixture of blood and sweat. It hurt worse than the bite marks in my shoulder and all I wanted to do was to let go. Instead, I grabbed the tether in the middle with my right hand to give my left hand some slack and unwrapped it a couple of times. Luckily for me my right hand didn't slip nor did my opponent turn around to see what I was doing. At that point, I barely held on to the strap, and I could have easily lost had he noticed. I quickly rewrapped the strap, but this time I included my wrist a couple of times before I returned it to my palm for a single circumference.

The bond felt more secure than it had to start with, so I flipped over onto my back. Then I spun on my butt until my feet pointed forward and I was in a seated position. I dug in my heels and Warrior's Cry tripped up on my intruding feet. And with that move, Warrior's Cry pulled me right up to my feet. After getting us ten feet closer to the knife, he was met with resistance again. The tribe cheered loudly once more.

I went to punch him in the head again with my free right fist, but he blocked it with his left arm, and with his free right, he grabbed me by the wrist. There wasn't enough slack in the leather strap for me to do anything with my left hand, so our arms ended up crossed above our heads. We started to kick each other in the shins. Some landed, some missed. We pushed, pulled, and shoved at each other.

I grew incredibly hot. It wasn't as hot as the "hellhole," but it was close enough when you have a man of equal strength and body temperature only inches away with the bright sun beating down. Fortunately, his grip on me loosened from the sweat, and I twisted my arm and spun my body and he lost his hold of me. I found myself in a terribly awkward position because my back ended up toward Warrior's Cry, and I felt him try to take advantage of it. I had to think fast on my feet.

It was only because of the tether that I felt him lower his hands to wrap them around my upper body. And I let him, because I thought that once his arms were at my shoulder level I could grab hold and flip him over my back. I thought wrong.

I felt a hand land on my shoulder, and then the second one grabbed hold of the waist of my shorts, and I was suddenly pulled backward and hoisted into the air high above Warrior's Cry's head. There was nothing I could do to prevent it.

Warrior's Cry let out a scream that curdled my blood. The tribe's cheers grew louder. I quickly looked around for a chance to escape my horizontal predicament as he carried me toward the south strike pole and the knife, but it happened so fast that I saw no opportunity to do anything except watch my fate.

Victory was soon at hand for my opponent, for as we neared the pole he threw me up against it. If I had crashed into the pole with the small of my back then I am sure that I would have been paralyzed, but because of the short tether and Warrior's Cry ill attempt, I spun in midair and slammed up against the pole with my stomach instead. The severity of it was the wind was knocked out of me, and I laid there, gasping for air and watched Warrior's Cry pull the knife out of the top of the smooth stump. As the saying goes, "Haste makes waste," and Warrior's Cry took the time for a pre-celebration with the mob of people who were exploding with excitement. He raised the knife up high to show everyone, to make the moment of the win last just a second longer, and that was his mistake.

I laid there at his feet, barely able to breathe, and watched his gloating. I did the only thing I could to stop him. I raised a leg, cocked it back, and in a last ditch effort to win, I thrust my heel directly into his groin. Warrior's Cry never saw it coming. His straining face went deep red and he fell to his knees, which brought the knife down to the ground next to me. I lunged for it.

Only one hand had a sure grip on the knife handle and it belonged to my adversary. As I tried to pry it from him, he gained enough composure to start to fight back again. We rolled over each other, again and again, with the sharp blade between us until we came to the circle of rocks in the center of the playing field. When our roll finally stopped, I found myself on top. The knife had worked its way up between our faces. Warrior's Cry pushed the blade at me, and I felt a slice open up in my cheek. I pulled back to almost a sitting position with enough force to keep him from cutting me more and his right hand came free. I suddenly had the advantage, and I used all my weight to slam his arm down on a rock near his head. I heard a sharp crack, which meant I had broken his arm, and he let the knife fall to the ground. We both looked for it at the same time, and we both saw where it landed. Warrior's Cry looked back at me, and I at him. I could see that he still had resolve in his squinty, hateful eyes.

I placed my left knee on his right arm and pinned him down. He bucked and squirmed to be rid of my weight upon him as I reached for the knife. His left arm was caught underneath him and couldn't move. I grabbed hold of the knife and brought it back into Warrior's Cry's sight. He bucked some more, so I placed the knife at his throat and he immediately stopped his struggle. He grimaced at first, but then his whole body relaxed, his eyes closed, and he stretched out his neck as an offering.

I placed the sharp edge against his skin and then hesitated. *What are you doing?* I thought.

I moved the knife down to the strap and sliced through it like butter. I had won.

As I stood up, free from my bond, the piece of leather still in my left hand dangled down to brush against my knee. I looked up from it to face the crowd, and they went berserk. The taste of warm salty fluid filled my mouth, and I realized it was my blood from the cut on my cheek. I spat it out to the ground in distaste of the whole event. If it were Warrior's Cry who stood before the tribe, then they would have cheered just as loudly. I felt as if I could care less. I just wanted my watch back. I walked over to the edge of the sea of celebrating faces to stand before Wood's Edge. The knife was still firmly seated in my right hand.

He stood and wound his way through the bodies to me. I didn't say anything. I didn't even smile. I just looked him square in the eye the whole time and as he drew close, I raised my left hand up and open. He stopped in front of me. Wood's Edge didn't say anything, and when he saw that I wasn't going to smile, his smile dissipated, and he handed me the watch very solemnly. I looked down at it resting in my leather wrapped palm. The picture of my dad's carport among the trees back on Bay Road showed in pictured relief. I closed my fingers around it, dropped the knife at his feet, and walked back to my hut.

The crowd didn't notice my lack of enthusiasm, or they just didn't care because they carried on with their own celebration as I passed through them. I don't blame

Wood's Edge for calling for the challenge to settle the dispute, and I don't blame the Wangunks for their excitement either, but at that point in time I no longer wanted to be with them. I wanted to go home, to my old home, back to my days.

Namoenee caught up to me as excited as the first day of the challenge, "You have won, my husband."

I continued walking and did not respond.

"Are you not happy?" she asked.

I stopped in front of our hut. "No," I answered and went inside.

Namoenee followed me in. I sat down on the bed and wiped the blood off of my face with a forearm. My bride came and kneeled on the reed mats by my side. "What's wrong?"

"When I held the knife to Warrior's Cry's neck, and he exposed it to me ..." I opened my fist to see the prize I had reclaimed and then paused in disbelief at the words I said next. "I wanted to kill him. I ... I don't belong here."

"Do not say these words James. We are meant to be," Namoenee said with certain conviction. She sat up on the bed with me and softly placed a hand on my face. She guided me to face her, and she winced when she saw the extent of my cut. "You did not kill Warrior's Cry. You could have, but you showed your kindness, and that is what I love about you."

She went to one of the woven baskets and pulled out a jar of salve. It was the same one used for my wrist and leg when I first arrived and a flicker of a smile passed my lips as I remembered it was her who took care of me. It was she who had the kindness she spoke of. When she returned to me, Namoenee started to spread the ointment into my wound, and all I could do was look into those caring eyes of hers. I felt lost in those eyes. Her eyes were soft and clear, gentle and affectionate, and their dark brown color, with a hint of gold mixed in when the light hit them right, eased my troubled mind. I knew I wouldn't leave her. I couldn't. She was right when she said we were meant to be.

I kissed her unexpectedly.

"Feeling better?" she inquired.

"Much better. Thank you."

"You are welcome my husband," she said and returned the clay jar back to its home. I looked at the watch again for a moment and then placed it in my pocket.

When Namoenee turned to me she had her fingers in her mouth as she sucked off the residual salve.

"How *much* better are you feeling?" she asked with a change of attitude from caregiver to vixen.

I undid the strap from my left hand and wrist and then nonchalantly let it fall to the reed mat on the floor. "I believe it's time to celebrate my victory," I answered smugly.

She stripped off her hides and with a broad smile on her face she undulated toward me in a very, very sexy fashion. I instantly became aroused, so I stood and tore off my jean shorts, and we met each other naked. We didn't exit the hut until the next morning.

*　　*　　*

I woke a second time with a revived sense of belonging. I was with the woman I loved, and I had regained possession of the time travelling watch. When I went to shave (with the straight edge of my knife) and bathe (with Wangunk soap naturally made from the surrounding elements) in the morning light, I was at peace with myself again. I waved to everyone I saw, and they waved back. I was happy.

Namoenee cooked us breakfast and then joined me in the water after we cleaned up. I gave her some more swimming lessons, which came along quite nicely. She gained the confidence to venture out a little way and swam on her own, and I was quite proud of her. It was only her second day of lessons, and she caught on quickly with her thirst for knowledge.

After lunch and some light chores in the hut and around the village, we went for a long walk around the lakes and ended up sitting on the rocky cliff that bordered the smaller lake on its southeast side. We talked about anything and everything. We talked about nothing. We enjoyed each other's company and looked over the water from a hundred feet up. From our vantage, I could clearly see where my father's cottage would be built in the future, and we could see faint smoke coming from the village as the others started their early dinners.

Namoenee excused herself because she had to urinate before we headed back. I pulled out the watch while I waited for her and popped open the cover. It told me it was five o'clock, and I realized that I didn't care. I'm not even really sure why I looked at the time other than it was an old habit that had returned. The Wangunks didn't care about time or whether they had to be anywhere or do anything at any given time. They *did* care about harvest time and when to sow the seeds, but when it came to daily time, they weren't interested.

The challenge was over and everything returned to normal for the Wangunks until Wood's Edge called for another tribal council meeting that night. It was time to prepare for war.

WAR

Each man in the tribe who had been in a skirmish of any sort had an eagle feather that they wore in their hair when the time came to face an enemy. Not only did the number of eagle feathers worn signify how many fights you had been in, but also what kind of fights as well, and the shape and color of the feathers determined the differences.

For instance, a white feather dyed black at its tip meant that the wearer struck at his enemy first. A white feather with black tip and a black band at its base signaled that the bearer had two such encounters and struck at both of his enemies first. A warrior could end up with four bands on his black tipped feather before he received another. If he was lucky enough to come away without any scrapes of his own, that is. If the feather was dyed all black, then it meant that an enemy wounded you without you causing him any harm, and if it were all black and split down the middle along its shaft, then you had received many wounds. A brown feather without any dye showed that you had killed a woman by accident, which was not a sought after feather by any means, but there were some who wore them. If you owned a feather, which was white with a black tip and had a black spot painted on it, then it showed that you had killed a male enemy. The more spots there were on the feather meant the more victims that had fallen under your prowess.

I knew the Wangunks were not the warring type because not many of the men had a lot of feathers to display. Only a noted warrior could wear the stereotypical war bonnet that consisted of fifty or more feathers, and there was only one person to wear such a bonnet in the Wangunk tribe. It was my father-in-law, Chief Tahadondeh, Wood's Edge.

Namoenee tied three feathers in my hair, which had grown just long enough in the five weeks I had been there for her to do so. I told her that the feathers would look silly with my length hair, but she insisted on giving me two white feathers and a third. The first had a black tip and black band, and the second one was similar, but instead of a band at the base, it had two black spots. It was an unpleasant reminder for me that I had killed, but I understood the reasoning for the symbolism. The feathers were pride for some, but they were mostly worn to show your experience to the enemy. If you met an Indian who had more feathers than you did, then you may choose not to engage him and vice versa. It led to a more peaceful existence. The third feather Namoenee gave me was a beautifully long brown pheasant tail feather with a black speckled pattern on it. My bride told me it had no significance other than she thought it would look nice. I robustly thanked her for it and then headed off to the tribal council meeting.

The Chief's tribal council, my second since my arrival, was far from mundane. The first one was just a back and forth, questions and answers. This second one came as a surprise to me because I had never seen the tribe so rowdily boisterous before. Wood's Edge had the all the males, young and old alike, in an uproar as he told them that the Podunks had sent word that they would wage war against the Wangunks. Against us. He said that it was not the Wangunks' fault that the Podunks allowed themselves to be so careless with their food supplies, and the fact that the white man was encroaching on their lands. I felt self-conscious when he said that last bit, though no one looked in my direction. Wood's Edge continued by saying that there was no room for negotiations and we would fight to the death to save our land, our supplies, our women, and our children. He stood tall above the mob within the center of the gathering hut between the two fire pits, and his shadow predominantly danced in many places along the walls of the interior. My father-in-law made sure to look everyone in the eye as he turned to face the warriors. He was a terrific orator. In my day, he would have made a good politician or pontificator. Though he boosted their spirits and pride and had the mass all psyched to save their way of life, he changed the mood somewhat when he asked for suggestions on how they should proceed. *What?* Some of the others and I were taken aback a bit because I (and apparently the others) had never seen or heard him ask advice from anyone before, not even from his daughter. Sure, he would consult the Powwaw, but never his tribe. And never about matters of war. He was their leader. Maybe because he knew some of his people were going to die, he wanted to hear their opinion on the matter. Whatever the reason, he gained more respect from his tribe that night. You could see it in their eyes, for they felt important.

My fishing buddy, Eagle Wing, was seated next to me, and he suddenly stood and said something to the affect of, "We should not wait for the Podunks to come to us. We should meet them in battle." He sat back down and didn't look to anyone for approval. He just looked to see what Tahadondeh would say next.

Wood's Edge scanned the crowd and paused a little too long in my direction. Was he looking for rebuttal suggestions from me, or an agreement to Eagle Wing? I did not know.

He Sings stood, "We should send out scouts to see when they will come, so we will be ready."

Others stood.

"We should build a barricade," one said.

"We should move out to the islands, for we will be better protected by the water."

"I agree with Eagle Wing," said another.

Wood's Edge looked directly at me again. His demeanor suggested it was my turn to speak, so I did, reluctantly. I wasn't going to, I admit, but he had a way of making people do things just by looking at them, and he was looking to me for a suggestion but wanted it to seem unsolicited.

There comes a turning point in each person's life—a benchmark if you will. Perhaps, for some there are many, but this was one for me that I will never forget. I wasn't fond of killing another human, of this I was certain, but given the recent events I knew that if there was going to be a war between the Podunks and the Wangunks, then I would fight tooth and nail to preserve my new way of life. So, in order to save my woman and her people—my people—I knew I would have to kill again. Only this time, I had a plan.

"I do not agree," I said as I stood, and the hut went immediately quiet.

I looked out over everyone in the hut and decided to take a chance and speak my mind. All they could do was laugh in my face if they disagreed. Without Namoenee there to translate for me, I know I left big gaps in my sentence structure, but I gave them what I thought was a good plan. "Let's be sneaky," I told them and told them how, and when I was done Tahadondeh looked to his people for an answer.

Warrior's Cry was the first to stand. He cradled his arm. *Oh no*, I thought. *He's the last person I want to hear from. He's probably going to oppose everything I said just because I beat him in the challenge.* I was shocked when he agreed that my plan

[153]

could work. Others began to stand and soon the whole tribe was in unison. We would use my plan of action, and I hoped that it would work because my life and the lives of others depended on it. I had a plan that would keep any Wangunk involved alive and well.

*   *   *

"How dare you suggest that I take the women and children and go hide while *you* and the men stay here and defend *my* people?" Namoenee glared at me with a sternness I had not seen from her before. She was full of surprises just like her father.

"Your father looked to me for a plan. I gave him one and the tribe agreed," I said quickly. I didn't really know what the problem was. "I thought you would be happy. I was trying to think of you and the other women," I paused just long enough to catch up with my thoughts. "I want you all to be safe until this is over. This is for the elderly and especially the children."

"And I am neither!" Namoenee paced the floor of her father's hut and then walked right up to him and stared him in the face. "I am your daughter. I am the sachem's daughter. Do you really want me to run and hide like a timid mouse?"

"Yes," he answered plainly.

"And why would you call for advice from my husband?" I didn't take her question personally. Even though we were married, I was the outsider after all.

"You have always been too curious."

"It is in my nature," she said sternly.

"It is really of no concern to you, my daughter, what *I* choose to do or not do, but if you must know then it is because when I go to see Hobomoko, the Great Spirit in the sky, your husband will become sachem. It is our way as you are well aware of. You are my only daughter and he is now my only son. I must start the tribe in trusting him or they will kill him after I am gone."

The tribe would kill me? I was finally understanding Tahadondeh, because I was a wonnux, a white man, it was unheard of for someone like me to become sachem of a Native American tribe unless the tribe knew I had an exemplary history that showed only interest for the well being of the tribe. That would be the only way for them to respect me and accept me in succession of their chief. It wouldn't matter if I were married to the Princess after Wood's Edge passed on; if they did not trust me to lead them, then they would overthrow me by assassination. Wood's Edge was wise beyond his years and I had serious doubt that I could ever succeed him even if I wanted to.

* * *

For three days, I was without the company of Namoenee, and life was boring and unromantic without her. All the males felt different without their companions, mothers, and sisters. The village just wasn't the same without my bride or any of the women, the weak, or the children to make us whole. The men who stayed and waited for the Podunks to show just moped about as lonely as I was. We didn't have the luxury of living our normal lives, and we couldn't venture much outside the boundaries of our village. So, we just waited.

We all helped each other with minor repairs to various huts throughout the village and there were some unenthusiastic games of hubbub in between chores to kill the time. Tobacco was shared after some of the meals, but there was no jocularity or relaxation involved in it. Individually, some of the male folk buried their personal items to keep them from being stolen, and others just sat in their huts and prayed all day. There were sixty plus capable males who stayed for the fight, and as we waited, we did these menial tasks to keep our minds off of the missing our women and children, but mostly, we kept busy to keep our minds off of the impending war. Waiting can sometimes be harder than doing.

Then on the third day of waiting, word came from our scouts that the Podunks would soon be on us. The enemy had decided to be early, but we were ready. Back at the tribal council I had agreed with He Sings to send out scouts, but it was my idea to send them out only so far. With the tribe's approval, the scouts camped on the tops of the hills that surrounded Lake Pocotopaug and waited for signs that the Podunks were coming. According to what the scouts had seen, the Podunks were only coming from the North, and they would approach the village along the Western shoreline of the lake. After almost three full days of boredom, tensions mounted, as it was time to take our positions.

The Podunks approach to the village was very slow and cautious though they had not been met with any resistance. As they reached the perimeter of the village, everything looked normal as smoke rose from the roofs of huts from recently built fires within, but there was no activity within the village. It looked deserted. The Wangunks appeared to be gone. The Podunks eased out from behind their concealment of trees and brush and stepped slowly out onto the grassy clearing. There were four dozen warriors in their party, and you could tell they didn't know what to make of the recently vacated village. They were bewildered. But with each step forward, they grew more confident in their belief that no one was there. They started to slip in and out of huts to make sure, but they found no one. Smiles appeared on their war painted faces, and after a while, they hooted and hollered because they thought they had a victory in their possession.

They thought the Wangunks had given up their land in order not to fight them. The Podunks thought they had won a war without the need to deliver a single blow. They thought that since no one was there to defend the village that they could relax and enjoy their spoils.

They thought wrong.

The Podunks gathered in the center of the village, and just as they let down their guard and began to celebrate their un-fought victory, a flaming arrow soared across the sky in a high arc above their heads. It was high enough for the Podunks to miss it, but low enough that for those of us who watched for it, even those that hid underneath the water along the shoreline breathing through cattail stalks, could see it. The arrow snuffed out when it hit the water sixty yards out from shore and that was the signal we'd all been waiting for.

Our attack began in waves.

First, ten men emerged from the water with their bows ready and they loosened their arrows without warning. Eight Podunk men went down to the ground with sudden injuries. When the remaining Podunks turned to see what had happened to their brethren, ten more Wangunks stepped out from the tree line opposite the shore and set sharpened spears to flight. Seven more Podunks went down. I signaled the five men in the trees to swing down from on high using wisteria vines that I had shown them how to use. Then we, the rest of the tribe as one unit, rushed the Podunks with weapons drawn.

The Podunks had no idea what had happened to them, and by the time they figured it out, it was too late. We had them surrounded and they laid down their weapons. My plan had worked, or at least that's what we all had thought.

Where is Gowanus? I thought in passing as I looked over the surrendered mob.

Suddenly, a shot was fired from a gun. It was loud and startling. Before the echoes of it could return to us from the surrounding hills, He Sings was catapulted forward. He lay at our feet with a nickel-sized hole in his back. He was dead, and then the mayhem ensued.

Everyone scattered as a second shot was fired. This time a Podunk was hit in the shoulder. The bullet went completely through. I say bullet, but as soon as I saw the size of the hole in He Sings' back, I knew it was a musket ball. The musket rifle was a single action shooter, which used wadding, powder, a lead ball, and a long steel shaft to pack them all into the three foot long barrel. The rifleman who shot first didn't have enough time to reload before the second shot was fired, so I knew there were at least two of them out there.

I turned in the direction of the gunshot and saw a white puff of smoke that rose and mixed in with the leaves in the trees. It looked like a vapor ghost that floated there among the living. I followed the smoke down to see a slight rustle in the bushes.

I found one of you. I switched my ball club over to my left hand and drew out my revolver from my waistband with my right and fired a couple into the bushes before I ran behind one of the huts for cover.

It was the hut next to mine, and it belonged to Fat Fish. He used to complain about my snoring until Namoenee moved in with me. Either I had stopped my nighttime vibrations, or Fatty, as I jokingly called him though he wasn't overweight at all, decided it best not to say anything about the husband of his chief's daughter. Maybe I had just stopped snoring when she moved in. The warmth of a woman can do wonders.

Another musket shot was fired. This time it was directed at me. It tore off some bark on the hut at waist height. I inched my way around the edge of the hut just enough to see the general direction and fired two more shots.

When I put my back up against the side of the hut, I saw a Podunk warrior rush at me with a spear raised up to his waist with both hands like a minuteman coming after

[157]

me with a bayonet. When the shots were first fired everyone had scattered and left the Podunks to be free again, so I raised my gun and shot him square in the chest.

I looked up from his body on the ground and saw the rest of the village in an uproar. Some of the huts were on fire and the Wangunks and Podunks fought hand to hand. I saw some of my new family struggling to survive even though at the onset we had an advantage in numbers. I fired my last cartridge when I realized I had left the two boxes of forty-fives in my hut. I didn't think I was going to be in a gunfight. *So much for my devious plan.*

The opening to my bark house loomed in front of me. I decided to make a quick sprint over the short twenty feet, but halfway there a Podunk tripped me up. I rolled into the fall and came up to face him in a crouched position. I was prepared to fight him, but another shot fired from the tree line dropped him for me. I finished the run into my hut just as the second musket rifle went off.

I laid my ball club and gun on the bed and grabbed the two boxes of cartridges. I spilled one of them out onto the black bear furs and grabbed a couple handfuls of bullets and placed them in my front pockets. I left six behind to reload with.

Just then, a body appeared at my doorway and rushed in. I reached for the club and raised it as I spun around. At first, all I saw was long black hair that made its way past the hide cover, and as I was about to strike when I heard, "It's me."

It was Namoenee.

I threw the club back down on the bed and we embraced. "What are you doing here?" I asked.

"I am here to fight by your side, my husband."

"Not only are you 'She That Is Curious', but you're 'She That Is Stubborn' as well. Is that it?"

"Among other things," she smiled.

"You're telling me," I smiled back. I couldn't argue with her. She was already there and I didn't have the luxury of time. I had to deal with the riflemen before more of my people were gunned down. "Okay," I said, "take these," and I handed her the second box of bullets. She tucked the box into a pocket of sorts located on the outside of her short deer skin skirt and then grabbed a bow and a fox quiver of arrows off of the wall.

I winced when I saw her do it. I didn't want her to fight anyone. That's why I had come up with the plan to send her away in the first place, but if she was going to fight, then she now had her choice of weapon.

The two shooters were careless as they both fired at roughly the same time, and it gave us the opportunity to exit out into the open before either one had a chance to reload. Namoenee followed close behind as we ran behind Fatty's hut. I fired twice as we did in the direction where the rifle shots were fired last, but I didn't know if they had moved positions while I was inside. As I peered around the corner of the hut, I could sense that Namoenee was keeping herself busy behind me as she sent arrows to targets of her own.

"Let us not just sit here," she said in an innocent way without any malice or sarcasm toward me in her voice.

I explained that it took approximately ten seconds for the shooters to reload, and since I didn't know the enemy's exact location, we had to wait for them to fire again before making another move.

"You need to know where they are?"

"Yes," I responded as I continued to sneak a peek around the corner to see any signs of the riflemen.

"I will find out for you, my husband," Namoenee said and then scurried off.

I quickly spun around to stop her, but she was already gone. *Damn it.* A musket shot went off with another loud report. "God damn it!"

BETRAYAL

Feral is the only word to describe the situation I was in. There were cries of victory on top of screaming defeats, and I saw firsthand that war is ugly. War was just downright sad, and I found myself in the middle of it. Men—myself included—fought for their lives and it was nerve racking. Smoke and fire were everywhere. Men lay on the ground as blood oozed from beneath their skin and turned bright red as it oxidized. Some moved in agony and most didn't move at all. Maybe the latter were better off.

I was pinned down behind Fat Fish's hut by two riflemen that took turns firing shots at me. My guess, at the time, was that they concentrated on me because I was the only one in the village that was firing back at them. Thus, they kept their biggest threat pinned down and hoped to hit me before they ran out of ammunition. And Namoenee left with my second box, so I was the one that was low on cartridges. I decided I needed a new tactic. My bride was out there somewhere and I had to find her. It wasn't just because of the bullets I thought I would need to finish this fight with, but I had to find out if she was all right. She left my side in order to help me find the hiding spots of the shooters, but it had to have been over a half an hour since she did. I didn't know if she were wounded or dead, so I decided I needed to force the enemy's hand.

I reloaded my pistol and three slugs remained in my left pocket. My right was empty. My hands shook as I closed the cylinder and I tried to ignore it as I took a deep breath and popped my head up to fire another shot off. Eight bullets remained. One musket rifle shot back at me. I quickly ducked down but not for long because as I wanted to see the spot where the spent gunpowder rose. I had to take a chance.

Because I thought I had finally nailed down the area where the first shooter was, I ran the length of the hut back toward my own. I took the corner at full steam and headed straight for the hidden sniper. I hoped I had caught the second shooter off guard and that he was still aiming at the other side of the bark house. Just before I reached the tree line, I had heard another shot fired from the second rifleman, but I remained intact and launched my body head first into a horizontal dive over the waist high underbrush.

My dive into the woods, like I was sliding into second base, was not the smartest thing I've ever done. The small trees that grew up in that particular spot gave way under my arms and weight, but when I broke through them to the heftier thickness of the wood, I landed in a precarious position. I was stuck within a bush, and I was upside down.

After shaking the cobwebs out of my head I regained my bearings and my sight fell upon the rifleman. It took me a while to recognize him, but he was the tall skinny colonist that had partnered up with the shorter rotund man that Tahadondeh had killed the night Namoenee was almost taken. I was not surprised that he had returned. He sat facing me with his feet only a yard away from my face. Because my head was so close to the ground position, I noticed he had holes in the bottom of his boots, and he wore brightly colored socks. If I had the luxury of time to think about it, I would have found that very peculiar. First of all, he still wore the same dirty clothes from the first altercation, but his socks were clean and didn't look like they were from that time period.

As I looked up and into his muddy brown eyes, I could see that the surprise had turned to fright as he scrambled to finish reloading his musket rifle. I could tell he was nervous that I was so near him because he kept looking back and forth at me to see what I was doing, and he couldn't get the stamping rod into the hole of the barrel. One could say that I was a lucky individual, but in that same instant I was having trouble of my own. Not only was I upside down, but my hand and revolver were stuck back up near my waist. In my haste, I had panicked and I couldn't get the pistol free.

I pulled hard against the bush as I watched the white man find the hole and shove the rod down to its bottom. I pulled even harder as he finished his quick three taps and began to pull out the steel rod. As I pulled harder still, I felt a tug on my shorts. I had to take the time to look at what I was stuck on. The hammer of my pistol was caught in the front belt loop of my shorts.

I immediately pushed instead of pulled and the hammer came free. The gun and my arm were still restricted somewhat within the saplings, but I was able to bring them down through the many mini-trunks to take aim.

When I finally looked back, I saw the long barrel of the rifle swing down in my direction. I took aim as best as I could through the bush.

"It's time you paid for your interference, you E.T.A. scum" he said.

We both fired.

The smoke from both guns eventually cleared, and my enemy gasped for breath. His breathing was labored and it had a thick liquid sound to it like someone trying to breathe through a throat full of phlegm. I had shot him in the right side of his chest and it didn't take long before both lungs were filled. He quickly began to cough up blood.

Moments later, he couldn't breathe at all and collapsed backward to lie on the ground.

He was dead.

With both arms now somewhat free, I jockeyed myself into an upright position to look down upon the man who would have given anything to trade places with me. His mouth was agape and his eyes were halfway rolled up into his head as the flies began to buzz around him. The fresh blood on his chin and down his shirt was too hard for them to resist. I felt no remorse as I sneered down at him. I was glad he was gone though I wasn't smiling about it.

Just then, I heard a scream come from Namoenee a short distance away to my left, and I jerked my head up away from the corpse in the direction of the blare. It didn't sound like she was in trouble. It wasn't that kind of a scream. What it sounded like was pure hatred. If the situation had been different, then I wouldn't have thought she was capable of such a blood-curdling scream, except I knew it to be her because she was the only female around within a mile of the village. With the adrenaline still pumping through my veins I took off running and what I saw next was a terrible sight.

I came upon her as she stood over a body, and she was covered with splattered blood from the waist up. Her deer skin shirt had been ripped off of her during the obvious struggle, her hands were completely covered by the red liquid, and she held them out in front of her in shock of her own power. She was still breathing heavy when I ran up to her, and I looked down to see a dead Podunk who had a musket rifle at his side. She had just killed the second rifleman by taking a stone and smashing it repeatedly against his head. The dead Podunk was Gowanus.

*　*　*

She had clearly been upset over the matter of killing Gowanus, and between taking care of the wounded and the burning of the dead; it subsequently took me several days to gently coerce the story from her. I didn't push her, but I knew that if she didn't talk about it, then she would have tormented herself with guilt until she drowned in it. She was withdrawn and solemn, depressed and angry, and scornful to anyone who tried to approach her—including her husband. For five nights, she slept on the opposite side of our hut.

I gave her the distance that I felt she needed, but I didn't let it go. I couldn't ignore the fact that she hurt inside because she was the only one that I cared for, and I had to help her through it without pushing her away. I prodded her gently at least once a day and said things like, "I know you'll tell me when you're ready," and "You'll feel better after talking about it," and "I want to help you, my love."

On the sixth morning before we ate, which she had all but stopped doing, I had had just about enough of her moping around, so I grabbed her arm as she tried to walk away from me for the umpteenth time. She struggled lightly against my touch until she knew I wasn't going to let go, and then she spun on the heels of her feet and started physically fighting with me. She punched and kicked me hard – just trying to get away – but I didn't react and I didn't let go. I stood there and took it because I wanted it out of her system. Almost as fast as she started up, she began to calm, and then she collapsed into my arms and cried like a little girl.

"I didn't mean to kill him," she said over and over between the sobs and gasps.

"I know," I said as sincerely as I could because I meant it.

"But I had to. He threatened to kill you and father if I didn't leave with him and become his wife. When I told him 'No,' he called me a traitor to my people for choosing to be with a wonnux." She gave a big sniffle before she continued, and I felt her body tremble. "When I tried to convince him what he was doing – to cause war between his people and mine—that it not good for anyone, he called me a … a moygoowog [bad witch, whore], and I just couldn't take his filthy words any longer. I screamed at the top of my lungs at him. He just laughed and that made me more furious. I rushed him in my anger, and we fought, but he was too strong for me. He

[164]

tore off my shirt and held me down. He tried … he tried putting his thing in me … and that's when I felt the loose rock on the ground. I hit him in the head, and he fell over. I jumped on top of him. I couldn't stop hitting him."

"You did what you needed to do to protect yourself," I said as I tried to look her in the eyes, but she wouldn't let me. She just buried her face deeper into my chest.

"I will understand if you wish to leave me."

"What!?! Why would I ever want to do that?"

"He rape me!"

"You said 'he tried to'."

"It doesn't matter. He tried to have his way with me and now I spoiled for you."

"Namoenee," I said in a soft, gentle, and loving voice. "There is no one, nor is there anything on Mother Earth that could ever spoil you for me. I love you. I will always love you."

She took my words to be true, for they were because I never lied to her, and she knew that. It cheered her up to the point that she was able to move on from there. Just as the rest of the tribe healed in its own way and time, she too had begun to heal—to become herself again.

*   *   *

The one day of war ended just before sunset and the Wangunk men outnumbered the Podunks almost two to one. The Podunk men surrendered. Much to everyone's surprise, Tahadondeh told the Podunks that they were now Wangunks, and he instructed that the Podunk women and children, and any possession that they wished, including any livestock, be brought back to our village. The Wangunk numbers almost doubled that day in spite of the death toll, which was many. It was the Indian way of survival to be greater in numbers.

It took two weeks before the village resembled the way it did before the war. Except now, it was larger. Everyone helped with the effort, including the captured Podunks, for the Podunks were glad to now be called Wangunks. It was their ultimate goal, after all, to join with us. Men and women alike were busy remaking clothes that had been ruined. They replaced food that had been lost, and damaged huts were torn down and replaced with new ones.

At first, tensions were high, but they eventually eased. It reminded me of when I first arrived here. I had killed, but they took me in. I was a stranger to their ways, but I was accepted. The Podunks were not any different than me. Just because the color of their skin was the same as the Wangunks, it didn't mean they weren't strangers, but the Wangunks took them in, and friendships began to blossom. Children innocently started to play games together. Food was shared, and a few sparks of love (at least flirtations) began to fly.

Namoenee became much better too as time passed. She forgave herself for killing Gowanus, and after two weeks of her father's and my counsel, she smiled and laughed again, even at my corny jokes. She even took the time to make me a leather vest. It was her way of saying "thank you" for investing the time to help her through her feelings. My bride learned how to put pockets on the outside of it too after she saw how much I used the pockets in my shorts. By all accounts, Namoenee was back to normal, but I knew deep down she still felt betrayed by Gowanus and of her own actions against him. I wondered if she would ever truly let go of those feelings.

Betrayal in war is childlike compared to betrayal in love. How quickly love turns to hate when rejected. It drove Gowanus mad, and subsequently, he wanted me dead, and he convinced his father to go to war with the Wangunk tribe because of it. I knew all this to be true because Gowanus' father, the sachem of the Podunks, was still alive after that deadly day and he told the three of us, Tahadondeh, Namoenee, and I, all of this over dinner one night a couple of weeks later.

"He let himself be captured twelve moons ago so he could be close to you," he said to Namoenee. "It was his plan to unite the tribes. He thought he could win your heart, and I went along with it. But as I sit here now, a humble servant to you and your father, I can tell where your heart is."

Namoenee turned to me and smiled. I smiled back.

I will never know that if I hadn't come into Namoenee's life if she would have ended up with Gowanus, but my instincts told me that she never would have loved him the way she did me. On one hand, I felt guilty because I was the catalyst of this war, and on the other, I had Namoenee's love, and that still made me the happiest man in the world. My thoughts of possibly having changed history soon faded.

HOBOMOKO'S WRATH

Part of Gowanus' plan did work in the end, but he just wasn't there to be a part of it. Under the direction of Tahadondeh, the two tribes had united, and after a short stint of time, life went back to the way it was before the merge. However, winter was forthcoming and preparations had to be made.

The tribe had doubled in size and Tahadondeh was concerned about the food supplies lasting over the snowy months ahead for all of us, so he gave everyone a role except for the very old. Men worked together in great hunting parties that lasted days at a time, and the women prepared the hides for clothing and smoked the meat for winter storage. Young boys, old enough to handle a bow and arrow, sought out the smaller game and young girls gathered nuts and wild vegetation like mushrooms, seeds, and berries to supplement the food supply.

The days remained warm enough in the sun to be bare-chested, but the early evening and night time temperatures dropped to the point where one was glad to be seated next to the fire or under the furs and snuggling with a loved one. I had been with the Wangunks for three months, and I guessed it to be past mid-October, past my birthday of the twelfth anyway. My birthdays have always been special to me, but this time it neither mattered to me that I had missed it nor that it hadn't been celebrated. I'm not sure if being in the past made me not care if it was my birthday or not, or if it was my being with Namoenee and her people—who never celebrated birthdays because they lived day to day like it were their last. I was in my glory. Whatever the reason, I let the idea of my being another year older slip away from me with a shrug.

It was around this time (after my short lived b-day realization) that all the available hunters decided to go fishing for the day instead of hunting for deer, caribou, elk, and the like. In past excursions, the tribe had begotten much bounty, but this time tragedy struck yet again against the Wangunk tribe.

*   *   *

The day started off overcast, a perfect morning to fish, and we set out in twelve canoes, two men per. I was teamed up with Dunker tei, What Ails Him, a scrawny, under developed twenty-year-old who joined us from the Podunks. He was a nice fellow though somewhat sickly looking. Apparently, as a child, he was bedridden for long periods of time with a coughing sickness that wouldn't go away. He told me in a quiet and reserved fashion, while we paddled to a favorite spot of mine, that he had never fully recovered from it even now that he was older. I suspected that it was asthma. He thanked me for allowing him in the canoe with me as no one else wanted to have him, and I felt sorry for him when he told me that the alienation from the others had been this way for all of his life. He was able to function as any other adult could, though winded at times, but he was somewhat shunned due to his lingering illness. Dunker tei was without wife and child because people feared what they didn't understand, and he was a loner because of it.

I looked out over the lake at all the other canoes. At all the friends who rode together. I wanted to tell Dunker tei that we could be friends if he wanted to, but that was not the way. We had to have proven times together first, so I kept silent.

As we came upon my trusted fishing spot, Dunker tei and I started hauling in fish, one right after another. I thought it was a sign of good fortune. Toward midday, as my belly began to grumble and grow eager for lunch, the slight breeze that we enjoyed all morning stopped to a dead halt, and I saw dark thunderclouds begin to form off to the West. I decided that our day of fishing would be better put off to another day since I had seen many a storm in my childhood start just the same way on the lake. We were the first to start to paddle home, but the storm came in too quickly and caught us out in the open water. It caught all of us out on the water.

The wind and waves made for slow going. Because I was in the back, I decided to steer us toward the eastern shoreline where we would wait for the storm to pass. I did not hear any arguments from Dunker tei as his urgency hastened with every stroke of his paddle. I saw the other canoes start to scramble toward home for safety in a similar fashion.

The skies grew terribly dark, and I tried to yell to everyone over the wind, "Head for the shore! You won't make it back to the village in time," but I was yelling to no

[169]

one since they were too far away to hear me over the fierce wind. Then the rain came down in sheets.

Dunker tei and I beached the canoe as the first lightning bolt lit up the dark afternoon sky, and it struck the water with a splash and sizzle a couple hundred yards away. Dunker tei lept out of the canoe and almost dumped our haul into the water. I shot him a glance of "don't be so stupid," but when I saw him completely and utterly frightened, hugging a tree for dear life, I couldn't stay mad.

I told him in his language as best as I could, "Let go of the tree and crouch down as close as you can to the ground."

He did as I told him.

I was about to get out of the canoe myself, but when I looked back over the water after a second blinding flash, I saw the closest of the other canoes tip over. I saw arms flailing about in the water as they tried to keep their heads above the high waves and regain possession of their canoe. They weren't going to make it.

I pushed off from shore and quickly pumped the paddle with my arms against the high waves in an effort to reach them—to help them. The storm completely surrounded us in minutes with deafening cracks of thunder and lightning that made the hair on my forearms and the back of my neck stand up. It felt like every breath I took was filled with electricity. I was petrified. As I neared the overturned canoe, I heard a yell come from behind me. It was Dunker tei and he was in the water swimming toward me. He screamed that he too wanted to help and that I should wait for him.

"No!" I yelled back to him. "Get back to land."

This time he didn't listen to me, or he couldn't hear. I squinted forward, took two quick swipes at my glasses to try to clear them of raindrops and saw another of our fishing canoes capsize. I looked back to Dunker tei. He struggled like the others in the rough water. The wind and waves were too strong for any moderate swimmer. I had to make a choice and Dunker tei was the closest to me. I turned the canoe around.

He went under just as I reached him. I threw my glasses to the bottom of the dugout canoe, dove in, and quickly remembered the lifeguard techniques I had learned in all my swim classes back in high school. I swam down until his knees were at eye level, grabbed him by the sides of his thighs and spun him around to have his back toward me. I then swam up, grabbed him under the armpits, and started to swim with him to the surface. He didn't react to any of my doings, and I took that as a bad sign.

I brought him up to the surface, but it was too choppy for me to try mouth to mouth resuscitation while we floated. I eyed the canoe and started to swim for it with Dunker tei in tow, but all my training didn't account for how difficult navigating high waves with another body during a thunderstorm would be. I had a hard time keeping my own head above the water. The canoe seemed miles away. I swam sidestroke with his body, all-be-it a little body, above me with my arm draped across his chest and my hand secure under the opposite armpit. By the time I reached the floating tree trunk, I was exhausted, and I couldn't lift Dunker tei into it. I felt helpless, but I did not give up.

I flipped him over, placed his arm and head into the canoe, and quickly swam underneath to the other side and struggled to get myself in. Between the waves that lunged the boat up and down and my three attempts at getting my body up high enough to swing a leg in, Dunker tei started to fall back into the water. I grabbed for his wrist just as he got loose and was about to go under for a second time. I pulled hard and got half of his body into the dugout before I grabbed hold of his breechcloth and hauled the rest of him in. I landed hard on the bottom of the canoe among all the water and dead fish, and Dunker tei ended up on top of me.

The rain fell down hard on our faces.

I started to give him mouth to mouth within the tight confines, but there was no reaction. I rolled him on his side and squarely smacked him on his back to force the inhaled water out of his lungs. That seemed to work because the water shot out like projectile vomit. I gave him mouth to mouth again, felt for a pulse, and found none. I tried CPR. I pumped on his chest just above the sternum five quick times in between each breath I gave him. I did this over and over as the canoe rocked its way across the white capped waters.

It didn't work. Dunker tei's lungs weren't strong enough to recover. He was gone and he would no longer suffer from his asthma, or from the alienation of his tribe.

I sat down in the water filled canoe—exhausted and furious that I couldn't save the young man when there was another flash of lightning and an instant crack of thunder overhead. It jolted me out of my depression and into action. There were still others who could use my help. I searched and found my glasses at the rear of the canoe in more than six inches of water, but when I put them on, I couldn't find a paddle right away.

I was clearly upset, from my failure to save Dunker tei, and because I was in the middle of a monstrous storm, I screamed at the top of my lungs, "Where the fuck are the paddles!?!"

A single paddle bobbed in the front of the canoe, but I panicked, and it took a moment for me to see it. I made my way over the body of Dunker tei to the front of the dugout and knelt down to start my way again. Half way to the first overturned canoe, the wind died down, which caused the waves to do the same. This made the progress easier and a little quicker, but when I reached the canoe I found no one there.

My better judgement told me not to, for I knew I would be a worse lightning rod if I did, but I braved standing up in the canoe. I needed a better vantage point to see across the water, but I saw nothing except two other canoes that rocked in the waves a short distance away and they were both unmanned.

I paddled over to each and found the same as the first. I found no one.

Maybe they swam to safety. I scanned the closest shoreline, but it was still too far away for me to see anyone.

* * *

The storm ended as fast as it had begun and fourteen out of the original thirty-four fishermen who had survived joined me out on the lake in search for the missing, but we came up empty handed. We were missing twenty of us. It was a devastating blow after the loss of so many in the war. We refused to give up our search. Even after dark, we paddled around with torches held high in the air. Those who did not search from the water searched along all the shores, either by land or wading along in the shallows, and hoped for a sign of life from someone.

We gave up the search after two days, without results, when Tahadondeh called for a tribal meeting to mourn the dead. The tribe gathered to burn the body of Dunker tei, and then we buried his remains. I ended up speaking for him, and told the rest of the tribe of his bravery in facing the storm to try and help the others. I saw some twangs of guilt creep into the faces of those who had treated him unfairly during his life. His mother wept silently. After his burial ritual was over, we gathered up the possessions of the missing and floated them out to the middle of the lake on a burning raft—the thought was that the dead could use them in the Great Hunting Grounds in the Sky.

Everyone sobbed with grief for the dead. Everyone took the loss to heart, which caused some to start to worry that the Great Spirit Hobomoko was displeased about something that they had done. The worry soon turned to rumors. I tried to down play those rumors and stated that not everything that happened, good or bad, was left to the will of any Spirit. Needless to say, I was met with opposition even from Namoenee.

Then the rumors became believable fact when people started to fall sick.

*　　*　　*

The Wangunks started to plead to the heavens, mostly to Hobomoko, to be merciful for they did not know what they had done wrong, but their pleas apparently fell upon a deaf deity. Four days after the bravest and strongest of swimmers, both Podunk and Wangunk, were taken to a watery grave, a terrible plague struck the tribe.

Within days, almost every hut had at least one sick person that resided within, so I suggested to Tahadondeh that he round up all of them and place them in the gathering hut, but he ignored my proposal.

It was a ferocious sickness. First, people grew very tired and they developed the shakes and shivers. The second symptom was that they couldn't eat or drink without immediately tossing it up with blood mixed in. An infected person died on or around the sixth day after the first symptom showed.

It was at this time that Traven showed his face to me again. I was taking a stroll in the woods, alone and solemn, trying to think of a way to save my new family. This time he was more welcomed by me, rather than his annoyances in the past.

"I feel so helpless," I said to him.

He responded, "I understand your desire to stay here. It's a simple life, so beautiful and serene, and you've made an existence here that you never had at home, but you can't change history. If the Wangunks were supposed to survive to your time, then they would have. You can't save them Jim. Even if you could, you should know better than that."

As a third person looking in, Traven's words may have made sense to me, but because I was so close to the situation I just couldn't see it. "I need to save my friends."

"I completely know how you feel, but even I don't know what the ramifications could be. No, it's best just to leave it alone and let history unfold as it did."

We strolled on a bit more and didn't say anything to each other until Traven piped up, "I know that you got the watch back, so why don't we just leave this place? Believe me Jim, you'll feel much better about it once you're back in your own time."

"I can't do that now. I'm too involved. I have to see it through. Besides, I ..." I was about to tell him of Namoenee and myself, but I decided I'd better not. I didn't need another lecture about non-interference.

"Besides, you ... what?"

"Nothing. It's not important."

"So you're staying here then?"

"Yes." I said, and with that I said goodbye to the professor.

Before he left, Traven said, "Oh, this isn't goodbye. I'm sure we will see each other again."

After Traven's departure, I started to head back to the village, and I decided I would give Wood's Edge one more try.

"These people are sick due to an illness and not from the wrath of Hobomoko," I tried to tell Tahadondeh. I reiterated to him that I thought we needed to separate the sick from the healthy, but he ignored me again. I had brought Namoenee with me to try and convince him, "Tell everyone not to touch the blood of the sick, or even their sweat. Better yet, if you confine the sick, chances are the rest of us will get through this," I explained. I wasn't really concerned for myself because I grew up with inoculations, which was a silly idea since I had no idea what everyone was contracting, but I didn't want to see any more of my friends die from a terrible sickness.

"Father, his words may be true," Namoenee said to him.

Tahadondeh, Wood's Edge, had heard enough. He stood and said firmly, "I will not forsake my people when they need me most. I will not discard them like the end of an evening meal. I will hold council, and together we will find a way to appease the Great Spirit. He will make them well again. Now go and tell all who are able it is time to meet."

"Why is he so stubborn?" I asked her as we exited his hut. "At the very least, let me go to a doctor at the nearest colony and get some penicillin." I didn't know if the closest settlements along the Connecticut River (what would eventually become Portland, Middletown, and East Haddam) had a doctor, and I didn't even know if penicillin was invented yet, but it didn't matter anyway because apparently I had said the wrong thing.

My bride stiffened, "We are Inchun. You are now Inchun too, my husband. We do not need the help from the English. I know you mean well, but my father will find a way. Believe me."

"But Namoenee..." It was no use. I couldn't convince anyone to go along with my ideas, so I despairingly went along with theirs. Namoenee and I did as her father asked and we gathered up all that had the energy to come.

* * *

"We must find a way," an old woman pleaded.

"We must do whatever we can to stop this," a man yelled out.

"Whatever means necessary, we must appease the great Hobomoko," someone else called.

"Yes, yes," people agreed in unison.

Suddenly the hut grew quiet as the Powwaw entered. He wove his way through the tribe like a snake, and waved tobacco fumes above everyone's heads while he chanted below his breath. Those closest people to him reached up and tried to scoop handfuls of the wispy smoke down to their noses as he passed. He then made his way to a small clearing in the middle of the circle of braves who surrounded Tahadondeh and sat down.

The sachem rose from his elevated chair to speak, "It must be that we have failed the great Hobomoko in some way, and he is angry with us. Why else has he spread so much death and disease among our people? We must find a way to have him smile down upon us again, but what will be done? And will we honor the decision without doubt?"

One by one the fearful tribe members stood and gave their allegiance to whatever the decision would be. I dreaded to have to do the same when it came to my turn because I didn't believe. I thought the whole Spirit thing was hocus-pocus, a way to explain the unexplainable, but Namoenee looked at me with her big doe eyes, and she squeezed my hand and pleaded for me to join in the decision. Reluctantly, I did. Then her father spoke once more as we all sat back down.

"It is done. Whatever is decided will not happen with interruption from any of us," Tahadondeh said with a sorrowful pride. He then looked down to the man seated in front of him, "Go then Powwaw. Go and consult your bones and perform your incantations. Speak with the Great Spirit and find out his wishes, so that he may be appeased and release us from his wrath."

The Powwaw stood and did several three-sixties with his arms raised. In one hand, he rattled a string of bear claws and in the other the tobacco smoldered. His motion caused the smoke to gather about him densely and made his face hard to see, but I could have sworn that when he looked at me, and at no one else, he had a look of hatred. *He knows that I don't believe in him.*

He left the gathering hut and soon afterward the tribe disbanded. I stood with Namoenee outside the large bark dwelling and watched him depart into the woods. He was alone, and he left in search for a vision and an answer.

"What will he tell us?" I asked my wife.

She replied hopefully, "The answer to our problems."

"From one man," I paused. "What if we don't like what he has to say?"

"We made a pledge to father to follow his decision no matter if we like it or not."

"That's what I'm afraid of," I said not trying to hide my feelings from her.

She and I held hands tightly as we walked back to our hut for supper and a restless night's sleep, and we all waited for the Powwaw to return.

A JOURNEY'S END

Two days after the Powwaw had left on his vision quest he returned in the early morning and went straight into Tahadondeh's hut. The news traveled fast and we all soon knew that he was back, and everyone grew more anxious. You could feel the tension mount as we all waited for the answer.

Namoenee was nervous. I was nervous too but for a different reason, for I was never a good follower. I didn't like the fact that one man's words would be listened to no matter what he had to say. The situation reminded me of Waco or of the Jones camp; because one man's voice, the supposed voice of God, told those people to follow him and look where it got them. Everyone died by either a botched ATF (Bureau of Alcohol, Tobacco and Firearms) siege at a paranoid farmhouse or by some poisoned fruit punch, but in this case, those that were sick were dying anyway and something needed to be done. I just didn't like the way that everyone believed this one man had the answer to his or her problems, but I was certainly outnumbered. I didn't have any say in the matter. Even Namoenee wouldn't listen to me seriously, and she was my biggest ally.

"Everything will be all right now," she said, lacking the confidence in her voice that I had grown so accustomed to.

Maybe my words had placed some doubt in her conviction, but I was tired of trying to convince her of my thoughts on the situation, "For the sake of the tribe, I hope you are right."

Namoenee fidgeted with a shirt that she was working on for me, but I could tell she wasn't really concentrating on it. She said, "I realize you have doubts, my husband, but you will see. The Powwaw has great magic, and if Hobomoko gave him an answer true, the tribe will be saved."

"Uh huh," I responded somewhat coldly. I couldn't tell her about science and viruses and modern medicine, and that with those things her people would stand a better chance of survival. I couldn't tell her that if she lived in the future, with me in my day, she wouldn't have to worry about this sickness, and it tore at my psyche.

Suddenly, Eagle Wing approached the door of our hut. "Namoenee, the sachem wishes to see you right away," he stated with an air of urgency.

She and I both stood.

"Just you," he said to her.

We both stepped outside and she kissed me, "My heart will be forever yours."

Eagle Wing and I watched her walk over to her father's hut. I felt wronged somehow because I couldn't go with her to hear the answer first hand, but my friend and fishing partner made me quickly forget about it. He said, "Perhaps after Hobomoko is made happy again, you and I can go fishing together like before."

I looked down to see that he had fashioned a new pair of leggings made from the leg portions of my jeans. I gave him a smile. I was getting better at speaking and understanding their language by then, so I replied, "Yes, I would like that. We did quite well that day."

"Join me in a game of hubbub?"

I looked at him sideways and said, "This is not the time for games."

"How about a smoke over in my hut?"

"No thank you," I said, and looked over Eagle Wing's shoulder at Tahadondeh's hut. I noticed some other men cross my line of sight as they gathered behind Eagle Wing. Something wasn't right. "What's going on here?"

Eagle Wing stood directly in front of me, "Jim, you are a good man. You are friend to Eagle Wing, but it is feared you will try to interfere."

I looked him straight in the eyes. "We are friends," I agreed as I counted three men behind him. "So tell me. Interfere with what?"

"With the decision of the Powwaw."

"And what decision would that be?" I didn't wait for an answer because I saw Namoenee exiting her father's hut. She looked stately as she stood there, upright and proud, her hands clasped in front of her just like the first day we met, but this time she did not look happy. She looked directly at me, and I started to walk toward her.

My friend raised a hand to me, "I'm sorry Jim, we can not let you pass."

At first, I thought the decision to appease Hobomoko was to get rid of me. I mean, the way Namoenee looked toward me with such sorrow, and the way I was surrounded, I thought for sure it had to do with me. Then I quickly remembered Eagle Wing telling me that they didn't want me to *interfere*, so it must have had something to do with Namoenee. I grabbed Eagle Wing's arm, used his weight against me to my advantage, and spun him around. Then shoved him off to the side, all the while my eyes stayed fixed on Namoenee. She still just stood there. I saw her reach up and brush her cheek. She was crying. I moved more quickly and dodged one of the three other men as he tried to tackle me. I didn't know his name because he was from the Podunks, and we hadn't met before then. The others rushed me. Eagle Wing reached up behind my head and held on to the neckline of the vest Namoenee had made as the others converged on me.

I fought back in a terrified frenzy. "Let me go," I screamed, but they didn't listen. Instead, they wrestled me to the ground and held on tight. I couldn't move.

I twisted my head around to look at my bride, and my hard breath kicked up puffs of dust in front of my face. Namoenee mouthed an "I love you" to me, then blew me a kiss and finished it with a half-hearted wave. Then she took off running.

"Namoenee!" I yelled out and struggled again against my restrainers. I felt someone's knee come down between my shoulder blades, and it forced my face down harder to the ground in an effort to hold me still. "Namoenee!" I choked out. Just before she went out of sight, I called for her one more time, and then she was gone. *Where is she running to? What is she doing?*

"This isn't right! Let go of me!" I pleaded to the four men who held me down, but they had their orders. They weren't going to listen to reason, so I lied and cried uncle. "All right," I said calmly. "I understand. I won't interfere," and with that I forced myself to relax my whole body.

The men slowly let their grasp on me ease to the point where I was allowed to get up off of the ground. Eagle Wing still had a hold of my arm only this time he was trying to help me. "It's all right," I said as I brushed myself off and calmly turned around to go back into my hut. After I got inside, I grabbed my loaded revolver and immediately went back outside. I pointed it at Eagle Wing and the others, and without a word, I made them back away from me. As I kept a watchful eye for anyone else who might have been in the mindset to stop me, I backed away from the four men, and kept my gun trained on them.

Eagle Wing took a step toward me with a look of worry on his face. I didn't know whether the worry was from a true friend or from someone who was concerned that I might spoil their plans, but I fired a warning shot at his feet anyway. They knew the power I held in my hand, and no one else ventured in my direction. As I came to the edge of the village, I looked off in the direction that Namoenee had gone, saw no one there to stop me, so I took off after her. I heard yelling come from behind me. They were following me because they still did not want me to interfere with a decision made by the Powwaw. I had no idea what I would be interfering with, but whatever it was, it involved Namoenee, and I had to try.

I ran around the Eastside of the lake along the path that Namoenee and I had taken strolls on many times before. It's the path that led to the rocky precipice where she and I had sat and talked, got to know one another, and enjoyed the most beautiful sunsets together. It's the place where I had given her a wampum shell necklace as a wedding gift.

I remembered her saying, "James, it's beautiful. Thank you. I love it and will never take it off for as long as we are together." I ran like my ass was on fire, but I couldn't seem to catch up to her. I started to believe she had gone off of the beaten path, but I trekked on.

As I ran, I thought that it didn't make any sense for the Powwaw to choose my bride to be the one to cease Hobomoko's wrath. If the Great Spirit were truly lashing out his anger at the tribe, which I knew to be ridiculous, then maybe he was doing it as punishment for the tribes uniting. *Shouldn't it then have been Namoenee's father that would have to pay for that decision? Or Gowanus' father? Is this how the sachem was to pay for his mistake, to exile his only daughter?*

As I got closer to where I knew the path ended, right at the cliff above the water, I saw a gleaming flash of light from the corner of my eye. It was off in the woods, ahead and to the right of me, and at the time I didn't think too much of it. I was too focused on my pursuit of Namoenee.

When I reached the bluff, I stopped dead in my tracks because there she was. I saw her standing on her tiptoes right at the very edge of the cliff. "Namoenee," I called out to her as I placed one hand on my knee exhausted and in pain from the two-mile sprint. My other hand reached out in her direction. I was relieved that I had found her, but she didn't respond to my call. She didn't even turn around to face me. I had no time to say anything else to her before she leapt.

"Nooooo!" I screamed. Birds flew from their perches as my yell stretched out and echoed among the hills, and Namoenee fell to the rocky bottom below.

And in a flash, a new memory formed in my mind that I had not known before. It came rushing in from a vast openness like a tsunami against a shore and it crashed over all other memories that I had of the lake … My dad and I were in his aluminum rowboat. I was eight. We were fishing in the early morning, and he told me a small tale. "You know, legend has it that it was right here, high above us, that the Princess of Lake Pocotopaug committed suicide in an effort to save her people."

I fell to my knees.

*   *   *

What brought me back to the awareness of my surroundings was the watch that I pulled out of my vest pocket without any notion that I had done so, and it caught my eye as the hot midday sun reflected off of it. This watch, which lay in the palm of my hand with beads of water that dripped down its antique face, had started it all. A watch so complicated in its nature, so complex with its inner workings, that I had no understanding of how it operated, or why Traven had chosen me to own it. It had brought me to a place where life was simpler than anything I had ever imagined in my most pleasant of dreams, and then suddenly, without warning, everything became horribly complex – a living nightmare. I never had peace in my life, but I learned from her, before her death, how uncomplicated everything could be if you just let it, but then, suddenly, I was without her, and my world was shattered. I was alone again.

I went down to the rocky shore, but I couldn't bring myself to go near her, because to see her lay there up close, face down in the water, unmoving, was too much for me to handle. My legs gave out from under me, and I collapsed a second time.

An hour and a half had passed since I saw her leap off the high cliff above me. An hour had passed since the men carried her body back to the village. She was dead, and it left me feeling empty inside. I stared down at the watch, and it seemed to mock me because I couldn't use it to save her. Traven told me I couldn't go back. He said that the user couldn't occupy the same space at the same time. I couldn't go back to overt the war. I couldn't go back to stop all the men from going fishing. I couldn't stop the plague that swept through the village. I couldn't stop myself from falling in love with a princess. *Or could I?* No, I couldn't travel within my own lifetime to prevent myself from accepting the watch from Traven, or even using the watch all together, but it was a thought.

I was stunned, perhaps even in shock, and I couldn't move for two hours. I just sat there and absently watched the minutes tick away on the pocket watch. Absently, I watched the waves lap at my feet, and I pondered the only question that rose up in my mind. *Did the Powwaw choose her to die because of me or was he punishing Tahadondeh?* It was one man's decision, and I hated him for it. The truest love of my life was gone, and I could do nothing to prevent it.

I gently closed the cover of the timepiece and rubbed the surface of it. My father's carport still showed in its relief, which made me look across the water to the opposite shoreline. *Four hundred years from now*, I thought as I spied something in the water. I stood, put the watch away, and took a couple of steps. The thing in the water was the necklace I had made for Namoenee. It was made of white and purple wampum. I waded over to it, scooped it up, and a distant smile touched my lips. She told me she would never take it off as long as we were together, and that's when the floodgates opened up. I started to bawl my eyes out. I outstretched my arms to the sky and screamed, "Why!?! Why her? What kind of God are you? Answer me! Why her? Answer me if you're such a Great Spirit."

Hobomoko did not respond, nor did I really think that he would.

I tied Namoenee's necklace around my neck, and it settled onto my shoulders. Then I headed back to the village at a very slow pace, and by the time I got back to my hut, it was nightfall. I spoke to no one, and no one spoke to me. When I entered the hut, I saw her lying there with a tanned square cloth that covered her face. At first, I thought maybe it was the Wangunk's tradition to cover the face of the dead like in my day when the morticians sowed the corpse's eyelids shut, or even before my day when they use to place coins on top of them. Both of which were done so as not to spook the surviving mourners. I thought that this was the case, except in past ceremonies that I had experienced, the dead didn't have any face cloths, so I willed myself to look at her one last time, and lifted the square of hide. I discovered that the cloth was there to hide the ugliness of her brutal death. She was so misshapen that I couldn't see her face at all. She must have landed on her head because her face was totally gone, and I was horrified. I wished then that I hadn't looked.

If anyone has ever wondered what it feels like to go mentally insane, I came close to it that night. I thought I was going to completely lose it. My mind reeled as I took in a couple of deep breaths, but I couldn't escape the grotesque image, or the sick feeling I had in the pit of my stomach. I felt alone in the universe. I wished Spencer was there with me, but I couldn't involve him this late in the game. He wouldn't be able to help me anyway, other than just to talk to. And I was too void of energy to even contemplate using the watch to go see him. I didn't know what to do, who to talk to, or what I needed to do next. Everything closed in on me, so I ran outside for some fresh air.

Tahadondeh stood slumped over outside my hut as I exited. He could see the horror and sorrow on my face. He placed an arm over my shoulders, and I let him. "Walk with me," he said. We walked to the shoreline and stood there a long while, his arm still around me. "I feel very proud of my daughter, and so should you."

I did not respond.

"Namoenee had a great love for her people, which was equal only to the love she had for you and me. She will be missed by all. We will send her to the Great Spirit at first light, and from then on, great tales will be told of her long after you and I are gone."

Tahadondeh continued as he took in the night air. "The moon lights up the sky. The wind has shifted. Hobomoko smiles down on us once again. I can feel it." I guess he could tell his words were doing nothing for me because he dropped his arm and stepped to face me. He looked me in the eye, but I couldn't hold his gaze, for it brought upon me a deep anger that I knew wasn't justified. I stared at his bear tattoo as he spoke, "Listen to me Jim Southland, my son, her giving nature is what saved us. It couldn't have been anyone else. Namoenee's love was the greatest to give. She knew that she might have been chosen, and yet she agreed in the gathering. So did you. So did we all. We all accepted the fact that if the Powwaw's vision called for any one of us to go to Hobomoko, we would have done so willingly. She explained this to you, no? "

No. No she didn't. She knew I would never have accepted that.

"She was a great friend to you, I could tell. She was a terrific wife, and a wonderful daughter. She treated all equally and gave everyone her love, so please don't dishonor her memory with hatred. That may spoil Hobomoko's good mood."

I finally spoke, "I won't."

Tahadondeh relaxed. "Good," he said. "Come morning we will celebrate her and send her on her way to Him. Come the rising of the sun we will begin again, and you and I will carry on. We will honor her every day for the tribe to see how proud of her we are, and we will rebuild. This tribe will be strong again."

No it won't. Maybe in the near future you and the tribe will survive but not far beyond that. You'll all be gone, and no one will give a damn. Your land will be sold out under your feet. You will be pushed off of it, and it will be built upon, polluted and spoiled, and none of the intruders will realize that you were ever here. And without Namoenee around for me to live with, it isn't worth staying. I made a decision, "I won't be staying after tomorrow."

"That is your choice son, but know this, you are always welcome here," Tahadondeh said before he walked away.

I just stood there and stared out into the night. "This is the worst night ever," I said to myself as I spied the funeral pyre being built off to my right. It looked ominous there in the dark—like an empty gallows that's waiting to be used. Four thick posts held up a bed of wood. Underneath the bed was a pile of fallen debris gathered out of the woods. I looked away from it and returned my thoughtless gaze back out over the water. I didn't want to return to the hut. There was no point. I knew I wouldn't sleep that night, and I couldn't bear to look upon my loved one's lifeless body. Eventually, my legs weakened from standing for hours, and I sat down on the ground until dawn.

At the first inkling of light, I knew it was time to burn the dead. It was time for the tribe to send her off to be with Hobomoko, and oh, how I was envious of him. Only He would have the pleasure of my wife's company, but I knew that He could not love her as much as I did. I was beside myself with rage, self-pity, and jealousy that she was gone and no longer with me. She was to be with Him. I hated Him. I hated the stupid superstitions that surrounded Him. I hated the Powwaw too, for the same reasons.

I heard people begin to stir in the village behind me, so I stood with a heavy sigh and meandered my way back inside the hut where I was met by her father, Eagle Wing, and Snow Falling. Snow Falling looked up at me with tears in his young round eyes and it broke my heart. I placed a hand on his shoulder and gave him a comforting squeeze. He leaned into me, and we hugged a while. Tahadondeh motioned to me to join him up at Namoenee's shoulders as Eagle Wing stood near her thighs. I could not look down to her covered face, so instead, I watched Snow Falling step to her feet. Without a word, we all lifted and carried her body outside.

Everyone in the village, including some of the ill that amazingly had started to feel better, gathered to see her off. Young and old, Wangunks and Podunks together in unison bowed their heads as we passed. Some of Namoenee's best women friends wept openly and reached out to her for one last touch goodbye. I could see that everyone loved her and that they were all going to miss her.

The four of us raised her up above our heads and on to the wooden pyre. Then her closest of friends, one by one, placed items beside her to be burned with her. The items were all purposely broken so that the spirits that were held within them could travel with her. A broken bow and a quiver of broken arrows, a broken clay dish, a dented brass bowl, some splintered wooden spoons and ladle, and torn clothing for all the seasons were placed beside her for her to use in the afterlife. When the procession of gift givers had passed, the Powwaw came into the circle, did a dance, and sang a song about her. It was a eulogy.

I could not look directly at him as he danced around the pyre, for the sight of him sickened me, but I can admit now that his song was beautiful. The words he sang about her told everyone just how special a person she was and of how she loved life and all that surrounded her. He even praised me for bringing her the love only a husband can give to his wife, of how she had waited for me her whole life, and of how it had made her the happiest person on Mother Earth. His words made me feel better about him, but not enough to let me look up from the ground.

The Powwaw finished up with the story of the appeasement of Hobomoko, and how Namoenee gallantly accepted her fate in honor of the tribe, and how the Great Spirit would ease their strife. He sang that all would be well, and everyone believed his words including me. I wanted to believe that her sacrifice would do some good.

One of the men came through the crowd and handed Tahadondeh a lit torch. It was normally the father's task to ignite the pyre if he was still alive, but Wood's Edge hesitated. Instead, he turned to me and said aloud so that all could hear, "My daughter has not died in vain—for she will live on in each of us." My father-in-law handed the torch to me, and in a softer voice he said, "Especially with you, my son."

I accepted the torch and boldly took a step forward. I stretched out my arm, the torch with it, and the dried wood immediately caught and quickly Namoenee and her items were engulfed in flames.

*   *   *

Ashes to ashes and dust to dust –that's all death really amounts to for the physical body as we return from where we came—Mother Earth. We live and then we die. In fact, the minute we are born we start down a path to the great unknown. We meet people along the way, and then they, or we, move on. Some say when we die that we move on to greater things, and others say there's nothing to look forward to. But those who watched the fire burn down to nothing with me that early morning would have sworn they saw Namonee's spirit escape the physical. They would have said it rose up to the heavens with the smoke.

I, however, saw no such thing.

During mid afternoon, two men came and removed the four posts that held up the funeral bed, and then the Powwaw collected up all the ashes. He placed the ashes, brass pot, and arrowheads, gently and purposefully on top of a ceremonial bear-hide that lay on the ground. I sat there, as I had all day, and watched him roll up the hide and sow the ends together so competently that none of the contents would have a chance of spilling out during our trek. With that done, it was time to take the remains to their final resting-place. As the able congregated for the four-mile walk, I gathered some of my things from inside the hut.

Tahadondeh led the funeral march of fifty along the west side of the lake all the way to the graveyard. He and I carried the hide bag between us – he at one end and I at the other. Neither one of us spoke a word. No one did, as it was a time for remembrance, self-reflection, and above all, silence for the dead.

As we came to an area of openness in the forest, I noticed a hole had already been dug into the ground. Someone, or more, had come at first light while she burned and prepared the sight. It was a shallow grave because there wasn't a need for a lot of room, given the contents we carried, and some medium sized rocks had been scattered around it. Wood's Edge and I set the remains down next to the grave and waited as the rest of the line gathered around. The Powwaw brought up the rear, and he came forward to perform his last ritual for Namoenee. He walked around the grave three times, blessed it by shaking both his string of bear claws and a turtle shell rattle then knelt beside the bear hide and chanted some incoherent grunts and gurgles as he cut the rawhide that held the ends closed. Carefully and patiently he then unrolled the hide and placed the charred relics and the ashes into the grave. When he was done, we watched the other members of the tribe come to the site, pick up one of the rocks and place it on top of the grave. After their task was done, again, one by one, they stood before their sachem and bowed their heads to him for a silent moment. Then they side stepped in front of me and did the same. I bowed my head in return to each one of them, and then they parted and started their walk back to the village. The Powwaw was the last to place a stone, and then he said, "Let no one disturb this place for no reason, or let Hobomoko have his way with them." He shook his bear claws once more and then departed. All that were left was just Wood's Edge and me. We looked down at the pile of rocks.

After a time, the sachem started to make his way back to the village like the others, but I stood my ground. Namoenee's father must have realized that I wasn't going to come with him because he stopped a few feet away, turned around, and came back to me. We just looked at each other a while, and then he reached out his right arm to me. I reached out to him as well and grasped him below the elbow. He took hold of me and we shook, one pump, strong and true. His eyes welled with tears, but he turned away before any of them began to flow. He walked away from me and never looked back. We never said goodbye. The Wangunks never said goodbye, for they didn't have a word for it.

When I was sure that he had gone, I pulled out the watch, opened it, and immediately pushed the right button. The trees ceased their rhythmic sway as time pushed forward slowly at first, and then it sped up. The forest didn't change as much as I thought it would. The trees grew a little taller and thicker, but near the end of the trip, I noticed two saplings grow to be medium sized trees at either end of the pile of rocks. Then, if I had blinked I would have missed it, I saw two very quick colors of motion appear, and a quiver shook my whole body. I felt sick to my stomach, and my head swam. I knew what was happening.

Traven was right. Even though I was just "passing by," I was so close to my past self that I felt the effects of it. All I could do was watch as some of the rocks, which Namoenee and her remains were under; suddenly moved off from the pile. I thought that I needed to slow down the speed at which I passed through time, and just like that, the rate began to slow. I had willed it to happen. In fact, it slowed so much so that I felt like I was there. I guess I really was in a way, though I did not fully materialize.

What an opportunity it was to see myself in the past. I was a wash of emotions, and I had to laugh even though I did not feel well. This was the grave Spencer and I had started to uncover when we were kids. I walked around the two youngsters and felt very nostalgic, when they suddenly reacted strangely. As kids, it was my older self who we had noticed as the "shadow in the woods." I was the eidolon, the protective Indian spirit—I was my own doppelganger. When I realized that, it made me laugh even harder, a big loud belly laugh. Then the kids started to run. I stayed close behind them though they were quick as hell, but I didn't intend to keep their pace. "Run, run, run away!" I laughed.

After they were gone, I willed the passage of time to resume its normal rate and then the sickness went away. At that moment, the fear I had for that place, the one place I vowed never to return to, but had done so often those past months, the place Spence and I unknowingly called the graveyard, dissipated. I had come full circle because it was the older me that had scared away Spence and I back then. I had done it and was glad he and I had been scared enough to stop our efforts to uncover Namoenee.

Then time began to slow. Everything solidified, and I was back to the year 2004.

I bent down and picked up a dozen or so of the rocks that had been disturbed by my younger self and Spencer and placed them back where they belonged. As I did, I felt Namoenee's necklace rock back and forth against the underside my chin. When I was done fixing her grave, I took off the wampum necklace and hooked it on a knot in one of the two trees that had grown to symbolize a head and foot stone for her.

"I love you Namoenee," I said with a lump in my throat. I started to walk away, but decided I couldn't leave. I turned back, grabbed the necklace off of the tree, placed it in my pocket, and walked away.

I absent-mindedly walked the path down to the road when a car passed and made me jump and hide behind a tree. At first, I did so because I didn't recognize what the strange noise was that approached me. When I did realize it for what it was I didn't want anyone to see me. If anyone saw a grown man come out of the woods dressed in cut-off jeans with the butt of a handgun stuck out at his waistline, a buckskin vest adorned with beads and fringe, and moccasins on his feet, it would have raised some serious questions. I hid until the car passed then stealthily slid across the road to the shadows of the carport and hopped into my car.

My wristwatch was still on the passenger seat, and I picked it up. It read, August 23, 2004, 4:40 PM. *I've only been gone for fifteen minutes.* I was gone only for the amount of time it took me to walk from the graveyard to my car. I pulled the gun out of my waistband and placed it and the watch on the empty seat next to me. The keys were still in the ignition, and I turned the engine over. I had left the radio on when I had shut off the car two months before, and it came on loudly with some incessant ad for my need to buy car insurance. The mind scrambling noise felt unworldly to me, and I immediately turned it off. At that moment, while I sat in my car, annoyed by such a common place thing as a radio, I felt as if I didn't belong. After being with Namoenee and her people for only two months, I questioned if coming back to my time was really the answer for me. Going back would not have been the answer either. I would have been miserable without my wife. Subsequently, I felt I no longer belonged in either place.

I couldn't think of any other option, so after a moment of sitting there listening to the engine idle, I threw the car in reverse, backed out of the carport, and drove down the street. I decided to go back to what I used to call home.

ANOTHER JOURNEY BEGINS

The first half of my ride home was excruciating. It was the start of a Monday afternoon rush hour, and everyone seemed to get in my way. I wanted to yell and swear in frustration at cars and their drivers as they cut me off, didn't use their signals, or tailgated me. One woman talked on her cell phone, and she swerved in and out of her lane in front of me as she drove oblivious to her surroundings – I wanted to drive up next to her and show her my gun, but I restrained.

Signs were everywhere—yield, merge, stop, speed limits—and they all blocked my mind from the thoughtlessness I sought. Bridges. Guardrails, and car after car. Ghastly grey pavement interrupted the lay of the land. There was a constant noise. They all broken up the natural and simple order of life that I had grown accustomed to. I was not happy to be back in this congested way of life, but then I remembered Namoenee's love for all things, and it calmed me down. I saw her silhouette against the evening sky. The way she caressed the cattails as she walked along their stalks. I remembered her love for all things. I remembered her love for her people. Her love for me. I remembered her smile. I remembered how she told me that everyone has a right to live their own lives and to do whatever makes them happy as long as it didn't cause harm to others. I remembered Gowanus and how his hatred caused so much bloodshed, so I let go of my anger. I still couldn't wait to be off of the road, but the thoughts of my bride's sweetness and innocence eased my road rage, and I made it home without incident.

A big sigh of relief and surrender escaped me as I pulled into my driveway. My tan, story-and-a-half cape was a welcoming sight tucked back away from the road. The dogwood tree and mountain laurel were in full bloom as well as the rhododendrons, and my rose bushes were full and luscious looking.

I parked the car, turned off the house alarm with my remote, left the six-shooter and wristwatch behind, got out, and went straight to the back door. Keisha, as always, was so happy to see me. She grabbed her outside tennis ball and wanted to play, but all I wanted to do was to hug her. I needed a friend. I knelt down on the driveway and did just that for a long time too. She must have been confused by my actions because she just saw me about an hour earlier, but for me, the sight of her again after two months made me realize just how much I had missed her. I gave into her attempts to squirm away and threw the ball for her a couple of times before I felt the desire to go inside. As I opened the storm door to let her in I heard someone from within my house give a deep-rooted cough.

I grabbed the dog's collar, eased her back away from the door, and then went back to the car for my gun. I checked to see that I had some bullets left in it, which I did, and then I placed the pocket watch into my vest pocket. *Why didn't the alarm go off? It wasn't disabled. I just turned it off. Why did Keisha allow someone access to the house?* I began to venture in when Keisha plowed right past me and ran inside like she had done on any other occasion. "Keisha, wait," I whispered.

I peered around the corner, and I could see that she ran straight into the living room. Her tags jingled enough to let me know that someone was petting her. I proceeded with caution, not willing to let my guard down just because an intruder had befriended my dog, and when I walked into the living room my eyes and my gun were trained on Professor Albert Traven.

"Hello Jim. Welcome home," he said, as he sat in my recliner and stroked Keisha's head between her ears.

I was about to ask him how he bypassed the alarm and got into my house, but then I recalled the first time I used the pocket watch. Locked doors were not a problem for a time traveler. They just let the house, over time, be built around them.

"What do you want?" I asked; the gun still leveled at his head.

He didn't care about the gun being pointed at him. "I wanted to congratulate you," he said, with a genuine smile that made the laugh lines around his eyes accentuate. He looked to me to be about ten years older than when I had met him at the Colt building. "You did remarkably well in not changing history considering all that you've been through."

Aesop's fable about the fox and the crow quickly came into my mind. In it, the fox sees a crow up on a branch with a bit of food in its mouth and because he was hungry himself, he says, "Oh what a beautiful specimen of a bird you are. You must have a beautiful singing voice too. May I hear it?" When the crow sang for the fox,

[193]

the food dropped out of his mouth onto the ground, and the fox snatched it up and ran away. The moral was that all flatterers might not speak the truth. Sometimes they just may want something from you instead. I felt that Traven wasn't there just to say congratulations. "What else do you want?" I demanded, but he was caught up in a one-sided conversation again.

"Granted, I did have to go back and fix some of the records. Imagine, a white man marrying an Indian princess in the fifteenth century."

"I don't care," I said, and with the thought of Namoenee, I lowered the gun and held it along side my leg.

"Oh, but you have to care my boy. You have to. If you're going to time travel, you have to care about history and make sure you do not change it."

"But I did change it." I reached across my body with my left hand, fished out the pocket watch from my vest, and then tossed it to Traven. He raised his hand from Keisha's head just in time to catch it, and then he looked up to me in puzzlement. I said, "I won't be time traveling anymore!"

Traven didn't take my exclamation seriously. He just stood up and said quite confidently, "I know you'll change your mind." Then his demeanor changed from cocky to unsure, "I mean, how else would we see each other again when you and … oh, sorry. Perhaps I shouldn't say that just yet." Traven looked down to the watch in his hand, and his mood changed back to seriousness. "So I'll just leave this right here." He placed the watch on my coffee table. "I must be going as I'm late already. We didn't really have any idea when you would return, so with that I must …"

"We?" I asked.

"Yes. We have had a very busy day and weren't sure when you would arrive back home. In fact, we've been here just about an hour. Namoenee was …"

I couldn't believe my own ears, "Namoenee? Namoenee is here?"

"Yes. She's upstairs taking a nap, and I must say that …"

I didn't wait to hear the rest of it but instead vaulted up the stairs three at a time in sheer excitement. When I reached the top of the stairs and turned the corner, I came to a complete stop. There she was. She lay on my bed, on top of the blankets, her face turned into the afternoon sun that streamed in from my bedroom window, and she looked angelic. I placed the gun quietly down on top of my dresser. My heart pounded in my throat as I turned and quietly walked over to the side of the bed.

She wore modern clothing that took me back a bit, but I soon forgot about it as I looked at her face. She had a faint smile as she slept. She was as beautiful as I remembered. I all but forgot the image of her misshapen face. Her long black hair was spread out behind her, which exposed her cute little left ear, and her body listed onto her right side. She looked very comfortable and at peace, and I didn't want to disturb her, but I slipped off my moccasins anyway and crawled in next to her. I rested my head down next to hers, placed my hand on her left hip, and I laid there just gazing at her.

After a short time, she stirred and rested her hand on my chest. She whispered without opening her eyes, "I've missed you."

"I missed you too," I almost cried.

We kissed, and it was blissful, like one I've never experienced before. We kept our lips pressed together for a long time. It was passionate and full of betrothal. It said everything I wanted to say to her at that moment without the need to speak a word. When our lips finally parted, I felt I had to say how much I loved her.

She replied, "I love you too."

After another kiss or two, she sat straight up with excitement. "And I love your house, all these amenities, and your animals! Keisha!" She called. We could hear the dog as she ran up the stairs, into the bedroom and then up on the bed to rest next to Namoenee. Her hands got drool all over them. "Someone just had a drink, didn't they?" She turned back to me, "I love running water!" She bounced up and down a little on the bed as she played with the dog. "Why didn't you tell me about all this?"

I was taken by surprise, "About all what?"

Namoenee's excitement seemed never-ending, "I knew you were holding back from me. You could have told me about electricity, and hair dryers, and toilets. Oh, and music! I love music, especially that bio-rhythmic jazz."

I had to laugh at myself. During the ride home I had such disdain for having returned home, but I realized, as I held my bride's hand, that it didn't matter where or when I lived as long as I had the right person to share my life with.

"Bio-rhythmic jazz?" I asked with a chuckle.

"Yes," she said. "In the future."

I sat up to face her, "How could I have possibly told you about all of these things? You never would have believed me. Besides, I was willing to give all of it up to be with you." The rest of her words took a moment to sink in. I had never heard of bio-rhythmic jazz before. "Did you say, 'In the future'? Who's future?"

"Ours, of course," she said with even more enthusiasm. "There are a lot of wondrous things to look forward to in the future. There's no more hunger or disease, no more treating people like the Native Americans were treated, but it will take a lot of work on our part to make the future as bright as possible. I know we can do it."

"Hold on. You're talking a mile a minute ... and with very good English I might add."

"Thank you," she said with a smile. "I've been studying."

"You're saying that you've been to the future?"

"Yes, my husband, Albert has shown a lot of things to me in the future and of the past, which, according to him, I am now ready to share with you."

I became heated at the mention of the professor, so I got up from the bed and started downstairs. Namoenee and Keisha followed close behind. I was tired of having to play by his rules and wanted some straight answers, so I walked into the living room, but he had left and who knew when he would return. I had a feeling that Namoenee knew, and because of it, a look of frustration fell upon my face. I wanted to confront him once and for all. I wanted to finally pin him down, but I turned to Namoenee instead, "Just how long have you been with Traven? And while we're on the subject, how is it that you're here and not dead?"

"Okay, I think it's best if I start with that last day on the lake," she replied. "I'm sorry I left you, but I had a duty to perform for the tribe."

I gave her a look of disbelief.

She caught the look and continued after she regained her train of thought, "I know, I know. I know now that things could have been done a lot differently, but back then I had no choice." She gave me her "Please don't be angry with me" look and my shoulders eased their tension. She decided to continue, "Anyway, I was running through the woods, and as I got close to the cliff, the professor grabbed me, pulled me off to the side, and told me to be quiet. I found his attire to be quite odd, and I was scared. I tried to fight him. But, when he pulled out a watch like yours, my curiosity got the better of me, so I did what he asked of me. He told me to hold onto his hand, and then he pushed the button on his watch and we traveled into the future to a time after I died, or like he says, 'supposedly died.'"

I sat down hard into the recliner.

"Again, I am so sorry that I didn't know better. I never meant to hurt you."

"I believe you," I said, and tried to take it all in.

"We ended up in this beautiful house in the future, and the whole time I was with him I felt an urgency to be with you. Albert explained to me that time takes on a different meaning when you have the ability to travel through it. I had no idea what to do next. It took weeks for me to understand that no matter how much time I stayed with him that he could bring me back to the very moment from when and where we left.

"It was a whole new world to me, James. One that Traven told me you were a part of, so during these past weeks, I learned all about your culture, and I slowly adjusted. I was miserable without you and only had the professor to trust, so when Albert said that he could fix it for us to be together again, I agreed to do whatever he had in mind.

"When Albert thought I was ready, he showed me a dummy he had in his basement where the time travel watches are made. That body was so real, and so lifelike. It had hair just like mine, a body with the same proportions as mine, but it wasn't real. It was made out of synthetic skin. But the face wasn't like mine at all, and Albert said he didn't have the expertise to make it look exactly like me, so he smashed it in. He said it would be more realistic due to the fall anyway. Then he placed my old clothes on it and even I would have sworn it was my body lying there if I hadn't been standing next to it.

"The professor told me his plan to switch the dummy for me just before you could reach me on the precipice, because you and the rest of the tribe had to believe that I was dead in order to save the time line. I don't know everything there is to know about that yet, but I believe he made the right call.

"So, we went back to the cliff and placed the dummy there. Albert said we had only about a minute before you showed, so he loosely tied some fishing string to the mannequin, and we hid and waited for you to come. And just when you caught up to me or the dummy if you'd prefer, Traven pulled the string and over the bluff the body-double went.

"I saw how distraught you were. I watched you go down there, and it just tore my heart to pieces. I pleaded with him to let me go to you, but he said that was impossible. Albert then showed me that some of the tribe had followed you, and if I exposed my real self, then it would have been worse than to let you suffer for a day. Just imagine how freaked out my father, the Powwaw, and the tribe would have been if they saw two of me suddenly there?" Namoenee chuckled.

"Somehow he knew that you would come back home. Don't ask me how he knew it, but here you are, and here we are, together again."

I sat quietly for several minutes and went over it all again in my head. I ended up being of two minds about it. I said, "While I appreciate the fact that he saved your life and that we are together again, and that I will owe him for the rest of our lives, this doesn't explain how it came to be that you have seen the future. How long were you with Traven before he decided to bring you back here?"

She told me, "A month." My whole body tensed, and she knew I was not happy. "Please don't be angry with him or me. For you, it was only one day. For me I was without the man I loved much longer. After I knew that he could bring me back to any place and time whenever I wanted, I wanted to know more. I wanted to be your equal, James. I needed to know what you know, so that I could live with you in your time."

"But, apparently, you now know more than I do."

"And I want to show you it all," she said honestly.

My love for Namoenee was the strongest feeling I've ever had, and I couldn't refuse her excitement. "Okay," I said, "but I don't want to have anything more to do with Traven. There's just something about him that rubs me the wrong way."

"Me too, a little, but he's gone now," she said as she picked up the pocket watch and handed it to me. "I think it would be a good idea if you showered and shaved before we leave for dinner."

"Oh? And where are we going?"

"I have a craving for duck in the south of France. Have you ever been to France?"

"Yes, yes I have actually," I said as I wrapped my arm around the small of her back and pulled her in close.

"Ah, mais vous n'avez pas dans trois mille dix," she struggled in French. Her learning new languages went way beyond what I knew she was capable of.

"I'm sorry dear heart, but just because I've been to France doesn't mean I know the language. I mean, I took a class a long time ago, but …"

Namoenee placed her hand to the side of my furry face and teasingly said, "I said, 'But you haven't been there in the year 3010'."

EPILOGUE

Alan Snyder, co-chair of the Earth Time Authority, found Professor Albert Traven sitting alone in the lounge of the building that housed the time traveling society, but he was reluctant to talk to him. The professor was greatly admired by all that knew him because he was a co-founder of their elitist group and often quite mysterious because of it, but Alan had volunteered to be the bearer of bad news. He swallowed hard and took a step forward.

A great fire roared in the field stone fireplace making it the focal point of the room, and Alan stepped in between it and the professor casting a shadow over a book that Traven was studying.

"Yes, what is it?" Traven said, without the slightest hint of annoyance in his voice.

"Professor," Alan started. "May I have a word with you?"

Traven looked up from his read to see a look of concern on the young Snyder's face. "Of course," he said. "Pull up a seat. Would you care for a glass of Sherry?"

"Oh, no thank you," Alan declined and slid into the chair next to the professor. In between them now was a round marble-top table, armchair size, and on it an antique Tiffany stained glass lamp stood like new. It was just one of many priceless items throughout the house and Alan found he had to lean forward in order to speak to the time traveler extraordinaire.

"What can I do you for Alan?" the professor offered.

"Well, sir," Alan hesitated. Even though he had rehearsed the dialogue in his mind on the way over from the time observation room he had a hard time getting the exact words out. A bead of sweat trickled down his temple. Alan wasn't sure if it was from the heat of the fire or if it was from his lack of nerve, but in mid-sentence he decided to switch gears. "Do you think Jim Sutherland is the best choice to be your apprentice?"

"At this point, in both space and time … yes. Yes I do," Traven responded. "Why do you ask?"

"I mean he is from the past, and we have no idea what kind of person he is or if he can handle the rigors of this club." Alan felt immensely better now that his feelings were out in the open.

"Yes, he *is* from the past," Traven agreed. "But he did superbly in his first two travels, and I think he'll do fine."

"But that's just it sir, you went back and helped him. You saved him and his wife. There …" Alan choked off his anxious words.

Traven waited for him to continue, and when it seemed like the co-chair wouldn't, he prodded, "Yes? There … what?"

Alan swallowed hard a second time. "There are many of us who think you've broken the first rule, of observation only and not manipulation."

Traven grew a little hot under the collar, but he didn't let it show. "So, you think I've crossed over and become a T-MEEP? Is that it?"

"No, sir. It's not like …"

The older Traven cut the younger Snyder off. "Let me tell you one thing Mr. Snyder. In my future, I chose Jim Sutherland to be my apprentice. I don't know why as yet, and quite frankly, I don't care. It *may* have been on the suggestion of our council. Have you thought of that? No, I don't think you have. I understand that this may seem confusing to you and to the others but look …" Traven slid forward having giving the subject a lot of thought on his own. He looked Alan square in the eye. "I trust the judgement of my future self, and as far as my present self goes, I knew that if I didn't save that woman, then Jim Sutherland would never travel again."

"And that's why I'm here sir," Alan still couldn't say the words.

"Yes? What is it then?"

Finally Alan came out with it, "Jim … Jim Sutherland's gone, Professor. It's like he was never born." And there it was—the bad news had been delivered.

Traven thought he knew who was behind this—they had joined up with the Podunks, posed as colonists, but the only question he had was; could he undo what they had done?

FROM THE AUTHOR

The part about my father telling me of a legend when I was a youngster is true, but I never knew the whole story until just over a year ago from this writing. Before I started research for the pages you've read, I questioned myself, "What was the reason for the Princess of Lake Pocotopaug's demise? What if *I* was the reason she killed herself? How would I travel back in time to meet her?" From there the world of James Sutherland was born, so, thank you Dad for being the catalyst for this tale.

I would also like to give a special thanks to the East Hampton Historical Society for spending time with me, telling stories, and showing me all of the memorabilia they have that describes the history of the lake.

Thank you to the Mashantucket Pequot Museum and Research Center staff for taking the time in answering all my questions. The Mashantucket Pequot Tribal Nation has done a wonderful job in celebrating, recording, and restoring their history, and I would recommend to anyone interested in finding out more about the Pequots that they visit their museum located in Southeastern Connecticut.

A big thanks must go out to my friends and family for their encouragement during this writing; so kudos to Alison Faye, Nate, Dani, Sam, Tone, Lisa, and to my beautiful and supportive wife, Jeannine.

And to all of the readers out there that have made this work worthwhile. Although I wrote this because I felt I had a story that needed to be written, it is you that makes it more of a cherished first child. Thank you, thank you.

But the biggest of thanks goes out to my best friend Mark, to whom I dedicate this work. He started me on this path of placing thoughts and words down on paper, and he has always been there for me through thick and thin. I am honored to know him and to call him my brother. "Grace under pressure!"

Jonathan Westbrook
www.westbrookdesigns.com

Breinigsville, PA USA
14 August 2010
243624BV00006B/17/P

9 781453 648889